Conversations in Heaven: A Journey Into the Heavenly Realm

Sue Campbell

Conversations in Heaven: A Journey Into the Heavenly Realm

Sue Campbell

RIVER BIRCH PRESS

Mesa, Arizona

ISBN 978-1-956365-84-9 (Print)
ISBN 978-1-956365-85-6 (Ebook)

For Worldwide Distribution
Printed in the U.S.A.

River Birch Press
P.O. Box 7341, Mesa, AZ 85216

I dedicate this book to God,
who provided the inspiration,
and to my husband, Will,
whose encouragement, sacrifice,
and love made it happen.

Table of Contents

Prologue

My manager Ray and I were closing the pizza shop around midnight after a very busy Friday night's business, and I had just watched the last employee leave. While Ray unplugged the Open sign, I started locking the front door when I was shockingly thrown backward and to the floor after the door was violently pushed open. The enforcers were back, and I had a bad feeling that Ray's problems had finally done us both in.

This time the two oversized Italian men, who reeked of garlic and cigarette smoke, were carrying large guns. When I looked into the eyes of the largest and meanest of the two, I saw a steely emptiness stare back at me, and I knew we weren't going to get out of this. They had repeatedly warned Ray to pay his $75,000 gambling debt to the Mob and, even with me helping him as much as possible, Ray couldn't get ahead quickly enough. We had run out of time.

After his partner locked the front door, he snarled at Ray and me. "You two, into the cooler and on your knees."

"Please, mister, give us a chance," I pleaded. "I'll sell my business. You can have everything. Go, take whatever is in the cash register."

"Sell your business? In this economy?" he laughed; the gun pointed straight at the front of my chest. Hurricane Katrina had wiped us all out.

"Please, I beg you, don't kill Julie. This isn't her fault." Ray was crying. "I'll work twenty-four hours a day for you guys. Please don't do this!"

"We have our orders, Ray, we gotta get this over with. Besides that, she's a witness." It was too late. There was nothing that could be done now.

A fear seized me at that moment that literally sucked the breath out of me. I was going to die for something I had nothing to do with. As I walked toward the cooler on legs that felt like rope, I looked around the room at the photos of my mom and dad taken with happy and satisfied customers, a testimony to the love that had filled this business. I thought back to the memories we had made over the years, culminating with my wedding to Bobby in the side yard many years ago. Now, the ghosts of us all would fill these walls.

As I knelt down on my knees, my entire body was shaking as I realized these were my last moments on earth. I ripped the locket from my neck that contained the photo of my son and his family. I looked at my granddaughters' beautiful faces one last time and began to pray the Lord's Prayer. The last thing I heard as I was uttering, "thy kingdom come, thy will be done, on earth…" was the deafening roar of the 9-millimeter that would catapult me from this world to my eternal home.

What happened next involved the most exhilarating ride I had ever experienced. I was flying through a tunnel that was completely surrounded by flashing, almost psychedelic lights. It was as if I were inside a kaleidoscope, safely tumbling like a colorful rock. The rush was unexplainable. I felt infused by exquisite music, and I could hear the beckoning call of my parents' and my husband's voices. Rather than feeling terrified, I felt intense joy and anticipation, similar to the birth of my son and my grandchildren. I could see a light up ahead that seemed to burn with the intensity of a thousand suns. It was heaven and I knew I would soon pass into its glory.

1

Julie Enters Heaven

". . . as it is in heaven" I heard myself say as my exhilarating tunnel experience came to an end. I had landed on what felt like a large table covered in velvet.

I had passed from my former life to a new one, and I couldn't open my eyes. The brightness was too much for me.

I knew instantly that I was in heaven and "the peace that passes all understanding," the peace that I had always heard about throughout my life was now a part of me. The instant calming effect I experienced was worth the amazing ride I had taken to get here.

"Have no fear, Julie. Open your eyes . . . slowly." It was a commanding yet soothing voice that had to come from an angel and it conveyed strength, comfort, and assurance. I felt I had heard it before.

Once I timidly opened my eyes, I gazed upon the most exquisite creature I had ever seen standing before me. Its shimmering presence dominated my sight, and I held my breath for almost as long as I had when I told my parents I was leaving college to go live in a commune. I was speechless with excitement and incredulity.

This angel had to be at least ten feet tall and wore a robe of fine-spun gold, encrusted with gems including sapphires, emeralds, diamonds, and rubies. His translucent skin was milky white, and his long, white hair hung down his back, flecks of gold sparkling throughout it. I saw kind, pale blue eyes like those of my father gazing back at me, and I was happy to be in the presence of such a beautiful being. There were constant waves of golden light emanating from him, and I could not tear my eyes away from such beauty. Truly, everything else within sight of him paled to his glory.

Once I slowly sat up and found my voice, I grasped my chest and said, "Wow, now that was a ride! And you, sir, are magnificent; however, had I seen you on earth, I most certainly would have fainted. Please tell me I'm in heaven and you're an angel, or else I'm having a very strange day."

A hearty laugh issued from his mouth, and with eyes that already knew me, he said, "Julie, I am Wisdom, your guardian angel. And, yes, you are now in heaven."

At the mention of that name, a huge grin spread across my face and all I could say again was "Wow!" I knew why something about him had felt familiar, and I felt immense love and tenderness for the guardian angel that had protected me forever. While in prayer, I would sometimes feel his presence, and a time or two, I swear I felt the flutter of feathers.

"Wisdom," I said with great fondness while checking the back of my head to see if it was still there, and I felt thankful when I realized it was. "I don't know how to thank you for what you've done for me. I know I put you through the wringer a few times."

He nodded his head and replied, "Yes, indeed, but thankfully we will have all of eternity to catch up. By the way, you have no idea yet what interesting is. On earth, you only get a taste of it. Here, you will learn more than you've ever imagined. Oh yes, and since the shooting in your pizza shop, the back of your head is back in place, as well as the eyeball, and good as new. So, how are you feeling, Julie?"

"How am I feeling?" I laughed. "Well, as you know, I have just been on the ride of a lifetime! As I was passing from my earthly existence, I heard my life's story being played inside my head from the time I heard the sound of the gunshot until I arrived here.

"The physical sensation I was feeling during the great ride was as if someone had poured melted honey all over my body, totally relaxing me, yet I was being pushed to a heightened revelation. At the same time, I felt myself being pulled to a radiant light that seemed to burn with the intensity of a thousand suns. I was totally infused with spiritual and soulful music I had enjoyed during my lifetime while flashes of color turned and twisted and darted all around me."

"Actually, those were welcoming angels, sent by the Father, to guide you safely home," Wisdom commented while I caught my breath, thankful I was still seated.

"I could hear my beloved husband and parents' voices calling to me, 'Julie, Julie, come home. We can't wait to see you. We're waiting. We love you.'"

My grandparents, uncles and aunts, and other family members and friends also beckoned to me, and I knew something incredible was going to happen. It'd been so long since I'd seen them in person, and I had wondered with much sadness at times if I would ever be a part of their lives again. I was overcome with joy at the thought that soon I would see those who had been such a wonderful part of my life's journey.

"Now that I'm here, I thought I would feel incredible sadness at leaving my family and friends on earth, but for some reason, I cannot for the life of me conjure up any bad feelings. I feel no regrets, no apprehensions, no sorrow or pain. It's as if those emo-

5

tions never existed. What I am feeling is even more love for them. I know my prayers here can do even more for them now."

"And, you won't have those feelings anymore, Julie. Heaven removes all bad thoughts and feelings the moment you arrive. These are immediately replaced with complete joy and utter contentment. You may equate it to some of the happiest days of your life, such as your wedding day, or the births of Bobby Jr., and the birth of your granddaughters, only it's yours for an eternity."

I recalled the scripture in Revelation that says,

God will wipe every tear from their eyes. Death will be no more; mourning and crying and pain will be no more, for the first things have passed away. It was all true.

As Wisdom helped me off the table, he said, "I have been a part of your life from your conception. As your guardian angel, sent from God, it has been both my duty and pleasure to protect you, guide you, and help you through life's harsh times. It was I who covered you with my wings at times when you were scared and dismayed and too tired to go on."

"I knew you were there; I could feel it. Wisdom, I am so glad to meet you."

"Here, take my hand, and let's begin your new journey in heaven."

Before we left the building I had arrived in and knowing that I was a curious sort, Wisdom encouraged me to look around. The cavernous room was pure white and had the consistency of warm velvet. It was comforting.

Several hundred white marble tables were scattered around the room exactly like the one I had found myself on when I arrived. Every few minutes humans of all backgrounds and ages appeared on these tables, and they were immediately assisted by angels like Wisdom.

Beautiful murals surrounded the room and stories of the Bible were presented with actual moving parts and full-sized live characters. Four walls portrayed different significant biblical events: Moses' parting of the Red Sea; David vs. Goliath; Shadrach, Meshach and Abednego in the fiery furnace; and Daniel in the lions' den. I was drawn to the intensity of all of those historic events.

My guardian angel then spoke. "Julie, now that you have arrived, our next stop is the Pearly Gates." As I looked at him in amazement, he grinned and asked, "Why does this always bring that look? Yes, Julie, there are Pearly Gates and Saint Peter will be there to hopefully (and here he crossed his fingers) locate your name in the Lamb's Book of Life and welcome you home."

"Wisdom, you ARE kidding, I'm in there, right?" I pleaded, and he just laughed. His smile was dazzling, and I again felt the sweet spirit of this splendid and kindred angel.

Now I was starting to feel a bit giddy, and I felt like dancing a jig. Wisdom laughed and said, "Dance, Julie, dance!" And dance I did, thankful that one of the best parts about me still remained the same.

2

The Pearly Gates

As we were leaving the building, I started taking inventory of the new me. Gone was my pizza outfit that I had died in, and it was replaced with what appeared to be a stretchy body suit made of the finest golden silk I had ever seen, covering me from my neck down to my ankles.

I was still the same height, but I had lost quite a bit of weight in the process and that suited me just fine as it had always been my lifelong quest to do so.

"Gee, this must really be heaven," I said, approving of the new me. Breasts were non-existent, and I saw no hair anywhere other than on my head. Also missing were the liver spots on my hands and scars I had carried since childhood. I wasn't even aware of a heartbeat or sweat upon my brow. It was as if I was just existing without worry, stress, or conflict.

There was no more concern about my weight, my thinning hair, and the fact that men's admiring glances no longer came my way. Gone was the dread I had experienced after losing Bobby, my husband and soul mate, to a ravaging disease and worrying about how to function in that world without him. I would no longer face fear, betrayal, or rejection, three things which in and of themselves have derailed many a life's ambition.

Just the process of getting here had changed my life in a heartbeat, and I was reveling in it and thankful to be a part of it.

Shoes were not needed as there was a constant comfortably

warm temperature and a smooth golden surface to walk on. In every direction, I could hear heavenly music and would be hard-pressed even to explain how it sounded. It seemed to be a blend of all the beautiful scripture songs I had memorized over the years, but which were now presented in such full and perfect harmony. *A choir of angels?* I wondered.

Curious to see if my face had remained the same, I asked Wisdom where I might find a mirror. Immediately, there was one in my hand. This was no ordinary mirror, either, as the back side was covered with sapphires and diamonds, two of my favorite gems.

The face that looked back at me was definitely mine but missing the wrinkles and lines that my age had dictated. Blue, sparkly eyes stared at me with delight, and straight, shiny, silver hair hung to my shoulders.

"Not too shabby, huh, Wisdom?" I asked, still studying my reflection.

He replied, "You are still the same person you have always been, just a little touched-up by the Master."

"Heaven and I are most definitely going to get along," I stated, as I marveled at my much appreciated regeneration.

"You know, Julie, God is not as concerned with the outward appearance as He is with a person's heart. Your heart is pure, and He loves that about you.

"Also, because God is a strong believer in order, there is a process that all must go through in heaven. There are several stages, each with more and more glory that you will experience before you enter into the ultimate reward God reserves for His cherished chosen, those who have devotedly served Him.

"Just as on earth, here in heaven, He still gives you the free will to choose. One may wish to experience all the glory that heaven offers, while another finds a comfort zone at a different level. Considering He made us all unique, He allows you to be who you are; you're just a more improved version.

"There is only one Judgment Day and once you are through it, all the pain and hurt that you have suffered is tossed away. Those who earnestly continue to seek Him will reap the greatest rewards. As has always been and shall always be, I will be there with you through each stage." This inspiring creature filled my soul with hope.

As we walked along inhaling exotic fragrances and witnessing a rainbow of colors so tangible, they almost resembled a Thomas Kinkade painting, I reminisced momentarily about my past and those responsible for helping me get here.

My parents, Antonio and Alejandra, had grown up in the old country, breathing in fresh salt air at the Gulf of Palermo in the Tyrrhenian Sea surrounding the island of Sicily. Their parents had chosen to settle in Palermo because of its rich history, arts, music, culture, architecture, and, naturally, its reputation for exquisite food.

My grandparents were not alone in this decision as their best friends, another married couple, joined them and settled there as well. They all grew up together and were extremely close. The two couples staked their future in the rich fertile soil that had been formed from volcanic eruptions over several centuries. Together they built a very successful pizza business in Palermo until the war changed everything, and they were forced to emigrate to America.

It was a natural progression that my mother would eventually marry her best male friend of a lifetime as they had been as close as their parents, caring for one another from birth, and there had never been a doubt in anyone's mind that the two would make that commitment.

I was the firstborn, arriving in the great southern city of New Orleans on a hot, sultry evening in 1943 in a small hospital in St. Bernard Parish. My birth was greeted by my ecstatic father and my naive mother, who had been deflowered by him nine months earlier in the back seat of his 1940 candy-apple-red Oldsmobile coupe.

Though too young to marry by American standards—he was only twenty, and she eighteen—they were madly in love, and with the knowledge of my impending appearance, a justice of the peace had already sealed their lives together in matrimony five months earlier, making my birth a blessed event rather than a shameful result of reckless passion.

In true Italian fashion, five more siblings followed in rapid sequence, making our small, three-bedroom, wood-frame house seem even smaller.

My three brothers shared one large bedroom wallpapered in vintage airplanes and packed with boy clutter. Completed model planes and cars were displayed with pride around the room, a testimony to time spent between sons and their father.

We three sisters were all about dolls and having tea parties, and we loved dressing up like grownups.

At night, the last things we kids saw before we prayed and closed our eyes were the glow-in-the-dark constellations and stars our parents had placed on our ceilings to remind us of God's big universe and how small each of us really is.

Although my father had inherited his pizza parlor from his parents, we were not considered rich, yet we never thought of ourselves as poor. As a neighborhood made up primarily of Italian businesspeople and retirees who had fled Italy during the Second World War, we were all in the same shaky, socio-economic boat together.

Wisdom soon brought me back to heaven. "Come, Julie, let us go through your first stage. I believe you will be more than pleased."

He then took my hand in his, and I again felt the warmth of its softness. You cannot imagine how incredible it was to be actually touched by an angel.

I was led down a heavily foliaged golden path toward an enormous sparkling lake, teeming with a variety of fish swimming in crystal clear, aqua blue water. Tall, stately blue herons and pink flamingos, most standing on one leg, peacefully inhabited their spaces, content with dipping their beaks into the water in search of small fish. Wide-winged, long-billed pelicans and flocks of seagulls effortlessly flew overhead, diving occasionally to feed in the shallow waters that flowed over flat rocks covered with moss near the shore.

Wisdom led me to the lake and had me lie down on a solid walnut beach style recliner with thick cushions close to the water's edge and situated under a towering southern magnolia evergreen tree.

"Relax, Julie, take some time and enjoy what He has created just for you," he encouraged. With arms folded and eyes alert, he stood closely by.

I briefly wondered if this was part of a settling down period after one enters heaven. I mean, after all, I was still a little stunned considering that ride through the tunnel, meeting a 10-foot-tall angel, and everything else I had already encountered. Nothing I had ever read or heard about had prepared me for what I had just experienced. How could I even anticipate what was coming next?

I then closed my eyes, leaned back and breathed in the lake's serenity and calming breezes, letting its intoxicating magic overtake me. Water had always fueled my soul, proving to be an antidote for whatever ailed me.

After Bobby died, I spent occasional evenings sitting alone on a park bench at the Riverfront in New Orleans, gazing out over the Mississippi River, wondering where the ships and boats that navigated her waters were headed. I could see lights twinkling over on the West Bank, and I often thought of those unique people who speak like someone from the Bronx.

I started thinking of how much I love the instrumental "Breath of God" by Saggio, a gifted, self-taught flute player and healing artist who offers musical sacraments to a spiritually hungry planet and whose music had touched me over the years.

As soon as I thought of Saggio's music, it began playing and infusing me with its beauty. I thanked God right then. "Father God, I want to thank you for the privilege of being in a place that provides the most peaceful existence I have ever experienced."

As soon as I said that I felt His calming presence, and I was quickly surrounded by a multitude of angels, their brilliance almost blinding me. Before I could fathom what had just happened, what transpired next completely astounded me.

Once my eyes adjusted to the brightness, they were drawn to the large lake, where I was sensing a vibrant, building energy. The water in the middle began to boil with turbulence, taking on a life of its own. While gazing in open-mouthed wonder over the lake, I saw an immense cloud of water rise up out of the water and form into the shape of a huge, yet gentle face that was looking straight at me. The face immediately moved closer, a soft and fragrant wind blowing from its billowy face and hovering not far from mine.

I felt no fear, only powerful love and acceptance emanating from this pleasant figure who expressed happiness in the fact that I was here. Even without a textbook or Bible, I knew it was the Spirit of God and His one-of-a-kind welcome into His joyous kingdom which had been prepared for me.

Next, I felt enormous wings totally encompassing me, their multi-layered and colorful hues softly fluttering all around, products of those magnificent angels sent to comfort me. I felt totally protected for the first time in a long time. I knew that I would never have to worry about balancing a budget, or struggling to keep healthy, paying my bills, or keeping my employees happy. I wouldn't have to be the strong one who kept the business running and watched out for the family anymore. This was the beginning of a whole new life without constraints or pressure.

Almost as soon as this all transpired, it was over—the lake settled back down and the angels disappeared, but I knew I would feel His power for some time.

"That was a powerful encounter, Julie," Wisdom stated.

"Yes, that was some welcome from the Holy Spirit," I agreed. I felt as if I were glowing like a 1000-watt lightbulb, and I probably was.

Wisdom had told me earlier that energy comes from the River of Life that flows throughout heaven from the throne of God Almighty. The air around me almost crackled with it. He also said that the closer one gets to the city of God, the more powerful the river is.

I checked out the area and I could see trees of every persuasion around the exterior of the lake: fruit trees, pecan and walnut trees, oak, maple, elm, and weeping willows with their graceful arcing branches hugging the shore as if bowing before a queen.

A massive garden was located adjacent to the lake and within eyesight, brimming with every imaginable full-bodied vegetable. Lettuce, tomatoes, cucumbers, squash, peas, onions, Brussels sprouts, and peppers, and items I hadn't ever seen, were growing there without any obvious attendant.

"Why the vegetable gardens and fruit trees? Do people eat here in heaven?" I asked Wisdom.

"Why yes, Julie, but usually as a means of celebrating, not for existing. I will explain more about that to you later. You require nothing here but to worship God—no food, no water, no sleep, no exercise; however, it is all available to you at any time.

"Heaven is such a beautiful place; you have to be introduced to it little by little or it would overwhelm you. This is just God's way of giving you a view of what you perceive as paradise. He knows that you loved gardening."

"I love putting my hands into the soil, planting seeds, then watching them grow into beautiful and nourishing plants. Funny thing, Wisdom, I used to say that my momma could plant a popsicle stick in the ground and it would flower. She was just that good!" We both laughed at that image.

My engaging guide and I didn't so much walk as we glided along the pathway, and I kept taking in all that surrounded us. Everywhere I looked, God's creations were blooming, bursting forth with abundance and sending out a fragrance that could certainly be described as heavenly.

I could see hundreds of others who were happily being assisted by angels after their transformation, chatting away with their new guides. I wondered if they were feeling as I did, comparing it to the way I used to feel anytime I returned home to visit my parents. I always knew I was in a safe harbor and glad to be there.

Wisdom informed me that I would have an opportunity to speak with others like me in the Garden of Tranquility, a place I would see after I passed through the Pearly Gates.

He continued explaining as we walked, "Julie, one is introduced to the glories of heaven as one can cope with them. It is similar to the growing process of brand-new Christians. Baby Christians are first fed the milk of the Gospel, then, over time, are fed the solid food, becoming mature Christians through Bible study, prayer, fellowship, and serving God and others."

"You're so right about that, Wisdom. You know, it just kind of dawned on me. I am actually walking in heaven and talking with an angel. Who would believe this on earth?" I still had a hard time believing it myself.

"I hope many would believe it, Julie; however, things that are not seen by the naked eye are sometimes a little more difficult to comprehend. That is why faith is so important."

As we neared the top of a hill, I could see the Pearly Gates. The two solid gold gates were enormous—about thirty feet wide and over one hundred feet tall. The two posts which held the gates were made of solid pearl, with an oversized pearl perched on top. The entire structure glowed.

Magnificent twelve-foot-tall cherubim angels were guarding both sides of its entrance, as no one would be allowed into the City of God without first confirming that his or her name was written in the Lamb's Book of Life.

These special angels were equipped with four multi-petaled silver wings and four faces (human, lion, bull, and eagle) which looked in every direction, their eyes intensely burning. These high-ranking messengers of God had guarded the garden of Eden prior to man's fall and also covered the mercy seat on the Ark of the Covenant with their wings. I was taken aback at first by their fierce intensity; they appeared diligent beyond duty.

"Wisdom, I never envisioned cherubim angels quite like this. For some reason, I thought they were chubby little angels that just flew around, playing harps."

"Some do," he laughingly replied, "but, believe me, they are not cherubim angels."

I quickly realized, much to my joy, that I had now gone from playing in the minor league to "The Show." I could not wait for what lay ahead in this new adventure.

A tall, wizened, weathered man with a long, white beard and hair flowing down his back was standing behind a golden pulpit with a huge, equally weathered book on it. A white robe with a gold sash adorned his body and his tall 6 foot frame confirmed what I knew from all those years of Bible study.

"St. Peter, The Rock, and Keeper of the Keys to Heaven," I said. I couldn't wait to speak with one of my favorite disciples who looked at me with a twinkle in his eye, grinned, and opened the massive gold-embossed book.

St. Peter ran his finger down page after page of the Lamb's Book of Life and then stopped, looked up at me, and, with exaggerated concern, he shrugged his shoulders, and said "I'm so sorry, Julie, I can't seem to find your name."

Upon hearing my sharp intake of breath and observing my

look of abject terror, he laughed and said, "Welcome to heaven, dear sister. You are now and forever home."

Needless to say, I felt extremely thankful and grateful that years of Christian service, love, and sacrifice, not to mention placing one's full life in Christ's hands, had paid off in such a wonderful way. However, had I been on earth, I most likely would have had thoughts of decking him.

I laughed in relief and said, "St. Peter, you had me going there. Thank goodness I can't have a heart attack up here. I did want you to know that you are without a doubt my favorite disciple, or, used to be," I finished with a grin.

"Come here, Julie," he said, and he hugged me, making me feel even more welcome. I was incredibly humbled by this gesture. "You are going to love heaven, believe me. No one can take anything away from you here; it's already earned. The more you wish to explore and learn God's plan, the more you will enjoy what He has prepared for you. So, be off on your new journey, and I will see you soon."

"So, three Hail Marys, and I'm good to go?" I asked him.

Both he and Wisdom were still laughing when we passed through those beautiful pearly gates.

3

Garden of Tranquility

Wisdom then led me through those magnificent golden gates encrusted with a plethora of bright, glowing gems, and we arrived at the garden of Tranquility.

At the entrance stood a pure, white alabaster, full-sized replica of a smiling Jesus, arms outstretched and designed to welcome new arrivals home. The statue glowed and pulsated inside, radiating a bright light outward. It was as if a heart were really beating inside, and I had little doubt it probably was.

All dressed like me, other heavenly beings of different nationalities and ages were standing nearby with guardian angels and gazing as well. The collective looks on our faces suggested none of us had ever seen anything quite like this work of art. I felt an unusual comfort among them, mindful that we were all at the same point here.

I was the first to speak. "How beautiful our Savior is!"

"Yes, and everything surrounding Him, as well," Wisdom replied.

The details of this perfectly crafted statue helped me appreciate the creativity of the one and only true Designer of the universe. I looked forward to the moment I would see Him face to face, with excitement now building within me. So far everything I had encountered in my journey through this new world had been perfectly crafted just as the statue. Heaven was without mistakes and, as Wisdom had pointed out, was designed by God Himself from within the Holy of Holies.

Wisdom took my hand in his, and I gasped aloud when I saw what lay beyond the entrance. This was a flora world like nothing I had ever experienced. No amount of imagination on earth could have created the plenitude of vibrant foliage that seemed to fill every inch of garden space. I could feel the garden's enchantment envelop me as soon as I stepped down the cobblestone path.

As a young girl I had been fascinated by the biblical account of the garden of Eden and its Tree of Knowledge of Good and Evil. How could Adam and Eve sin against God in such a perfect place I had wondered, especially being tempted by Satan in the form of a lowly snake? Perhaps it had been God's gift of our free will that eventually did us all in.

Now I was introduced to its heavenly counterpart, a place bursting with fragrant flowers and plants and fruit trees laden with apples, bananas, figs, coconuts, blueberries and cherries, pears, kiwi, lychees, and many other unidentifiable fruits. There was no spoiled or soured fruit lying on the ground—every piece was unique and without blemish. *Again, this is evidence of a perfect world*, I thought.

"Wisdom, if I weren't so excited to see what heaven is all about, I just might enjoy hanging out here for the duration," I stated, a smile gracing my lips.

"I had considered that, Julie," he replied, "knowing how much you enjoyed time in your own garden."

Melodic harp music and the bubbling of numerous fountains created even more peace and tranquility as we walked along. I felt myself begin to understand the purpose of heaven and its peace that knows no limits. Along our winding path I could see that every species of flower was present with a multitude of roses, lilies, buttercups, petunias, daisies, daffodils, irises, pansies, orchids, and hundreds more that I cannot take the time to name. Sunflowers as high as six-feet tall grew everywhere, stretching their happy faces toward the sky.

Throughout the garden, fountains of every size bubbled over with pure water, and at the far end of the garden, a 300-foot waterfall cascaded down into another dazzling pool filled with an interesting array of oversized koi and water lilies. A number of large frogs croaked in the distance, and bees flew by, amazing me still with their ability to fly.

Colorful butterflies and hummingbirds fluttered around blooms bursting with nectar, drinking their fill. Doves, cardinals, blue jays, and red robins flitted above, occasionally landing in one of the groupings of large and healthy trees.

Golden gazebos trimmed in soothing pastel colors were located all around the massive garden and contained oversized and comfortable cushioned chairs. I could see small groups of people talking quietly among themselves in these gazebos and many more transformed beings like me were constantly arriving through the entrance. Relaxing harp music was played by cheerful, small angels, and it emanated throughout, allowing the groups to speak with little effort.

"This is where you will meet and get to know others who have just arrived. I know you will find their life's experiences very interesting, Julie. This will be the place for you to settle in and grow accustomed to your new surroundings. There is a table over there with fresh fruit, juice, and water if you wish to partake.

"Next, you will enter into the second phase of your acclimation after we sail over the Sea of Reconciliation to the Other Side. This is one of the most important phases, but first you will meet other members of your group."

I followed Wisdom to one of the gazebos, and he instructed me to take a seat where others would join me, which they soon did. I was relieved actually to see regular folks like me, not that I expected someone with an eye in the middle of their forehead. I couldn't wait to hear their stories.

I also hoped that the Other Side was what I thought it to be—a place where I would see my loved ones who had come here before me. Just the thought of touching and hugging my husband, mother, and father again was heartwarming and provided me with incredible contentment.

Our group was made up of five of us, and although our dressed bodies were exactly the same, our individuality would soon be evident.

The first to introduce himself was a tall, handsome black man who was well over six feet and carried a large body frame. He certainly commanded one's attention. Had he not had kind eyes, he might have looked a bit foreboding. I wondered if he had ever played football.

"Hello, everyone, I'm Tiny."

We all laughed at how ridiculous the name was for such a large man. One of the females we had yet to meet burst out with, "Boy they grow 'em big in your part of the country. Geez, Louise."

"I know, I get that a lot," he laughed. "Anyway, I have to say this. The trip through that tunnel was amazing. I'm still pretty much in total shock." We all nodded in agreement.

"Although I left my family prematurely, I'm thankful to be

here and ready to embrace this new life. I'm also looking forward to getting to know you all better," he finished.

Next was a young, striking woman with thick, red hair down to her waist; she looked to be in her late twenties. Her skin was interestingly pale and almost delicate. Her fingers were so long and slender, I wondered if she might be a musician. When she smiled, you saw not only a beautiful smile, but also a certain grace for one so young.

"Hi, I'm Abbie. Looks like I got here a little prematurely too since I'm only twenty-seven, but I am thrilled to be here myself, for soon I will see my darling husband, Andy. I truly am thankful that I have been spared some hard earthly experiences, and I can't wait to hear what you all have to say."

"The name's Sophia," we heard next, "and I have to tell you, I am just a little shocked to be here. I'm a Messianic Jew, which is good, 'cause, hey, I'm here. But, sheesh, the stuff I've done. And, Tiny, I'm with you on that tunnel. Best ride I've ever been on!" Sophia's expressive face had us all laughing. "Anyway, nice to meet you guys. I guess we'll all be hanging out together, huh?"

"Looks that way," I commented. Sophia was short with curly brown hair and was probably in her fifties. She had a strong personality and I imagined she would regale us with some interesting stories.

"I am Rashid. I am the miracle. When you hear my story, you will be very surprised that God allowed me to come here. Also, I am understanding what you are saying in your language, yet I never learned it because I am from Pakistan, and I speak Pushti. Heaven is quite interesting already, if I do say so myself. I am happy to be with you all." When he bowed from the waist, we bowed back, not entirely sure what to do.

I figured the black-haired Middle Easterner of average height to be around Abbie's age, and I liked him already as he had one of the most compassionate faces I had ever seen.

It was my turn.

"My name is Julie. I have to say, on earth, we would be considered an odd lot but here, everything flows with ease, and I love that there's no judgment or pre-conceived notions. We are all now a part of the family of God.

"Abbie, I too look forward to seeing my husband, Bobby, and most certainly my parents. I will enjoy exploring this beautiful new world with you all."

We were starting to forge a bond that would only increase over time.

Wisdom then spoke. "I will be leaving you for a while to help others. For now, get to know one another and eventually you will all be allowed to share your life's story. Just remember, we are here for an eternity, so relax and enjoy your time together."

I was again reminded that there are no clocks, watches, timetables, schedules, quotas to meet, irrational bosses, or anything that made us all so stressed on earth. I had never known anything like this in my life before. I was thankful that everything in heaven operates in total balance and peace.

Conversation and laughter for the five of us was effortless, and we all shared the thrills of the phenomenal trip through the tunnel to get here, each of us with a little different tale.

I was still amazed that we all understood Rashid as his Pakistani background did not include speaking English. I could not wait to hear how others had lived their lives and what had happened that made them reach out to Jesus. As a social worker, I had always wanted to know the reasons people behaved the way they did, and this was right up my alley.

"Who is going to share their story first?" Tiny asked.

Rashid immediately spoke up. "Me, please let me go first. I have a story you will not believe."

"Go right ahead," Abbie encouraged him. "We can't wait to hear it."

We all voiced our agreement and then sat back in our comfortable chairs, and with the beauty of God's garden surrounding us, listened with open and unhurried hearts.

4

Early Life in the Mountains of Pakistan

And so Rashid smiled and began his story as soon as everyone was settled ...

I grew up in a small village outside Chaman, a small, mountainous town in Pakistan, right at the border of Afghanistan. Chaman is an important trade route in the Balochistan region between my country and Karachi, as well as a major supply route for NATO forces in Afghanistan.

I was the oldest of seven children, and my family was very poor. I was named after a famous Taliban soldier my father admired, and from a very young age, much was expected from me with regard to fighting for the cause of Islam.

Our one-story baked mud house was located on the side of a high, rocky hill with an unobstructed view of tall, snow-covered mountains and a sandy, windswept valley that stretched as far as the eye could see.

Our primary source of food came from the goats we raised and a few vegetables (turnips, potatoes, onions, radishes, peas, tomatoes, lentils, and herbs), feebly grown in the small garden behind our house. We also had no electricity or running water, counting on lanterns and a stream nearby to supply us with both.

The region we lived in was quite mountainous and contained very little fertile soil, but my mother, Latifa, was quite inventive and would cook typical Pakistani dishes on her *bok-*

hari, a small stove—dishes such as *Quabelli*, a rice dish with nuts, orange peelings, raisins, and boiled meat, and *Manto* which was a meat with sour cream and spices cooked inside the dough she had kneaded and prepared.

We were all quite healthy and maintained a close bond with our mother that was never present with our father. We all slept together on a large mat, and in the summer, it would be quite uncomfortable as we had no windows through which the breezes could blow. Thankfully because we were in the mountains, our temperatures didn't reach the one-hundred-twenty plus heat that existed on the flatlands during the summer season. Plus, one grew accustomed to it over time.

Quite honestly, I greatly feared Abdul, my father, as his temper was well-known among everyone in our village. He was an imposing figure at over six feet four inches tall, he was strong as a bull, and the most intimidating human I ever met.

I never understood how my parents had so many children as I never saw kindness pass between them, and he was insufferably hard on her, as was the custom with the men of our tribe. Their marriage had been arranged by both sets of parents. Latifa had never even met Abdul until their wedding day.

It is believed by us Pashtons that the more children a man has, the more he is admired by other Muslims. Whether he could care for them or not was something of another matter.

My mother always wore the stifling hot burqa when she was out in public, but she was allowed to be unencumbered when she was in our home, preparing our meals and taking care of the younger children with her long, black hair flowing down her back. More than once, I heard her sobs after she had been beaten by my father.

"You are lazy!" he screamed. "You need to do more for your sons. You spend all day worrying over your daughters, and they are as worthless as you!"

"Mother," I said to her after he stormed out of our hut, "why do you allow him to do that to you? How can I help you?"

"Please, we cannot speak of this now. Go to sleep," she pleaded with me, and I did as she wished.

Later I would realize that he was trying to make an example out of her to develop the soldier in me and toughen me up. Upon hearing her cries, I would clench my fists and cry into the ground, knowing I could not help her even if I wanted to.

I learned at a very early age that discrimination between the sexes in our culture is tolerated—even admired. When I asked my mother why, she replied, "Young girls and women are looked down on and chosen by arrangement only for our ability to care for our husband and to birth sons. Daughters are barely tolerated and mostly ignored. It is our culture. We have no choice."

"I find this custom repulsive," I had replied, barely able to control my voice.

"Then do something about it," she said, then hurriedly walked away, almost like a mouse scurrying back to its hole. I would do anything to protect my three sisters from the same fate our mother suffered.

"My son," she said one evening after the children were asleep, "you know you are the only loving and caring father these children will ever have. I know this is a heavy burden for one so young to carry, but you are tried and true, and they love you."

I now felt the pressure, but it was a good kind, and I felt completely needed.

We all looked forward to our father's forays with his band of soldiers when he would be gone for weeks at a time. I began training Omar, my younger brother, to become the head of the house so that he could take over when my mandatory military training began. He was only twelve and already was absorbing everything I taught him, a fact that gave me a little more peace about leaving home for military duty in the future.

"So, Omar, do you have any doubts about handling things when I am gone?" I arrogantly asked, goading him a little.

"The only doubts I have, my brother, have to do with the abilities of my teacher," he kiddingly replied, while throwing a fake punch at my stomach. He was a good little brother.

Omar's training included instructions on how to load, shoot, and clean a rifle; how to protect the home from invaders of both the two-legged and four-legged type; and how to tend to the goats and procure oil for the lanterns. I also taught him how to slaughter, skin, cook, and prepare goat and lamb in several variations.

During my last year of freedom before conscription, I was occasionally taken by my father to the tribal meetings, or *Jirga*, where important decisions were made by the tribal leaders.

In these meetings, as we drank *dood-patee*, stories of previous wars and battles were shared with other warriors around the campfire. I found myself thinking on more than one occasion that maybe these were just embellishments meant to impress others participating in the cause. I noticed that the dark brown eyes of those sharing would take on an almost maniacal shine to them as if killing hordes of innocent individuals was as natural as performing their daily prayers to Allah.

The one thing that did impress me was the camaraderie shared by everyone who had fought in the jihad. These were definitely a different breed of men, and their intentions, though misguided, were powerful.

I, however, quickly tired of their bravado and boasts of killings. I wondered why we couldn't all just live in peace and harmony and not worry about the other religions of the world. Had I expressed my feelings, however, I would have been severely punished as one did not judge the actions of the elders, and I did not wish to incur my father's fiery wrath. I had no choice in the matter as I knew he would somehow blame my mother for my weaknesses, and she couldn't take much more of his rantings and punishment.

I was raised a devout Muslim and, as one, I faced Mecca five times a day, donned my *qualie*, kneeled on my *jahnamaz*, and prayed to Muhammad, observing *Kalima*, the Muslim profession of faith to Allah, the one true god in our minds. This, of course, was after we had performed our absolutions and cleansed our bodies and minds of any impurities. I also held my *tesbah* (prayer beads) while praying, as was our custom.

I had never known any other god but Allah, having been taught how to worship him from the time I was old enough to understand. My family believed that one must believe in a higher being in order to go to heaven, and I just went along with them. It wasn't that hard to do considering my father would not have tolerated abstinence from my prayers anyway.

5

The Taliban Years

Rashid continued his story after a few of them adjusted their seats . . .

As soon as I reached fifteen years of age, I received the call to fight for the Taliban, delivered through my father. It was a day I had dreaded since I was a young boy. I did not share their enthusiasm to annihilate every infidel in the world, as I was more interested in peace than war, a common goal both my mother and I shared.

I remember the pain in my mother's eyes as she hugged me goodbye before we left for the secret new recruits training camp in South Waziristan, Afghanistan. I wondered if I would ever see her again, and the thought was so horrifying, I quickly put it out of my head. Omar was now the designated protector of our family in my absence, and he was proud to take my place. I felt as if I were deserting those who needed me, and I hated my father even more.

Due to the fact that no one in my family had ever received any schooling, we could not read or write. I only learned how to read the Koran later through the aid of the mullahs, those who teach and call the people to prayer and jihad. There would be no way to communicate with my family while I was away, and I had no way of knowing just how long that would be.

It was a dark day for me, but I never let my father know

my true feelings as we walked away. He saw that I never looked back, and it might have impressed him.

"What are you thinking, Rashid?" he asked. "You know you are a man now, and it is your time to serve. You must be strong, for our people do not tolerate weakness."

All I could think was, *He knows nothing about me. He doesn't realize I ran the entire household while he was gone for weeks at a time. If that doesn't convey strength, then what does?*

However, what I said was, "I will not disappoint you, Father. I have much to learn, but I will be dedicated." It was now just him and me, and I prayed we wouldn't kill one another. I had to keep the peace, and I would make it a point to stay out of his way, just like I always had.

I was both in fear and awe of the Taliban leaders at first. Their passion was inescapable, yet I felt that I could never kill innocent people, especially over religion. I was a member of the Pashtons, however, a highly regarded group of Sunni Muslim warriors who had been fighting for centuries. I had to do what was expected of me for *Pashtonwali* (honor) is above everything in the tribe, and to bring shame on my father would also dishonor my mother.

Days were long and hard, and sometimes the heat was unbearable. In the training camp I was taught how to load artillery batteries, carry ammunition, and infiltrate military installations. I later became proficient with the mighty Kalashnikov, an AK-47 assault rifle mass-produced and supplied by our new friends, the Chinese.

I also trained to load and shoot a rocket-propelled grenade launcher. The first time I ever operated one, I found myself thrown flat on my back just from its sheer energy, an incident that brought laughter from the older soldiers and anger from my father.

"Hey, Rashid," one of the soldiers called out, "Whose side are you on, anyway?"

I could feel my cheeks burning from embarrassment as others joined in with laughter while I jumped up and shook off the dirt from my clothing.

I could already feel the backside of my father's hand that would most probably land on my face before I turned in for the night. I wished he would just learn to relax a little more and find something else in life that would bring him as much pleasure as war did.

In addition to strapping a bandolier of bullets across my chest, I now wore fatigue pants and matching jacket when fighting or the simple off-white pajama-like clothing of the *jamay* and a black turban, a symbol of the Taliban and one that Muhammad had worn. When not fighting, we wore little white caps called *pakols*.

Young men were not given the choice of whether or not to fight for to refuse meant certain death. Deserters were executed, and many times their bodies were left to decompose in sight of all other members of the group as a warning.

The *mullahs* also trained suicide bombers at our camp. I never desired to give my life in this way, but I respected the fact that these young men were providing for their families in the only way they knew how. Rich Arabs provide large sums of money to the families after a bomber's death, and they are honored forever as martyrs.

Those of us who regularly fought in jihad occasionally

received monetary payment, and we were provided food, clothing, and armaments while fighting. I found it ironic that the vast majority of the money that was used to purchase the latest and greatest in military supplies was funneled by American politicians to the Pakistanis who, in turn, supplied us with the weapons we used to kill and maim American soldiers. Although non-educated, I could figure out the stupidity of that plan for myself.

Part of our training involved complete indoctrination in the purpose of the Taliban. This group was developed and supported by Pakistan to fight against the Americans and NATO. The Taliban wished to create what Muhammad had done over 1000 years ago—a perfect, isolated Muslim world, involving man's search for purity, for God and eternal life or the hereafter, which included seventy-two virgins as a reward when he earned his way to heaven. The Taliban would kill anyone who got in their way, including other Muslims, a fact that greatly disturbed me since nowhere in the Koran were such actions sanctioned.

We studied the Koran, then memorized it, and this greatly pleased our superiors. I found myself at odds with their thirst for blood and carefully avoided getting involved in their hours-long plans of destroying everything non-Taliban. I began to question who I was and how I was going to survive this madness.

Occasionally, a Taliban soldier is allowed to go home for a period of rest, and I looked forward to doing so probably more than any other soldier. I very much enjoyed being with my family even though my mother was starting to get frail at this point, and I worried about her poor health. There was now no doctor in our small village as our only one had died of old age. Any younger, hopeful candidates were fighting with the Taliban or had escaped to cities far away from the fighting.

During my visits, I always stopped at a farmer's market on the way to pick up fresh vegetables and fruit for her and sweets for my brothers and sisters at another small store, luxuries she could ill afford and which I hoped would cheer her up a bit. I also purchased a lamb for slaughtering from a close friend and neighbor, trading part of my soldier's stipend for it.

Naturally I insisted on cooking, and my dear mother would let me pamper her in ways in which she was not accustomed. Her favorite meal was slow-cooked lamb over a wood fire, my special lamb curry, and fresh salad. Afterwards, I topped off the meal with *Gajar Ka Haleva* (carrots cooked in milk, then fried in butter).

On cloudless clear nights, we would find ourselves crowned with thousands of twinkling stars and in awe of the spectacle above us. So inspired, we would sit outside around our fire and sing beautiful songs of our country until the younger children grew sleepy and were put to bed. With no interruptions, Omar and my mother and I would have time alone to discuss things of importance.

I always began our discussions with, "Mother, I am concerned about your health and well-being." She was now so thin she seemed to be disappearing from my sight.

She replied, "Why, Rashid? I'm still living, and you know Omar is doing things right. After all, he was trained by the best. Please, don't worry," she would say, while gently patting my hand.

As I gazed into her tired eyes, I was saddened to see that so much of her sparkle had died, yet I knew that her heart was daily strengthened by the needs of her children.

We ended most evenings with Latifa gazing into the fire and praying for the souls of her children. With so few resources, she still managed to forge an unshakeable bond among all of us that would help us survive the hard days ahead.

6

Fila

After refreshments were passed out to us, Rashid continued his story . . .

It was during one of these trips home that I met Fila, a striking Afghan woman who was twenty years of age to my eighteen. Her aunt was hiding her in our village when she fled Kabul after witnessing the brutal atrocities inflicted by both the Mujahedeen and the Taliban against the Afghani women. She sought me out as a trusted friend for her niece after discussing it with my mother, and I gladly complied. Naturally, the aunt would supervise all meetings between us, as was our custom.

Over a period of time, Fila, this beautiful creature, started trusting me some, little by little opening up a Pandora's box that contained so much evil that even I, a Taliban soldier, was shocked and horrified to hear it. What made her tales even more compelling to me was the fact that, prior to joining the Taliban, I had never ventured beyond a few miles in any direction of my home.

Stories I had heard over the years around Taliban campfires paled in comparison to what Fila shared as, being located in Pakistan, we were a remote faction of the entire organization, receiving very little information about Kabul and its atrocities.

I would later understand why her parents chose this Afghan name for their daughter. It means "to love strength," and I knew of no woman stronger. I was totally taken with this tiny but spirited young woman with long, silky hair and large brown eyes like a doe. For the first time in my life, I fell in love, and Fila became my heroine.

Fila had shown great promise as a writer and journalist before being forced to leave her school during the Mujahedeen occupation. Armed now with only pencil and paper, she would painstakingly chronicle everything she witnessed throughout those years of war and the reign of terror to educate the world about the suffering of the Afghani women.

This is what she shared with me:

Our horrors in Kabul, Afghanistan, began in 1984 when the Mujahedeen and Russians went to war, and we suffered relentless shelling and attacks on our city. Entire innocent families would be wiped out by the 500-pound bombs that rained down on us at all hours of the day and night. We were not even safe in underground shelters as these weapons of destruction would find their way there. I would later learn that close to two million Afghans died during this time.

In 1989, the Russians left Afghanistan with a puppet regime in place under President Najibullah. The Mujahedeen, who were heavily funded by the United States, then swept in and took over. President Najibullah immediately went into hiding at the U.N. Embassy but was later captured, castrated, and cruelly hung in the Square with his brother.

The Mujahedeen were vicious, evil mercenaries intent on rape, brutal beheadings, and the torture of everyone not associated with their organization.

In 1995, the Taliban, an Islamic terrorist group, began to bomb Kabul, and government troops forced them back. However, it would be nine months later that the newly organized, heavily funded radicals would take over Kabul and things would change drastically overnight. It was the beginning of Sharia law and a relentless new form of terror, especially for females.

Women were immediately banned from work outside the home. This applied to teachers, engineers, and many professionals as well. Education for women was forbidden, and schools were shut down immediately.

This saddened my mother more than anything else as she and my father had always encouraged me to receive an education, fulfilling my dream of becoming a professional writer and journalist. Only boys were allowed to attend school and their total education involved studying and learning the Koran. All other information was deemed useless by the Taliban.

Only a few female doctors and nurses were allowed to continue to work in Kabul's hospitals, and they would quickly become overwhelmed. Women were no longer allowed to be treated by male doctors, and many died from a lack of medical care.

With no jobs available for women anymore, families began to face hunger, and fear became widespread and prevalent in the seized city. Because the streets were patrolled constantly by vicious and cruel soldiers, citizens were afraid to venture out even to find rations for their families. We all felt trapped and doomed.

Females could not walk freely in the streets and must

be accompanied by a *mahram* (a father, brother, or husband). Cosmetics, high heels, and laughter were prohibited, as well as brightly colored clothes and flared pants. At my age, this was a particularly difficult law for me as, being thoroughly enchanted with fashion, I had always dressed in the most current style.

Music, sports, international news reporting, and kite flying were prohibited. Taliban storm troopers burst into my father's twenty-two-year-old kite shop one day and smashed every kite in stock and then threw the cash register through the front plate glass window. My father was enraged, yet he could do nothing, for only the Taliban were allowed to have weapons and "he would have lost his life over a few kites" my mother would wisely point out later after he calmed down.

We now had no income except for funds my mother had quietly squirreled away for over twenty years. We were also lucky to have storage bins packed with carrots, onions, and potatoes, and a cistern on the roof filled with clean water. Apple trees in the backyard were bursting with ripening apples so we were set with provisions for the time being.

We dug our heels in as a family and started rationing our food and water and forming a plan of survival. As Afghans, we are proud people, and we would not desert our city. We would find a way to fight the enemy, but we would have to use our wits as we had very little else to fight with.

We felt the dragnet begin to tighten over the city as we were fighting an ignorant faction of people whose primary goal was to destroy every last one of us if they needed to, and we were ill-equipped to fight them.

One of their requirements that I despised the most was that I had to wear the full-length, uncomfortably hot burqa when outside the home. Every part of a female's body is covered in this heavy cloth, and only the eyes are seen through a small screen. One faced harsh whippings, beatings, and verbal abuse if any of us were not clothed in accordance with Taliban rules.

Women were even publicly whipped if their ankles were exposed, and adulteresses were stoned to death. I was dragged across the street by a Taliban soldier one day to witness one such death by stoning. Afterward, I lifted up my headdress and threw up on the officer's shoes, and he pushed me onto the ground in disgust. It was that day that I was thankful to have on the burqa for, had I not, this evil man would have seen the hatred burning through my eyes toward him.

As the Taliban's stranglehold on the people of Kabul became even more crushing over the years, my mother and father became extremely involved in the underground organization RAWA (Revolutionary Association of the Women of Afghanistan.) This group of dedicated and brave souls fought valiantly to assist the endangered women of Afghanistan, often at great danger to themselves and their families.

The group's tireless efforts included raising much-needed funds for school supplies used to secretly educate young girls and women in safe houses located away from the prying eyes of Taliban informants. Money was smuggled in through couriers who travelled to other countries, raising funds by sharing the plight of the women of Afghanistan. Pamphlets were also secretly distributed by male and female members throughout the country, encouraging despairing women not to lose hope.

As news of the group's efforts spread to the Taliban, public executions were increased to discourage Afghan men and women from bucking the new system, and a high bounty was placed on all RAWA members' heads.

I became involved in RAWA in spite of my parents' protests as I wanted to help change things as much as they did. I missed going to school and to parties. I yearned to fly kites once more from the roof of our home with my father, and to sing and run through the streets without a care in the world. It had been so long since we had experienced unbridled joy and freedom, and I was determined to give my life, if need be, to help bring our sane and happy world back to us.

I was used as a courier for members around town, hiding documents under my burqa. I didn't attract attention, as I appeared to be just a harmless young girl out for a walk with her brother.

I was just thankful to be doing anything rather than sitting around in a darkened house with nothing to do. I did all I could to increase the movement's membership and help in its fundraising efforts. It was at this time that I also began keeping a daily journal, even back-dating events that had happened leading up to that time.

With the Taliban's increased scrutiny and escalating violence over time, two horrific life-changing events happened to me in quick succession that necessitated my rapid, secret departure from my home in Kabul.

The first incident was when I was notified that Niki, my best friend for a lifetime, had jumped to her death from her parents' six-story balcony rather than face being raped by the five Taliban officers who had blatantly invaded their apartment. The parents would have been forced to witness their daughter's rape, and Niki could never have lived with that shame.

While still suffering extreme shock, I was notified later that same night that both my parents had been beheaded in the public square as a warning to others in RAWA. Taliban informants who had penetrated the RAWA organization had targeted my parents as leaders in the movement. The only satisfaction I had at all was the fact that my parents died as they had lived—passionately involved in their cause and together to the end. I was overcome with grief.

Without the protection of my family, I was now in grave danger. Our entire family had been put on the Taliban's hit list. I was never allowed to see my parents' bodies or to attend a service for them as close friends immediately smuggled me out of the country inside a grain container traveling into Pakistan. That is how I came to hide out here at my aunt's house. I knew my life would never be the same in Kabul.

It is my pledge that I will stay in hiding until I finish my expose´, then I will travel throughout Pakistan, the United States, and other nations to spread the truth about the Taliban and to avenge the deaths of my parents and best friend. I will also work nonstop on behalf of all who have needlessly perished at the hands of these despicable, heartless people who are so blinded to love that they know only hatred.

When Fila finished, she was trembling, and I reached for her tiny, smooth hands. The sad look in her eyes reminded me of the same look in my mother's eyes.

"Fila, don't worry, I will do whatever I can within the Taliban system to uncover information that might be helpful to you. We will work together to do what we can to help change and improve the situation for women in Afghanistan. You're not alone."

Obviously, my very existence as a Taliban soldier now sickened me even more, and I feared for her due to the fact that a local might reveal her hideout, and she would be taken back to Kabul to face her accusers. Her aunt's life would be in extreme danger as well if that happened.

Over the next few years, Fila, a fugitive from her beloved country, continued to write her story, and I continued to fight for a cause I had no use for. She became the bright spot in my life and made things a little easier to handle. However, as long as the war continued, I had no choice but to fight.

Our friendship blossomed, and I also enjoyed being a sounding board for her writings. Fila began also to teach me how to write simple sentences, which opened up a whole new world for me.

"Rashid," she commented one evening, "you are learning to write very quickly. Am I that good a teacher, or are you that smart?"

"Yes," I replied, and for a moment she looked puzzled, then she burst out laughing. I enjoyed making her laugh. "Fila, you know there is no good answer to that question."

I was proud of myself, and she was proud as well to be a part of my metamorphosis.

Death of a Soldier

The group took a break from the horrors of Rashid's story and gathered back together in a short while to hear more. Rashid continued:

In April 2009, we received word that my father had been killed in an intense firefight known as the Battle of Now Zad at Nawsad in the Helmund Province of South Afghanistan. Parts of his limbs were scattered around, the result of a direct hit by the bomb that blew up the second floor of the building in which he was located.

His identifiable remains were secured in a body bag and taken by fellow soldiers to our village for cleansing and burial. My mother had known this day would eventually come and had mentally prepared for it. She wasn't, however, prepared for how he was presented to her, and I was thankful to be there to provide moral and physical support.

Once family members cleansed Abdul's parts, they were shrouded in a *kafan*, a simple and modest plain white cotton cloth used to respect his dignity and privacy. For a few hours, several Taliban officers and soldiers filed through our small living area to pay their respects, and villagers came simply because he was one of their own. I thought it odd that no one seemed repulsed by the fact that only part of my father was actually lying there, later reasoning they were most likely accustomed to it.

We then gathered on our property at the burial site where my uncle placed my father's remains inside the grave that had been prepared. His body was placed on its right side, without a casket, and aligned perpendicular and facing Mecca.

After the service, the Muslims of our village gathered to offer their collective prayers for the forgiveness of my father and supplications for him and mankind, as was our custom.

Thankfully, I would be able to spend the next week at home to observe the three-day mourning period and to take care of family affairs. I would treasure the time with my mother and siblings, not knowing it would be the last time I would see them on earth.

I was also delighted that I could spend time with Fila again as I was enchanted and amazed at this young, strong woman who had stirred the budding manhood inside of me.

I had mixed feelings about my father's death, and I shared them with her one night.

"Fila, I am ashamed that I have not cried once since my father died. I tried but all I could muster up were memories of cursing, ridicule, and beatings by him. Secretly, I was happy he would no longer terrorize us. I feel my mother might have the same thoughts, although she has never voiced them. You know my mother has never known the love of a devoted husband. The only bright spot in her life has been her children and a few close female friends."

Fila reached for my hand, reminding me I was still in shock and not to worry about it.

Finally, with the blessings of Fila's aunt, and because she too had been in love once, the two of us were allowed to sit outside her dwelling for an hour or two at night. We were able to speak privately and did so in hushed tones. Fila's voice sounding like a scared little girl's.

"I think I'm suffering from survivor's guilt, Rashid," she confided. "Why was I spared? I'm also constantly fearful for others who were left behind. I can't sleep, and the worse thing is, I'm having a difficult time writing. I miss my family so much, I feel it might be consuming me. What am I to do?" she asked, with pleading eyes.

"Write! Fila, write!" I exclaimed, with a passion that revealed my heart. I believed in her; I treasured her.

I grabbed her arms, stood her up, pulled her to me, and held her with the neediness of one of love's newborns. "Take your guilt, pain, deep anger, and your fresh grief, and tell the world the truth. You are the voice of your people, Fila! You were saved for a reason."

We stood holding one another for what seemed like hours but was in truth only a few minutes. I found them to be the best few minutes—ever.

Looking up at me with a smile on her face, she replied, "Thank you, Rashid, for reminding me about that, and the promise I made to myself for my family. This will be revenge against those who have turned Afghanistan into a barbaric and savage country."

She looked to the skies, punched her fist into the air, and said, "I denounce you, Allah, for turning your back on your people. You let them kill my mother, my father, and my best friend. You destroyed everything I ever wanted, and you never heard our pleas. You do not exist, and you never will."

I was a little shocked at her outburst, but I too had harbored long-held doubts. With all she had been through, she had certainly earned a right to her opinion.

It was on the last night before I would return to my unit, and Fila and I were standing and holding hands, looking over the plains below us. We were both caught up in our own thoughts about my next day's deployment. No lights twinkled in the distance; however, a quarter-moon provided just enough light to illuminate her sad and downcast face. How I hated to leave her.

I looked at her with yearning burning inside of me, tilted her chin up so that her eyes met mine, and blurted out, "I love you, Fila. I have for a long time. Please wait for me; please say you'll be my wife." I then reached inside my pocket and presented her with a hand-hammered silver ring made in my village that perfectly fit the fourth finger on her left hand. She looked at it as if it were the first piece of jewelry she had ever owned, and I was sure it was.

Expelling her breath, she grabbed me, saying, "Oh, Rashid, yes, I want to be your wife. I'll wait as long as it takes. You are the love of my life." She was literally beaming.

We felt our hearts blaze with an even stronger love now, and we planned to marry once I was released from my military duty. Together, as man and wife, we would travel to America and begin the process of publishing and promoting Fila's eye-opening story. Our families were ecstatic, and we all privately celebrated the news of our engagement with a festive dinner and much joy.

When I returned to my unit, I found that a great many Taliban forces had been killed at the Now Zad battle where

Abdul had died. This victory by the U.S. Marines, or "The Great Satan," only served to rile up our forces even more. I watched as the Taliban stepped up its recruiting, stealing young boys from villages throughout Afghanistan and forcing them to the front lines where they were taught to destroy villages and burn houses.

I witnessed more massacres during this time than ever before, as village chieftains and *mullahs* tried to discourage this practice, doing all they could to protect eleven-year-old and twelve-year-old boys from conscription. In response, beheadings and rapes by soldiers were common, and innocent blood ran like water through the land. I was sickened by it and now began to doubt the Allah I had been forced to serve. How could a "loving" god condone so much misery?

8

Captured!

The group got up and stretched their limbs after Rashid's revelations. Soon they gathered back together, and Rashid continued his story.

The night that I was captured by the United States Army will be forever burned into my memory. Ten of us soldiers were out on night patrol in a mountainous area south of Kandahar, and I was the designated leader.

The moonless skies were as dark as black ink, and we had neither heard nor seen any of the enemy for quite some time. We started to let our guard down and relax a little; we soon discovered this was a big mistake.

As we came around a bend where the bush was extremely thick, we were immediately surrounded by American soldiers who seemed to rise up out of the sand like giant iguanas. Night vision goggles and M4s stared at us, and one of the soldiers shouted commands in Pashto, "Throw down your weapons and lie on the ground with your hands behind your head!" With no hope of escape, we immediately complied with their orders.

It was the first time I had seen the enemy up close, and I was impressed with the amount of gear each wore in such a hot climate. I had heard how professionally trained these soldiers are, and I wondered what would happen next. Would they execute us immediately or would they first torture us for information and then kill us? Perhaps they would force us to lead them to our base camp, something, quite frankly, I feared more than execution.

While prone, our hands were tied behind our backs with plastic ties, and hoods were placed over our heads. We were then herded into the back of a large military truck and driven for several hours to another location. We dared not speak among ourselves, as we had no idea what these men would do to us. All I knew was that all of a sudden, I was hungry, thirsty, and in need of relief for my bladder, but I kept my mouth shut. I could hear my fellow compatriots praying quietly to Allah to deliver them.

Yeah, good luck with that was all I could think.

Once we were unloaded, our blindfolds were removed, and we were escorted into a large tin building inside a military camp in the middle of the desert. We were then instructed to sit on the floor with our backs against the wall. Our temporary jail was a huge room filled with at least ten metal desks occupied by military men and women in light, khaki camouflage uniforms. Overhead fans only served to stir the dust that was prevalent everywhere.

There was a great deal of activity going on, phones ringing, people talking to one another, and others coming and going throughout the room. Along with color-coded, wall-sized maps of Afghanistan and Pakistan, a huge American flag was tacked on one wall along with a photo of the President of the United States. I had taken all of this in rather quickly as a Pashtun does not permit his gaze to last too long in another man's direction.

I realized what a rag-tag group the Taliban is when compared to this mighty army of professional soldiers. What keeps jihad alive are the loyal and fierce devotees it inspires to blindly carry out its destruction.

I had seen the consequences of a loveless religion in the rubble and remains of once-stately homes and buildings throughout Afghanistan. I suffered nightmares, haunted by dark, empty eyes that stared back inside heavy shapeless burqas, pleading for someone to make things right. The prayers of the suffering were going unanswered, and I could feel the loss of the souls of our two countries.

Maybe after I served time in an American jail, I would be able to return to Fila, and we could make things right. My thoughts were interrupted when one of the officers—a tall imposing figure who wore a beret—strode purposely into the room and asked, "Who is the leader of this group?"

I bowed my head, and he almost laughed when he saw it was someone who looked as young as me. I was soon jerked to my feet and led into another room where a translator was sitting and waiting to interrogate me.

True to the Pashtun culture, I kept my eyes averted from this man who was from my region, and I answered his questions as honestly and truthfully as I could.

The one time when I felt the American officer thought I was lying was when he asked me to point out the location of our training camp on a map of the region. I had felt his eyes boring into me throughout the interrogation, and I found it unsettling.

"We change them often, sir, as our *Maulavi* does not want the American satellites to locate us. I am sure they have already relocated the camp because we did not return as expected."

The look this officer gave me could have melted a glacier. Realizing I needed to do something quickly to redeem myself, I asked if I might point out our last known location. "Mr. Eyes of Ice" made note of it, then he turned away and instructed another soldier to take us all to a building that was heavily guarded. We were still alive!

We were then searched thoroughly, fed a bowl of rice and beans, and offered bottled water. I used a toilet for the very first time and marveled at its workings.

My fellow soldiers—these young men who had trusted me to keep them from harm—began plying me with questions: "When will the Taliban rescue us? Do they know we have been captured? Will we be hung and left to rot by our enemy?"

I replied, "Men, just say your prayers, and try and get some sleep. Right now, we are not going anywhere, and we are all more than exhausted. Have you not thanked Allah for keeping us alive?"

This brought negative comments from a number of them, which didn't surprise me. That night I slept better than I could remember, right there on the floor, feeling safe and secure for the first time in a long time.

The following day we were all assigned separate cells with a small cot, a toilet, and a wash basin with a bar of soap and a towel. We were then provided with an orange jumpsuit and slippers and ordered to put them on. It had been a while since I had felt this clean.

A small window with bars was our only connection with the outside world. Daily interrogation was performed on different members of our group without any torture tactics.

There was no need, as we supplied what limited information we had in the overall scope of things. We tried to explain that we were small cogs in a very large wheel.

As I had been the designated patrol leader, I was questioned constantly about different things: the size of our organization, names of the leaders, weapons suppliers, supply routes, training methods, the morale of the soldiers, and many other things. I felt safe in supplying anything they wished to know as I knew I would not be returning to the Taliban. In that small 10 x 10 cell, I felt more liberty than I had felt since joining the jihad. There would be no more blood on my hands.

Still, five times a day, all of us prisoners faced Mecca and, though without our customary religious accoutrements, we did what we Muslims have done for centuries no matter where we are—we prayed to Allah.

However, it now felt different as the god I had grown up with all of a sudden seemed quite remote and indifferent to my prayers. I began questioning my faith in him, now agreeing with Fila's courage and conviction to denounce a deity who clearly didn't deliver what he promised. I had also seen way too much death and destruction performed in his name.

After a few days of captivity, I was visited by U.S. Army Chaplain Dominic Menichella, an Italian American who spoke Pashto. I guessed him to be in his fifties. He had a full, white mane of hair and a stately appearance. I was impressed that he was impeccably dressed, with polished shoes and belt buckle. *Some outfit* was all I could think.

As a safety measure, he handcuffed my right hand to the bedpost, sat down at the other end, and checked me out for a few seconds. I was doing the same to him. It might remind you of two boxers who size up one another prior to a fight.

"Are you being treated fairly?" he asked in a light, non-threatening voice. It was almost soothing to me.

"Yes, sir, I am."

"Why are you addressing me as if you are an American soldier?" he questioned.

"Sir, I appreciate the fact that this army is quite different from mine. I am impressed with the professionalism of every soldier in every rank. It has been one of my strengths over the years to observe everything around me, something I learned as a young man with a big responsibility. Quite frankly, I have been better treated by my enemy than by those who are leaders in the very cause I served."

"Much wisdom from one so young," he replied. "Let me guess, you grew up in a small village, your father left the family for weeks, sometimes months at a time. As the oldest son, you had to shoulder the load, juggling man-sized duties; bending, but not breaking, under the weight."

"How do you know me so well?" I asked.

"You are a good person, Rashid. I have seen no evidence of violence in you. You apparently have a better relationship with your mother than you had with your father. I don't see a soldier's heart in you. Let's just say, we share a similar background." I couldn't wait to hear more.

I asked him, "Why are we being held in the desert when there are larger prisons in cities nearby?"

He explained, "Those facilities are already overcrowded

so you will be held here until other prisoners are transferred or released." That made sense.

He asked me how I had become involved with the Taliban, and it was then that I began to tell him my life's story, and it fell from my lips as easily as a ripe orange from a tree. No one had ever asked about me and my life before. Operating daily in a harsh environment had almost destroyed what tenderness there was inside of me. Something about the way he asked me kindled a sort of hope that there are indeed good people still left on this earth. I also noticed he had kind eyes.

The release I felt at the end when I finished with my father's death was followed by huge tears which unashamedly fell down my face onto the floor.

"This is the first time I have wept for him and for the father/son relationship that should have been. I wish he had known how to love us."

I was at once mortified to cry in front of another man yet was relieved. As I sobbed quietly, he placed his hand on my shoulder and began to pray for me. "Dear Father, let these tears provide a cleansing in Rashid's heart that will begin the process of healing it. Send your angels to comfort him."

I embraced the sincerity with which he prayed this, and I was ready to learn more.

This religious man became my mentor. He expressed a true hunger to know even more about Islam so that he could better understand it. I was beginning to hunger as well for this new, unfettered religion called Christianity.

We started comparing notes. I shared with him, "There are ninety-nine names for God in Islam."

He said, "They stopped at ninety-nine? Seriously?"

We laughed and then he replied, "There are about one hundred fifty Christian names for God." I was impressed.

I explained the concept of an "earned" life in the hereafter and the myth about seventy-two virgins. He shared heaven and its promise of "unearned" everlasting joy and eternal life for believers, minus the virgins, of course. As a Muslim male, I couldn't understand the sense in that concept; that had been one of the Taliban's selling points.

When he asked me how Muslims view hell, this is what I said: "God told an angel to have an angel from hell to bring a date made of fire to earth. The angel said this date would annihilate the entire world. The pit would do the same as would a grain of wheat. It is greater than all the nuclear power in the world and all the arms."

"As you know, Captain, Muslims live in constant fear of hell and that is why we pray five times a day, never missing prayers unless we are ill."

I was now beginning to worry a little. That didn't sound too good.

He then explained Judgment Day this way: "God will judge everyone who dies. Those who have believed in Him will be categorized as "sheep," and they will enter into heaven. Those who did not believe will be categorized as "goats," and they will enter into hell. Entrance into heaven is not determined by one's works on earth but rather by one's faith and belief."

He continued, "Christians should be as devout as Muslims in their prayers, not praying out of fear like you but out of total faith that our prayers will be answered." He felt it should be a yearned-for effort, in other words.

Each day this marvelous man visited me, and we spoke at length of all things religious, including being "born again," a concept that I had a hard time grasping. He laughed and told me, "You are just like Nicodemus, a member of the Jewish ruling council when Jesus was preaching. When Jesus had said, 'No one can see the kingdom of God unless he is born again,' Nicodemus had replied, 'Surely he cannot enter a second time into his mother's womb to be born.'" Obviously, this was a metaphor, but the meaning was not lost on me.

I had asked him to explain again what this meant, and he told me, "We are born into sin, and at some point in our lives, we are given the choice to surrender our will to God's. Then He will fill us with His spirit, allowing us to kill the 'old self' and be 'born again' as a new creation. We are made brand new, and all our sins are forgiven. God wipes the slate clean."

I began to see that this God is one of unconditional love, and I was beginning to feel a new kind of peace.

I thought back to the Taliban's thirst for blood and its unmoving stance on Islam, and I started realizing that this Savior that the Chaplain was talking about might be someone that could actually love me and forgive me for all whose lives I had taken. I was already profoundly affected by the positive influence of this simple man of God.

For several days, I read entire chapters in the Bible and began memorizing verses from it that my new teacher had given me. This allowed me to finally begin to understand the one true God. Nowhere did I see threat or hatred directed at me from these teachings.

Each day we prisoners were allowed to walk outside our cells in the sunshine for one hour with soldiers watching our every move. I tried to share what I had learned from the Chaplain with my comrades in captivity, but they laughed at me and scornfully said, "Rashid, you have finally lost your mind, have the Americans beat you senseless? You have forsaken Allah? You will surely burn in hell."

After that day, they no longer spoke to me, and I could only feel sorrow for their future destiny. I was now a pariah to them, yet I had a true peace they could not understand.

Now even more alone in my captivity, I was hungry to know more about the Christian faith, and my eagerness pleased the Chaplain.

My new spiritual father taught me about the significance of water baptism and the taking of Communion, things I had never heard of. Over time, I found myself thinking of Captain Menichella as the loving father I never had, and my days on earth were now counted by the hours I spent with him.

In the second week, I felt comfortable enough with him to share Fila's story, and he openly wept when I finished. "I have heard about some of the horrors in Kabul but not to this extent. Rashid, I will pass Fila's story on to all the soldiers in the camp, and funds will be donated in her parents' names to help the RAWA organization."

I was touched by his offer and eagerly accepted on Fila's behalf. He assured me he would give the funds to me upon my release in the future.

"How can I help? Is she safe?" he worriedly asked.

"She is hidden in my village, and I worry constantly for

her safety. The Taliban are always looking for her; she is a threat to them. If they catch her, I fear they will torture her or kill everyone in the entire village in retribution for hiding her."

"I will arrange for one of our undercover agents to go to your village, posing as a Taliban recruiter who needs to meet with your mother regarding Omar. He will stay in a small hut in the village for a while and travel to nearby villages under the guise of checking out young boys who will soon be soldiers, while keeping an eye on Fila and her aunt. He will also serve as a courier between you, your mother, and Fila. She can begin feeding her stories to the world. It's a beginning."

"An excellent one. Chaplain, I am humbled by such a kind gesture. This man, he won't be in harm's way, will he?" I was now the worried one.

"No. He's the best at what he does. He is a Mossad agent, working in conjunction with us, and a big believer in equal rights. It will be his privilege to protect the woman who will one day become a national treasure. This is to go no further than the three of us, agreed?"

"Sir, you are the only friend I have right now, and I would certainly never do anything to dishonor you. I certainly agree."

I asked him one day why he was always so cheerful and kind to me; after all, I had been responsible for many American deaths, a fact I was now ashamed of.

He explained, "Jesus, the son of God, came to earth and became man in the flesh, to understand our ways, then to die for all our sins; it was the ultimate sacrifice. People sacrifice their lives every day for a cause they believe in. Our cause is freedom while the Taliban's is a relentless attack against it."

He shared about the crucifixion and the resurrection, and that Jesus now sits at the right hand of the Father in heaven and is forever in a position to intercede for those of us who still exist on earth, helping us to live a better life, and to prepare for heaven.

I hung my head and told him, "I felt so horrible about my life as a soldier that I don't see how God can forgive me and welcome me into heaven."

The Chaplain then shared the story of Paul, one of the greatest apostles in the Bible and what kind of life he had led as Saul before his encounter with Jesus on the road to Damascus.

"The very fact that Saul was determined to wipe out all Christians from the face of the earth and that he had actively sought out Christians to arrest and have murdered prior to his transformation that day should give you hope. You see, Jesus found it in His heart to forgive Saul, even changing his name to Paul. This former murderer became a strong and mighty man of God and preached the love of Christ until his death many years later," he finished.

I was deeply moved by this story, and I finally mustered up the guts and asked him, "How do I come to know this Jesus you have made so real to me?"

It was then that he asked me to bow my head and repeat what he would say. When we were through, I felt as though one thousand tons had been lifted off my shoulders and I knew that I was a different man and all that I had done as a Taliban soldier had been forgiven. My captor had now allowed me to be set free!

It couldn't have come at a better time. A few nights later,

as the camp was settling down, I heard several loud voices shout, "Allah Akbar!" right before heavy rocket and mortar attacks began raining down on our outlying section of the camp, destroying everything in sight. This attack was carried out by the very Taliban we prisoners had so religiously served. Looking back, I find it ironic that both my father and I died similarly.

As for me, my new Christian identity brought me here and I now look forward to finding Captain Menichella—my *Andawal,* my true friend.

I really don't know what will happen in my future, but I am certainly ready for it. Thank you for taking the time to listen to my story. I am your *Andawal,* forever. He then bowed again, and we followed suit.

"What a story, Rashid. Man, that one sure tops mine," Tiny exclaimed.

"No doubt," I chimed in.

Wisdom had stood at the back of the pagoda the entire time Rashid was sharing his story. I was still in awe of his beauty and majestic carriage. He appeared human, but with effervescence and a bright and amazing aura constantly surrounding him. This angel had watched my back during my entire earthly life, and now he was closer than a friend. At that very moment I experienced a warm feeling and the faraway sound of my family beckoning. I knew now that I would see them very soon.

"Thank you, Rashid, your story is quite a testament to what happens when someone like Captain Menichella doesn't give up on you. Over time you will all have the opportunity to share with one another. We have many things to do," Wisdom related to us, and we could only imagine what was now in store for us.

Captured!

"Everyone ready to cross the Sea of Reconciliation?" Wisdom asked, and we were on our feet immediately.

9

The Disciples' Walkway

"Now, my new friends, you will cross the Sea of Reconciliation to the Other Side. There you will find your loved ones—those who have waited for you with joy and watched as your heavenly home was prepared for your arrival. Once you have finished with your visit, we will return here and then share more of your life stories."

We began laughing and hugging one another, thrilled that this was going to happen. My heart was full to bursting, and, for the first time since I had arrived in heaven, I found myself crying tears of joy.

I wondered how everyone would look. Would they be in the same bodysuit as me? Would they look younger, age lines gone like mine? I couldn't wait to feel my husband's strong arms wrapped around me and to share familiar moments with him I'd never forgotten. I was feeling the magical pull and strength of my loved ones, and I was thankful to be in heaven.

"Come, follow me," Wisdom instructed, clearly enjoying his role. In great anticipation, we followed him down a golden winding pathway, bordered by thick and massive palm trees that were filled with large, rich green fronds and surrounded by colorful orchids of all sizes. A variety of tropical birds—parrots, macaws, cockatoos, cockatiel, canaries, and parakeets—filled the air with their animated conversations.

We passed under a gem-encrusted golden archway with lettering that identified this area as Disciples Walkway, and I eagerly wondered if we would meet any of those incredible servants and devoted men of God along the way.

Brilliant and glowing yellow, red, white, orange, and multi-colored hyacinths exploded all around us and flocks of gray and white doves cooed and flapped their wings at us as if conveying a secret bird greeting. As I breathed in the air around me, I detected a combination of scents from my favorite perfumes, bath oils, and candles, and I was strangely comforted and at peace with this new world called heaven.

"God thinks of everything, doesn't he?" I asked Wisdom and he smiled and nodded in agreement.

"Heaven is designed to surround you with all the things from your earthly life you loved and cherished and to offer new opportunities for blessings in your new existence. Look up," he instructed all of us.

A pale peach and sea-foam green sky was highlighted with bright artwork in a style akin to the explosively talented artist, Jackson Pollock, the abstract features so spectacular, they took my breath away. We watched in total wonder as God flung the colors into the sky, each fling a little more bright and vivid. The colors glowed with such intensity, none of us could do anything but stand in awe of their beauty.

"An ongoing work by the Great Artist," Wisdom informed us. "Creativity is His specialty."

"And, all this time, I thought Pollock was crazy," Sophia said, and everyone laughed.

Spaced alongside and throughout this golden path were full-sized, exquisitely designed bronze statues depicting Jesus' twelve disciples: Peter, Andrew, James, John, Bartholomew, Thomas, Matthew, James, son of Alphaeus, Thaddeus, Simon, Philip and Judas. When I looked at Wisdom questioningly, he explained.

"Judas asked for God's forgiveness before he hung himself. He truly loved Jesus but was tempted by Satan. If you recall, Jesus also forgave the thief on the cross, the promiscuous woman at the well, and the great King David, who not only committed adultery, but who also arranged another man's murder. He even forgave Peter, his disciple, for denying Him three times before His death. He is a loving God."

All I could think at that moment was how easy He makes it for people to get it right. We just have to want to.

Overwhelmed with gratitude, I asked Wisdom if we could stop a moment and pray. Delighted, he replied, "Why, yes, Julie. Prayer is a huge part of heaven." I then prayed this simple and loving prayer that flowed from my lips and out of the depths of my heart:

"Dear God, thank you for your grace and for making it possible for me to end up here in the most beautiful place I have ever seen. Thank you for overlooking all my imperfections and bad decisions and for your gift of forgiveness and this new eternal life. I love you, Lord. Amen."

Even before I opened my eyes, I sensed Jesus was standing there as the light suddenly became brighter and I could feel a force that was very powerful. Waves of unconditional love and acceptance were already flowing from Him into me. I fell to my knees, overwhelmed by the fact that HE was standing right before me. When I could look up, I wasn't surprised to see him as I had always imagined him.

He was over six feet tall, with full and straight brown hair to his shoulders. A brown trim beard adorned His square-jawed face, and he was a ruggedly handsome man. I realized then how charismatic he had always been and why twelve men had forsaken their own livelihood and families to follow him and why so many of us believers have loved him and had faith in him throughout history.

Jesus was clothed in such pure white silk, it was almost blinding, and I saw the crucifixion scars upon His wrists and His feet. As I looked into those transparent, blue eyes, I felt as though He were allowing me to pass through the windows to His soul. I could see compassion, acceptance, forgiveness, and an almost intimate expression of love, but not in the earthly sense, and then I saw His smile, and it was directed right at me.

"I love you, too, Julie," he said in a voice that sounded like smooth honey, "Come here and let me see you."

He held out his hands and I stood before him and placed mine in his. I was in total awe and speechless. In that instant, I felt washed in his glory. I could feel myself entering into a new phase of growth and I was vibrant and alive like never before.

That smooth, velvet voice spoke again. "You are now in a safe place and one which you have justly earned. Your life has been a life of service to me and to others. By faith you always trusted and believed in me. Now is the time for you to receive your heavenly reward, and it is well-deserved."

"Oh, Jesus, thank you for never leaving me even when I felt you had forsaken me. Thank you for your pure agape love. I know the price you had to pay for me."

At that moment, a chorus of hundreds of angels, clothed in white robes, appeared in the sky, their wings perfectly layered with iridescent ivory-colored feathers and dusted with a range of turquoise shading. This magnificent choir sang their praises to Jesus and my four new friends found themselves also kneeling in worship to the King.

As Jesus moved among Abbie, Tiny, Rashid, and Sophia, welcoming them in the different ways comfortable and familiar to them, I walked over to Wisdom, who had also knelt before Jesus. He was smiling at me, and I asked, "So, was it the prayer?"

Wisdom chuckled, "Yes, Julie, simple, huh? How easy it is for us to communicate with the Master. It is His desire to comfort you through the bad times and rejoice with you in the good ones. He wanted you to know that many times when you prayed so fervently, He was there, standing right beside you.

"He cannot always grant everything you pray for; if He did, there would be nothing to build your faith. The difficult situations you endure and overcome throughout your life help mold you into a stronger individual. You have to understand that all things are a part of God's bigger plan." The difficult times were beginning to make sense.

I remembered when Bobby and I received the grim news about the cancer they had found in his pancreas. He immediately began a program of chemotherapy and radiation. When that didn't work, it was suggested that he try an aggressive drug "cocktail," utilizing a combination of chemotherapy and some new drugs that were being tested.

The doctors explained to us that this treatment would most probably extend my "gentle giant's" life for only so long. After praying about it, Bobby opted out and we slowly began the process of learning to live with dying and getting my husband's affairs in order.

We had decided to keep our attitudes extremely positive and live each day as if it were the last.

In that incredibly short time with Bobby, I spent many hours on my knees crying out for God's healing powers, knowing that as much as I wanted to keep my brave husband, God must want Him more. I prayed for my best friend not to have pain and he didn't.

Through prayer, I was able to make peace with the whole process as I could feel the love of Jesus surrounding me and giving me the strength to get through it each and every day. He was there. He helped me get through it, recover from it and He led me to where I am today.

It seemed that almost as soon as Jesus had shown up, in the blink of an eye, he was gone. We heard his voice ring down from the sky, not so far away, "Go in peace and welcome home." It was a unique exit and not one you see every day.

"Better get used to it," Wisdom laughed, and we joined in. "Come, let us go to the Sea of Reconciliation," our trusty guide informed us, and we dutifully followed him down the balance of the pathway, still in shock over our encounter with the Master. Wisdom later explained that Jesus is omnipotent and can reach out to many heavenly beings at one time.

Earlier in life, I had put that in the same category of wondering how Santa could make the rounds of over two billion homes in one single evening, delivering enough toys in one large bag for every kid, and ridiculously counting on flying reindeer. It was also puzzling to me how that big boy could make it down a chimney.

I never doubted God heard my prayers; I just figured since He had so many of them to deal with, some just took longer to answer.

When we arrived at the shores of the Sea of Reconciliation I stopped and held my breath at the radiant view stretching before me.

10

The Sea of Reconciliation

Many shades of turquoise and aqua green water shimmered as if covered by a blanket of blinking stars. This breathtaking body of water stretched as far as the eye could see and sailing boats of all designs were transporting hundreds of others like us from our area to the Other Side, their sails fully extended and aided by a light breeze.

A magnificent Chinese junk boat, measuring about thirty feet from bow to stern, was sitting at the water's edge, gently bobbing in the water, without the hint of an anchor. Its teak sides were hand carved with Chinese symbols, which I imagined portrayed stories about China, and large delicately embroidered sheets billowed above us in the wind. This centuries-old boat had always been one of my favorites, and I figured we had found our ride to the Other Side.

As we walked down to the junk, the sand appeared to be ground gold, which was soft to the feet and a little cooling. I stopped and closed my eyes, feeling the soft wind caress my face. Again, the voices of my loved ones, sent their familiar cries out to me. "I'm coming, I'm coming," I replied, and that thought alone filled me with tingling anticipation.

We loaded onto the boat I had been admiring, and Wisdom instructed us to find a seat and relax.

"Relax?" Sophia said while looking at the rest of us. "This guy, he's kidding, right? As a Jew, I don't have any idea if anybody will be waiting for me over there. I don't have a relaxed bone in my body. Actually, do I have any bones in my body?" Sophia asked, and we all burst out laughing.

I was about as relaxed as a girl could be and looking forward to the feel of the boat on the water and the wind blowing in my face and through my hair. More than that, though, I was ecstatic that I would soon be in the company of those who had always loved me. The excitement I was feeling could not be equated to anything I had ever felt before. I prayed I was not going to wake up tomorrow like Dorothy in *The Wizard of Oz* and realize this was just my overactive imagination.

Once we were all firmly seated, Wisdom walked to the front of the boat and slowly lifted up his arms and the boat began moving away from the shore. The movement was so smooth and soundless, you would never know you were on a body of water.

The smell in the air was salty and brought back memories of growing up near the Mississippi River and the Gulf of Mexico and the few times my dad shut down the pizza shop and went fishing. I recalled the time we went crawfishing in the backwater bayous around New Orleans and how I disliked the aggressive little critters yet later delighted in the joy of eating platters of them with potatoes and corn. Poppa also served them in the shop, and we would stay packed every night during crawfish season.

Our large family would also venture to the beach at Grand Isle once or twice a year, and our mother loved baking in the sun while we frolicked and snorkeled in the water nearby.

As we settled into a smooth glide, I looked at other boats on the water. There were schooners, sailboats, Boston whalers, houseboats, trawlers, and many other styles, making it a fascinating spectacle to see.

Wisdom explained that heaven is filled with the best of everything God has ever created. "It is His pleasure to make His children happy," he stated, and I had to agree.

Rashid cleared his throat and said that he had a funny story he would like to share. "It is totally clean, sir," he said, looking to Wisdom for approval.

"You couldn't share anything dirty if you tried, Rashid. Your soul has already been cleansed of any evil intent. Let us hear this story," he pleaded, and we all encouraged him.

Rashid looked at Sophia, cleared his throat, smiled, and said, "Miss Sophia, I hope you enjoy this as much as I do." Again, he cleared his throat, breathed deeply, and plunged in.

A fleeing Taliban, desperate for water, was plodding through the Afghan desert when he saw something far off in the distance. Hoping to find water, he hurried toward the oasis, only to find a little old Jewish man at a small stand, selling ties.

The Taliban asked, "Do you have water?" The Jewish man replied, "I have no water. Would you like to buy a tie? They are only $5."

The Taliban shouted, "Idiot! I do not need an over-priced tie. I need water! I should kill you, but I must find water first!"

"Okay," said the old Jewish man, "It does not matter that you do not want to buy a tie and that you hate me. I will show you that I am bigger than that. If you continue over that hill to the east for about two miles, you will find a lovely restaurant. It has all the ice cold water you need. Shalom."

Cursing, the Taliban staggered away over the hill. Several hours later he staggered back, almost dead and said, "I don't believe it; your brother won't let me in without a tie."

All of us, including Wisdom, held our sides we were laughing so hard, but Sophia was hysterical. I had to admit, that was one funny story, and I began to really care for Rashid. He was like no one I had ever met.

"That was excellent, Rashid. Now who would like to share their story next?" Wisdom asked.

"I will be happy to, Wisdom!" Abbie exclaimed, and we all settled in to hear her story.

11

Santa Monica

Abbie took Rashid's place, smiled at everyone, and began her story.

I grew up outside the sunny California city of Santa Monica in a huge tri-level home located on a cliff overlooking the Pacific Ocean. When I was a young girl, many nights I would sit outside on our wraparound balcony, gazing at the Milky Way, and wishing I could see God's face appear. I would imagine myself playing hopscotch among the stars and chasing moonbeams across the sky.

It was there at the tender age of ten that my dreams, aspirations, and sophistications began to form inside my spirit. I decided even then that I would live life on my terms, and I would do it well. I also knew I was destined to succeed.

I had the coolest parents in town. My Scottish father, Greg, is a respected entertainment attorney and dedicated golfer and my mother, Gisele (of French descent), is a chef, housekeeper, landscaper, chauffeur, physician, coach, psychiatrist, teacher, designer, and scheduler. Oh yes, and quite the charming social butterfly. Many of her friends said she reminded them of Simone Signoret, another beauty with the same accent.

I was the middle child, with one older sister and one younger brother, and our ages were exactly two years apart. We also looked so much alike, there was no mistaking to whom we belonged. We were a very tight-knit Scottish/ French family.

We had quite an unusual house as my parents had designed it, with architect Frank Lloyd Wright's passive-solar semicircular home in Hawaii inspiring them. The entire back of our home facing the ocean consisted of tempered glass windows, and our view was unobstructed. The sunken living room had several rectangular skylights, which infused the room with pleasures of light, and a regular overhead show of pleasant seagulls calmly swooping down.

A pearl white Steinway baby grand piano, a gift to me when I was eight, stood in one corner of the room, its top festooned with photos of a family that was well-traveled and fond of one another.

Having grown up in the large and prosperous floral shop her parents owned, my mother always appreciated the beauty of plants and flowers. As a tribute to her Parisian parents and her roots, she designed a twenty-foot spotlighted atrium to showcase her extensive collection of exotic plants, flowers, koi, and birds. It also served as a rather large and commanding entrance to our 8,000 square-foot home. A circular walkway comprised of handpicked stones wrapped around a two-story gilded bird cage, its occupants twenty different species of small parakeets called *conure*, imported from South America.

A large portion of our entire huge downstairs area was set up as an entertainment center, and it was my favorite room in the house. One end of the room was stylishly designed with a couple of stain-proof sofas and chairs and the largest television my father could find, complete with a VCR and over one hundred movie videos for our viewing pleasure.

The arcade area was made up of a billiard and ping pong table, and a Wurlitzer Vintage 850 Peacock Jukebox, a replica of the extravagantly designed 1941 model with a selection of over 2000 tunes and music for all tastes.

We kids had our own small kitchen with a sink, stove, microwave oven, and refrigerator that we kept stocked with soft drinks, water, snacks, frozen pizza, and lots of ice cream.

A large, private, well-insulated room and half-bath were located at the very end of the house and served as a place where my father conducted his business. He affectionately referred to his office as "the belly of the beast."

He explained the concept of his in-home office this way: "Some of my best wheeling and dealing is done down here. It's a place where two men can see eye-to-eye and discuss important matters in private, without interruption."

When I once had told him, "You know, Dad, you're nothing more than a glorified snake oil salesman," he had roared with laughter.

After a meeting, my father would invite his clients to our arcade area and challenge them to a game of their choosing. More times than not, he won.

My mother rarely visited his office, but she could certainly whip up some dandy dinners in her state-of-the-art kitchen worthy of Wolfgang Puck, another family friend. She was always running out to cooking classes somewhere, and we were amazed at her stamina. It seemed like everyone who came to see her brought her the latest cookbook.

"Gelly," as I loved to call her, enjoyed having theme dinners, and somehow, with her charming and wily ways, she always conned us into participating. One month she would serve us an Oriental-style dinner in a silk tight-fitting sarong, her hair knotted on top and held by colorful ivory chopsticks.

We donned sombreros and fake mustaches for Mexican night, with mariachi music blasting away in the background. Mother wore a Mexican-style peasant dress with a flower behind her ear.

As Scots, we couldn't help but dance the Highland Fling while attending the Highland Games once a year. We twirled madly in our tartans, flinging our arms up in the air, our feet madly prancing to the sounds of the bagpipes. You couldn't, however, pay us enough money to experience *haggis*, a dish of sheep's stomach for which none of us had any fondness. Our dear mother substituted it with shepherd's pie, thank God, one of her specialties.

After having fallen in love with Janis Joplin's music at the age of twelve, I made up my mind that I was going to be a rock star, and everything from that point on was planned with fanatical precision and with the exact intention of fulfilling that desire.

Once I convinced dear old dad and mom that I seriously wanted to be a rock star, they signed me up for guitar, voice, and dance lessons in addition to the years of study I had under my belt on the piano. It was my plan to be my teachers' greatest pupil, the "feather in their cap," and I went about my musical education with great vigor.

Thankfully, God had blessed me with a beautiful singing voice and an uncanny ear for music. I first performed "The Via Dolorosa" at thirteen at the United Methodist Church I grew up in. While singing the song, I closed my eyes and imagined Jesus carrying that heavy cross all the way to Calvary. Something deep inside me swelled and a heart-wrenching cry came out of me that brought the captivated audience to its feet. I finished the song to a rousing standing ovation and witnessed the tears on my parents' faces. My musical journey began that night in our small, close-knit church and I knew it had God's stamp of approval upon it.

Upon graduation, I auditioned for and was accepted at The Juilliard School in New York, and it was there that I would fine-tune my talents and learn music technique. Musical composition, ear training, literature study, and the materials of music and its history were all a part of my classroom curriculum.

It was an honor to be accepted in the over one-hundred-year-old school of performing arts and I was in awe of the other talented musicians I shared class time with. Although my father expressed his displeasure at my lack of interest in a college education (or "real" education as he was quick to point out), he was resigned to the fact that I was following my dream, and he and my mother strongly supported me. After all, my father had made his fortune by assisting people who were the very type of entertainer I was destined to become.

12

The Juilliard School

The boat we were on was jostled by a passing boat and everyone got up to see what was happening. Soon Abbie got their attention, and they all took their seats once again. She began sharing.

New York songwriters Irving and Eileen Steinberg were clients and close friends of my parents and, to help us out, they located a one-bedroom furnished apartment for me near Juilliard. They promised to show me the New York City ropes and assured my parents they would watch out for me in my first venture away from the innocence and safety of my California roots. They had always treated me like a cherished Jewish daughter, and I was delighted and thankful for their special kindness.

New York City can be a very threatening place to most people, but I found myself enjoying the vastness of it and the amazing opportunities it offered to explore different streets and avenues and communities of amazingly diverse cultures, cuisines, music styles, religions, and ethnicities.

I was in awe of the hustle and bustle of Times Square, alive and pulsing with its own rhythm. I roamed Broadway and Off-Broadway, the entire area lit up with bright marquees that advertised a tantalizing array of plays to choose from, featuring well-known and lesser-known actors.

With over two million works of art gracing the walls of

the Metropolitan Museum of Art, I was spellbound the first time I traversed the interior of the ¼-mile-long building which occupies over 2,000,000 square feet of building space.

I became a regular at The New York City Library with its fierce and stately lions guarding the entrance. Saturdays I spent checking out "starving artist" sidewalk art shows and drinking lattes and cappuccinos at Starbucks with new city friends and classmates while surfing the Internet.

Sometimes we would play Frisbee, or touch football, or fly kites in Central Park while dogs happily ran nearby. We were free to be and loving it!

On the other hand, Gelly, my over-protective mother, was convinced that I was going to be murdered.

"One day I'm going to be watching 'The Today Show' and I'll see your dead, lifeless eyes staring up at me," she whined. Where had that come from? You would think she was Jewish.

"Mom, aren't you over-stretching a little?" I asked. "Come on, give me a little credit." She finally was convinced by Irving and Eileen that I was firmly indoctrinated in the ways of a big city, that I was fearless, and that I was doing quite well on my own. The phone finally quit ringing every single day, and I was now on solid and independent footing.

Eager for our personal street education, a group of us students formed our own rock band, "Righteous Rags," and we began playing classic rock covers at small clubs in the SoHo district. I was the lead singer and played rhythm guitar. A local music critic once referred to me as a singer with the raw energy of Janis Joplin and the rich, raspy vocals of Stevie Nicks. These just happened to be my two favorite female entertainers and I was genuinely flattered.

Additionally, we had a drummer, bass and lead guitarists, and a keyboard player who sang solo at times and harmonized with me on a few songs. We played every weekend to packed crowds, took very short breaks, kept our music pure, and our reputation quickly grew. So also did our desire to break ground and try new things.

Although I had grown up in a Christian household, I found myself drifting away from my faith and I began experimenting with marijuana, and, like my parents, I also developed a taste for fine wine.

I had dedicated my entire high school existence to preparing for stardom by spending the majority of the week on lessons and practice and more practice. Obviously, schoolwork came first, and I studied hard to achieve membership in The National Honor Society, which I knew would look good on a college application.

I met my future husband, Andy, in 2005 after a gig at Underground Village, a live-music venue that is housed in the basement of what was once the legendary Gerdes Folk City on Third Street in Greenwich Village. Such memorable entertainers as Simon and Garfunkel; Bob Dylan; Peter, Paul, and Mary; and John Lee Hooker had all performed there. You could feel history hit you the moment you walked through the cigarette smoke that swirled out to greet you and walked into the dimly lit interior.

The place was reminiscent of the underground smoky jazz and blues clubs in Midtown back when Sinatra, Bennett, Hendrix, and other music greats hung out and spent all night jumping from club to club, always in search of new and interesting talent. These clubs were where many well-known musicians got their start. Underground Village was "the place" for live music, and we wanted to put on the best show we had ever done, a performance that sizzled.

"Okay, guys, this is our most important gig yet. Let's take it over the top!" I enthusiastically yelled while high fiving the rest of the band. "Let's rock the house!" we all screamed and then we ran onto the stage with the energy of newly pumped football players. One never knew who would be sitting in that audience. Three hours later, when the crowd went wild and begged for more, we knew we had the magic.

Andy had hung around the backstage door to meet me and the band afterwards and to compliment us on the show.

"Unbelievable sound. Man, you totally bring it. It won't be long until you're sitting at the top of the charts. You, Abbie, are amazing; the total package." He was clearly infatuated and not hiding it.

"And you are?" I asked him, with a twinkle in my eye. He was a nice-looking guy and came off very sincere in his efforts. I decided to give it a shot. Why not?

"Andy."

"Well, Andy, wanna go get a bite to eat with us? There's a quaint little all-nighter not far from here. The food is greasy, but good, and the jukebox can get on your nerves, but it's dark and nobody bothers you."

"No problem. I'll just call and cancel my dinner plans with Madonna." This brought a laugh from all of us.

I liked him immediately; mesmerized by his boyish good looks and great personality. Needless to say, I hit it off with this tall, slim, blonde-haired, brown-eyed, charismatic person who wore tight jeans, a leather jacket, and Tony Lama boots. Not to mention he was wearing "Obsession," one of my dad's favorite colognes.

Considering we were still on a high after such a rocking performance, I was starving and ready for some ham, eggs, and biscuits.

I turned to say something to the other band members and realized they had all abandoned me and left me alone with this tall, handsome stranger.

How dare they? I wondered, and then I smiled.

Andy and I stole away to one of the restaurant's dark corner tables and talked until the place closed, covering each other's background, the show, and hopefully what the future held for "Righteous Rags." I felt I could gaze into those brown eyes forever.

Andy was a professional drummer who had done a lot of studio work and also played with some pretty big musical groups. He was looking for a full-time gig and a talented band to hook up with. Once I heard him play with such precision, impeccable timing, and unbridled enthusiasm, I wanted him to join our group. He auditioned for the other members, flawlessly playing a drum solo patterned after John Bonham's recognizable riffs.

We voted unanimously to replace our current drummer with Andy, and I was left with the job of doing it.

Andy and I became a couple, and after setting up some ground rules and mutual considerations, he moved out of the fifth-floor walk-up apartment in Queens he had shared with another musician friend and into my apartment with me. He was my first serious boyfriend as I had dedicated every waking moment up until then to my plans of making it big in the music world. I had only had time for one close friend. It was my first time actually to live with someone besides my family, and I was a little terrified at first.

Also, my parents were not aware that Andy now lived with me, so most of his personal things were hidden in the attic in case they surprised me with a visit.

Oh, what tangled webs we weave kept popping into my head.

After shopping with Eileen at Bergdorf's one evening and watching her nonchalantly drop two grand on a Givenchy silk jacket, I later confided to her over dinner, "Eileen, I have a serious boyfriend. In fact, we're so serious we're living together."

The look on her face and the fact that she almost dropped her martini gave me a little insight into how Gelly would react should she find out.

"Seriously? You just moved here, child. Oh, Lord, you haven't told your mother, have you?"

"Eileen, you know she's the last person I want to know about this. That's why I'm telling you. I'm sorry, maybe I should just go." I got up to leave, and she asked me to stay. I sat back down.

"You know, I feel responsible for you. Gelly is one of my dearest friends. Oh, what's a good Jewish mother to do?" she asked, while frantically patting my hand and fanning herself with the menu. "Do you love him?"

"Yes, from the moment I met him. Is that bad?" I asked.

"Time will tell. Irving and I, we've had forty years of continuous celebration. We know how to live and enjoy every minute of every day. We've had our ups and our downs, but the ups outweigh the downs. We're two happy clowns."

"So, can you be happy for me?" I begged, while squeezing her hand.

"Yes, you young fool. Go, and may *Yahweh* go with you."

In June 2005, I graduated from Juilliard at twenty-one with a bachelor's in music. My entire family, Andy and the band, and Franny, my best friend from high school, were in attendance.

My dad took a liking to my "friend" Andy, and they enjoyed talking baseball together, Andy wowing him with his statistical knowledge of the New York Yankees and all the baseball stadiums he and his dad had visited over the years.

It was a glorious and beautiful day as we all hung out together, celebrating the occasion and our family's love for one another. I had not realized how much I sincerely missed them and the education in life they had already given me. I knew how blessed I had been to be born into such a loyal and devoted family.

13

Righteous Rags

It was time for everyone to get a good stretch and walk around the deck a bit. But intrigued by Abbie's story, before long everyone drifted back to their seats, eagerly awaiting to hear what happened next.

After graduation, Righteous Rags continued to play in and around the Big Apple, and our reputation was getting pretty strong. We had added original music to our repertoire, and I was enjoying writing lyrics, with Andy providing the musical composition. We were an unbeatable pair, and our band was discovered on a breezy September night by an RCA Records talent scout when we were invited to play again at Underground Village. Little did we know that someone who would change the course of our lives was present that very night.

Lionel Whitworth, a well-known and respected agent in the music industry, was over six feet tall and richly tanned, with thick, wavy, brown hair and a pleasant face with perfect teeth that were most likely implants. Smooth, tapered, manicured hands protruded out of a tailored, French-cuffed silk shirt, monogrammed with initials that matched the handkerchief peeking out of his left breast pocket. He was always impeccably dressed in one of the latest New York or Italian fashionable suits. He wore only Bruno Magli shoes and carried himself with such sophisticated dignity you could have easily mistaken him for a New York statesman. It was reputed this man managed more multi-million-dollar careers than anyone else in music history and could charm the spots off a leopard. He certainly captured our attention.

"I cannot tell you how delighted I am with your fresh sound. You are one of the tightest groups I have seen and heard in years. You know, the manager called me after your last performance and said I needed to get down here and see you for myself. Here's my card. I would very much like to represent you."

"You're talking about the entire band, right?" I asked.

"Absolutely. You guys are really good."

"Okay, I'll have my father, Greg McIntosh, call you," I said, while looking at the gold-embossed lettering on his black card. Very impressive.

"Greg McIntosh? The entertainment attorney in LA?"

"The one and only," I replied.

"I met your father at one of the many Hollywood awards shows we feel compelled to attend. We had both ordered scotch at one of the walk-up bars and struck up a conversation while waiting for our drinks. I liked him straight up and look forward to seeing him again." I knew Gelly was going to knock him off his feet.

Within the week, Lionel and I flew out to my parents' home in Santa Monica. As I predicted, Gelly bowled him over. He was struck speechless by her breathtaking atrium, then later asked her to marry him after eating her signature meal of *Bouillabaisse de Marseille*, French pot roast, and a fresh garden salad with French salad dressing of her own making.

"I told you she could cook," my dad boasted, and he and Lionel toasted to that.

Later, over cigars and brandy in the man cave, and after Lionel handily beat my father at a game of chess, the deal was sealed. My father would legally represent our band to help ensure our future success. and Lionel would open the doors to assist in making it happen. They had a strong mutual respect, both having survived decades in the same cutthroat industry.

RCA began laying the groundwork for our first introductory album, and we started the studio work immediately. We would use eight of our originals and two current and popular songs that would help hook the listener. We were in the hands of the pros and ready to rock and roll! God had answered many years of serious prayers, and I thanked Him for what He had done for me in so many areas of my life.

Our first album was entitled "Fire in the Hole," which reflected the heat of our music. Seven cuts on the album were hard-hitting rock and roll and three were love ballads. Within two weeks, our first released song, "Out of Darkness" (written in honor of my parents) went to the number one spot on Billboard, and we were well on our way to stardom.

With Lionel's help, Andy and I bought a small two-bedroom condo in Greenwich Village with our first record advance, and we started our lives together, brimming with excitement at what the future held for us. Gone were my reservations about living with a man without the benefit of marriage as I was now twenty-two and Andy was twenty-seven. To me, that qualified me to make adult decisions, but I found myself drifting even further from God. My parents were still not aware that I was living with him, and I hated deceiving those who had stood by me my entire life. However, the passion between us was undeniable. We were swept up in it, and I didn't want to let go of it.

After missing my second menstrual cycle, an in-home pregnancy test revealed that I was pregnant, and neither one of us was happy with this bit of news.

"How are we going to tour and promote our new album if I'm carrying a baby? How will my family react to a child born out of wedlock?" I wailed when I saw the results. "What was I thinking?"

"We'll be okay, Abbie, I'll take care of you." Andy's words comforted me, and he held me close.

Before anyone else heard the news, I would lose the baby through miscarriage a week later, and through the pain, I crawled my way back to God. I was humbled, totally sobered, and ready to serve Him once again.

Andy was bitter at the loss and did not share my enthusiasm for God, and we began quietly pulling inside our own empty shells. I was torn between my innocent love for him and my love for God. I prayed daily for Andy to find the joy and contentment I now possessed. Even though our relationship was strained, and offstage I was suffering from some serious depression, our band continued to pack the crowds in, and we began to plan our United States tour to promote the new album.

Money began flowing in, and I was thrilled with the record sales. It was really weird to hear our number one song being played continually on the radio.

My parents came to visit me soon afterwards and were shocked to see that I was living with someone they had met only once. Although Andy and I had separate bedrooms by this time, they were not happy with the arrangement.

"We are a little surprised that you would buy your first home without our blessing. It's not that we don't think you're capable, we just would have enjoyed being a part of the process," my mother explained. "You wouldn't have needed a partner to share half of the price." There it was. I had been waiting for it.

"Look, Mom, I'm grown up and my freedom is very necessary for what I do. Andy and I are a writing duo. Sometimes we stay up all night until we get the lyrics and the music to jive. It also isn't unusual for New York City women to have male roommates. We feel safer."

Once they were sufficiently satisfied that ours was nothing more than a platonic business relationship, their intense feelings eased somewhat. At least for now that part wasn't a lie.

A few evenings after their departure, I found Andy reading my Bible, totally unaware I had entered the living room. He appeared to be spellbound, and I was reluctant to breathe or move for fear that I might hinder God's gentle persuasion. When Andy's head dropped into his hands, and I could hear the sobs racking this man's soul, I knew he had been touched by the truth. I held him until it felt as if both our hearts were melting.

When I saw where the Bible was opened to and that Andy had been reading about Christ's crucifixion and resurrection, I knew everything was going to be all right.

"Oh, Abbie, I'm so sorry I've been so hard on you. I never realized what I was doing to you. Please forgive me. I need peace right now. I need someone bigger than me. Please help me understand this man Jesus."

Throughout the night, we talked about God's plan for us, and we welcomed the next day's sunrise on our knees, thanking Him for His grace. I saw a new man in him, and our love flourished from that day forward.

We agreed to keep our relationship strictly friendly until we married as I desired my parents' blessing on our union. I also decided to be totally honest with them and as hard as it was, I called and shared what had transpired with the loss of the baby earlier. Although they were shocked and hurt, they forgave me. After speaking with Andy, they welcomed him into the family.

Gelly later confided in me, "I had a premonition that things weren't all that good. I'm sorry I wasn't there for you." She continually amazed me.

The next few months were a whirlwind as we rehearsed and prepared for the grueling twenty-five-city tour to promote the new release that would begin in New Jersey at the famed Stone Pony at Asbury Park, Bruce Springsteen's launching pad. We would end the tour at the seventy-year-old Apollo Theater in Harlem, home to such Motown greats as Diana Ross and The Supremes, Sam and Dave, Smokey Robinson, James Brown, The Four Tops, The Temptations, and so many others.

Promo photo shoots, newly designed elaborate costumes, and difficult dance routines for me were also a part of preparation for the tour. By the time our launch date rolled around, I was both exhausted and exhilarated.

The night before we were set to perform, Andy surprised me with an intimate dinner at the eighty-year-old Russian Tea Room on West 57th Street, which had been opened in 1927 by the Russian Imperial Ballet. We dined on filet mignon and lobster in the Main Dining Room, afterwards sipping brandy in the Bear Room with its fifteen-foot revolving crystal glass bear, its Fabergé-inspired Venetian crystal egg tree, and a vividly painted ceiling. It was a wonderful surprise as I had always wanted to dine there, and I gawked at its beauty like a Florida tourist.

Andy later provided another surprise when he asked me to marry him on the observation deck atop the Empire State Building. Spreading his arms, he shouted, "One day, I am going to be king of this city, and I'm going to need someone strong to reign beside me. What do you say, my princess? Will you be my queen?"

I passionately exclaimed, "Yes, a thousand times yes, a million times yes!"

He then presented me with an oval diamond engagement ring, and we immediately called our parents who were thrilled and anxious for a wedding date. Naturally we were going to wait until the dust had settled after the tour.

The tour was even better than we had hoped for as we played to sold-out crowds in most of the major U.S. cities. We also sold out of CDs and t-shirts at the largest venues and enjoyed the adulation of fans of all ages. Our sound was unique, kind of a blend of classic rock and roll and a little bit of hillbilly, considering Andy was from the mountains of Tennessee. Whatever you classified it, it worked, and we also enjoyed success, especially from the I-pod downloads that were now very popular.

Our manager was ecstatic, our record company loved us, and my dad was helping keep things straight legally. He also set up a trust fund for both of us and began wisely holding on to the excess financial windfall that, without some careful savings, we surely would have foolishly spent.

We began to plan our overseas tour to Japan and China that would begin in nine months.

⋙ 14 ⋘

Our New Life Together

Abbie took a deep breath after sharing about their life so in depth. Rashid went and got her a glass of water while the rest of them talked quietly among themselves. Feeling revived Abbie took her narrative up again.

Needless to say, my mother began planning my wedding as if it were her own, and nothing gave me more pleasure.

On a beautiful Saturday in the fall of 2007, with the glimmering Pacific Ocean as a backdrop and a vibrant sunset casting its glow on the close of the day, we shared our vows in the side yard of my parents' home, with the Methodist minister of my youth performing the ceremony.

My Vera Wang pearl white wedding dress brought smiles from the two hundred guests assembled as it was worn off the shoulder, was hemmed in the front, and had a small manageable train cascading behind me. The custom design was covered in rhinestones, and my white rhinestone cowboy boots completed the package. I wore my hair long and loose, with flowers intertwined throughout. I proudly carried a bride's bouquet that included precious flowers from my mother's atrium—a rainbow of colorful roses, day lilies, and orchids. I was definitely going to preserve such a loving and thoughtful gift that my mom had made for me.

Andy almost made me swoon when I saw him dressed in tight jeans, a white shirt with a bolo tie, and a white cutaway tuxedo jacket with a homemade rose boutonniere, compliments of my mother. He was so handsome in his trademark Tony Lama boots and Stetson hat—a modern-day cowboy.

My best friend, Franny, was my maid-of-honor, and my sister was my bridesmaid. Andy's dad stood with him as his best man, and my brother was a groomsman. It was the best day of my life yet, and I remembered to thank God for bringing such a wonderful man into my life.

For the reception, we dined on Kobe steak flown in from Japan, Sockeye salmon, Maine lobster, and truffles, one of my mother's favorites. The obligatory toasts were capped with champagne, and the video that was later shown depicted some of the poignant and funny moments in our lives.

Our four-tiered wedding cake was decorated as a drum set and was the hit of the reception. Bailey, our other vocalist and keyboardist, and Ronnie, who played lead guitar, brought the house down with crowd favorites, and I was hugged by so many celebrities, I felt like I was one.

Andy, who was a much better drummer than singer performed a song he had written for me called "I Found an Angel." The lyrics were touching, and I would bet there was not one dry eye among the whole bunch of us at the end of that song.

All of us younger members of the wedding partied into the wee morning hours when most of us wound up in the heated swimming pool. Naturally, everything was perfectly orchestrated by my mother, the soul of our family.

The next three years proved to be an unbelievable experience as we had hit after hit . Both of our new CDs and videos shot to number one on Billboard and MTV respectively. We bought a touring bus and outfitted it with all our favorite comfort foods, CDs, and DVDs. Our king-sized bed was located in the rear of the bus, and we also had our own private bath. The band members slept on custom-built bunk beds in the middle of the bus and shared a communal bath and shower.

"Guys, can you knock it off with the "Jackass" stunts?" Andy asked in exasperation late one night. I had to admit, some of those pranks were well-executed, though highly stupid. A lot of foolishness went on constantly with them. All in all, though, it was a great experience, and we didn't lose a single member of the band because of it.

Every year our road tour swept us through the heartland of America, and we were featured on "The Today Show," "The Tonight Show," "Letterman," "Oprah," "The Rachel Ray Show," and naturally, "Saturday Night Live." We were thrilled to perform at the Grammys to celebrate our platinum record, "Fire in the Hole," and 2007's "Best Song of the Year."

We had finally made the big time, and we couldn't get enough of it. The money was pouring in, and our future was set. We also had a great road and concert crew, and we took extremely good care of them, as they were the backbone of our success.

I bought Andy a Harley-Davidson Touring Road Glide Custom bike, emblazoned with fire and flames tendrils to celebrate that first hit song, and together we decided on a well-appointed 10,000 square foot beach house on Long Island in the Hamptons.

"I bet the price tag on this beauty is more than the entire national debt of New Guinea," Andy had whispered during the tour. I figured he was probably right. However, money was rolling in and my father wisely began investing it.

Now we were rubbing elbows with famous movie stars, writers, and directors, and some of the elite of New York City. We began to talk about starting a family and considered the next year to be a great time for that. God's blessings were on us, and it seemed like nothing could go wrong. My life with Andy was so rich and full, it was like eating key lime pie every single day.

~~ 15 ~~

A Fateful Flight

Abbie stopped a minute before she plunged into the next part of her story. The rest would be hard to share, she knew, and shot a quick prayer asking for help to get through it before she began again.

In the first week of April 2010 Andy received a call from his dad in Clinton, Tennessee, telling him that his mother was going to have surgery the next day in Knoxville to remove a malignant tumor in her breast. Andy was visibly shaken by this news and booked his flight immediately.

As I kissed him goodbye at the airport security area, I held him a little longer than necessary, feeling his heartbeat and the strength of those muscled arms around me.

"Andy, I'll be praying for your mother. She's a strong woman. It's good that you'll be there for your dad as well. Call me the minute you arrive. I love you so much."

"I love you too my darling wife," he replied, holding me closer than normal as well.

We prayed together for his mother's surgery and kissed passionately once more before he boarded.

It would be the last time I would see my precious husband as his plane crashed when a flock of birds flew into the engine of the Boeing 757 while on approach to the Knoxville airport. The plane struck a fuel truck upon impact, creating a fiery inferno that caused both fuel tanks to explode. There were no survivors.

I was notified in person by the local police before the news hit the cable and network shows. Thankfully, they stayed with me until I called my parents, who immediately assured me they would call other family and friends. My mother then told me that my father would book the first available airplane charter to New York.

Within minutes, Eileen and Irving checked in and informed me they were on their way over. I found myself walking around in a daze, numbed by the news, finding it hard to believe that a lifetime of dreams had crashed along with that jet. I kept listening for my cell phone to ring with Andy assuring me that he was all right, they were mistaken about the crash, and it wasn't his plane.

Once Irving and Eileen arrived, Irving took charge of calling Lionel and the band members and local friends. Eileen ran a hot bath for me and proceeded to locate information that would help organize Andy's memorial. I told her where our documents were and where to locate photo albums that his mother had given me, chronicling his life.

While numbly lying in my garden tub, I could hear folks arriving and the sounds of muted sorrow. I looked at the fullness of the water and thought how easy it would be just to end it all immediately, but God's spirit in me would not allow it. I thought of the serious consequences of such a selfish act and of how many people would be adversely affected by it.

I needed my mother now. and I wanted to feel my father's strong, protective arms hold me and make the bad things go away. I knew it would be hours before they would make it from the West Coast, and I realized I had to pull myself together for those who had stopped in to comfort me.

Our huge house seemed so empty now, even with people, flowers, food, and conversation filling every corner of it. I kept looking around, hoping to see Andy, wishing it so much that I thought it just might happen.

"Lionel, please tell me I'm dreaming this and that I'll wake up and laugh at such a stupid nightmare, just like Bobby's death in the TV show *Dallas*. Andy will hold me, kiss me, and assure me that everything's okay, right? How will I live without him?"

Lionel put a protective arm around my shoulder and said, "It's been four years since I lost Victoria to breast cancer. It truly takes time and, even then, the pain never leaves you. I'll be here for you whenever you need me."

My parents flew with me the next day to Knoxville to meet with the airline officials and others who had also suffered human loss from the plane crash. Somehow, the fact that I was not alone helped me cope a little better, even though we all looked like zombies. I had seen people in shock before but not to this extent. There were only charred remains and no bodies to identify and very little luggage had survived. Actual identification would come from dental records at this point.

The love of my life was gone, and for the first time in my life, I felt truly alone.

Andy's oceanside memorial service was held three days later and attended by hundreds of people, many whom I did not know. The parasitic news reporters, trucks, and cameras were everywhere, and I just wanted to shout to the imposters to leave. They didn't know my Andy. They were only on the fringes of our lives and could not possibly report accurately on such a horrible event.

My band members were with me constantly, and they were grieving almost as much as I was.

"What do we do now?" they asked me. "Keep the band? Not keep the band?"

"Look, guys, I'm gonna need some time to figure this out. Just sit on your money for a little while and hang tight with me. We all need some time off."

They agreed and then took turns hugging me. We were more than a band; we were more like a dysfunctional family. I couldn't even think about a replacement drummer right now. I couldn't think at all, I was such a mess.

Andy's parents were loving and supportive even in their own state of shock. His mother's cancer surgery was postponed until the week after the service. I prayed my mother-in-law would survive this horrible experience, and I vaguely remember her reassurance that she would do just that, in memory of her only child.

With my siblings having flown home after the service and my parents needing to return to California a few days later, I was left in a mausoleum with nothing but a ticking clock to remind me that I was still in the land of the living. Only thing was, I didn't want to be there. I wanted to be with Andy. Thankfully, abject shock had carried me through the arrangements, the visitation, and the memorial service. The hard part was yet to come.

Once everyone was gone, I crawled into the hot tub and

turned the heat as high as I could stand it, hoping to burn the pain out of my heart. I vaguely remembered well-meaning friends and family who had told me, "Be brave," "You're still young, you'll find another person to share your life with," "Andy's in heaven now, waiting for you," and so many other senseless ramblings. What everyone didn't understand was that nothing they could say would bring Andy back. Nothing would fill the emptiness in my heart where Andy had been. I appreciated their concern, but it just didn't help.

Now, it was just me and reminders everywhere of what our lives had been together. There were so many happy photos of us performing with our band; me, the biker chick, on the back of Andy's Harley; playing on the beach; relaxing at home, and special moments with our families. I had called him a "pig on a hog" once while taking his photo. He had liked it and shared it with his Harley riding friends who nicknamed him "Pig" from then on.

There were signed record albums, photos with other close musician friends, Andy's first Yamaha drums, his clothing, shoes, and his favorite colognes. I remembered the day RCA had presented Andy and me with our first platinum record for "Out of Darkness,"engraved with the words "Song of the Year 2007" on it.

A cut-out photo of a golden retriever, the dog he wanted to buy, was still propped on top of the mantel. His collection of signed Major League baseball caps was still hanging on the special cap rack he had built, a testimony to a fun-filled life with a dad who had shared his passion for baseball. I made a mental note to give the caps to his father, the rightful new owner.

Over the next few days, I left messages on all my phones that I would be taking a break for a while; then I shut all electronics off, closed the drapes, and didn't answer the doorbell. Sleep and hunger eluded me, and I became numb with grief. I tried to pray many times and found that the words stuck in my mouth like sandpaper, and loneliness, my new enemy, began quickly swallowing me with its icy chill.

I felt such profound loss that I couldn't even cry and walks on the beach did nothing to help mend my shattered heart. In desperation I called Eileen, asking her if she had any medication that might help me make it through this horrible experience. Andy and I had long given up smoking weed or doing anything like that, as we wanted to stay healthy and have a baby.

Eileen came over immediately, bringing a small overnight bag so that I would have some company, and she could keep an eye on me. The deep concern I read in her eyes confirmed my suspicions that I looked pretty bad. Had I looked in the mirror, I would have been alarmed to see the deep dark circles ringing my eyes and tangled hair that hadn't seen a brush in a few days.

She provided me Xanax for my depression and Phenobarbital, and she held me as I cried and grieved for the love of my life until I finally fell into a sound sleep, the first I had experienced since Andy's death. She checked on me throughout the night, served me breakfast in bed the following morning, and before leaving, gave me strict instructions to see her physician. She had already made the appointment for the next day. I made her promise not to call my parents.

Dr. Guggenheimer was a kindly, old, bespectacled Jewish

practitioner with an office on the top floor of a high rise building on Madison Avenue. He was gifted with a bedside manner that put me instantly at ease.

"Such a young woman to lose your husband. It must be very difficult for you. I am so sorry."

"Thank you, doctor. Is your wife still living?" I asked.

"Yes, sixty-two years we have been together now. She's a good woman to put up with me."

"I'm sure she is blessed as well."

I could feel tears beginning to squeeze out of my eyes and he could sense my depression. We talked for some time, and he provided me with a prescription for sleeplessness, another for depression, and the third one for anxiety.

"Please be mature about taking these types of drugs and do not mix them with alcohol."

I couldn't see where that would be a problem. I prayed they would numb me or put me to sleep, and I wouldn't have to deal with anything.

In the beginning, I moved around the house in slow motion, a stranger to my new drug regime. For a while the drugs worked by temporarily numbing the pain; however, I knew that, not too far in the future, I was going to have to communicate with my parents and my friends. I just wasn't there yet and the daily messages I left for them on my answering machine kept them all at bay.

Most days I sat on the back deck, facing the ocean, praying God would heal my broken heart. I couldn't even listen to CDs of our music, as the memories were so heavy, they settled like concrete in my heart. Many times, I cried out to heaven, but I felt heaven didn't hear me. I tell you this, grief is something that takes everything out of you, and it lingers for a long time.

One evening I was packing Andy's clothing and shoes to be given to a Goodwill store the following day. Occasionally, I had to stop and wipe the tears away after smelling Andy's cologne on his clothing. More than once, I clung to a particular item, laughing at the memory surrounding it.

When I opened up Andy's leather overnight bag to empty it, I saw a baby blue blanket designed with baby bottles and rattles, and the softest teddy bear I had ever held. A small silver picture frame, which would have held the photo of our newborn baby, was also included. These must have been items Andy had picked up over time to surprise me.

I grabbed the bear and held it to my face, realizing fully now that our dream of having a child together would never materialize. The flood of tears came for what would never be, and I thought I could possibly die and join him in the afterlife at that very moment. Tears that had been so hard to shed before now flowed freely.

"No, God, no," I cried, while rocking back and forth. "I miss you, Andy. I'm dying here."

After lying on the floor in the fetal position for a couple of hours, I vaguely remember walking to my car and driving to a liquor store where I purchased two 1.5-liter bottles of cabernet sauvignon, mine and Andy's favorite red wine. Tonight, I would drown my sorrows and tomorrow I would try to start the process of getting over the pain of his absence.

I'm not sure what actually triggered the act that took my

life, but I remember lying on our king-sized bed, holding my husband's tattered workout tee shirt (the last thing he had worn before leaving the house the morning of the plane crash) and the soft little teddy bear I had found.

I drank both bottles of wine, and, because my mind was now fuzzy, I inadvertently mixed up my dosages of the trifecta of pills I was taking, accidentally overdosing. All I remember is going to sleep and waking up in this beautiful place.

My greatest joy right now is that I will see Andy and our baby once again. Thank you for letting me share my story.

We all stood and hugged Abbie, even now more anxious to hear about each other's journeys through life.

16

Receiving the Family Coat

Wisdom then walked to the cabin located at the bow of the boat, opened the door, and disappeared inside. A few minutes later he returned, carrying several large robes and sashes.

He held up a rich deep purple silk robe which was embroidered on the back with my family's coat of arms. A smaller replica was located where a pocket would have been on the front in the upper left area. The sleeves were beautifully embroidered on the cuffs as well. I couldn't wait to wear it!

"This is your family's coat of honor—the family you were born into, Julie. You will wear this on special occasions or whenever you wish. The tasseled sash represents the coat of honor of your husband's family, and it should be worn around your shoulders. All those in your family line wear this same robe."

As I put the robe on and belted it, I could almost feel the history of generations that had preceded me since the beginning of time. I would wear it with honor. The sleeves fell down to my wrist and the length hit around my calves. It was made of delicate, finely woven silk, and I breathed in a blend of my favorite fragrances that lightly rested upon it.

My son, Bobby Jr., would one day wear a robe like this. What a blessing he had been to his father and me! He was very well liked at school and church and never disappointed us with his conduct. He was a star baseball pitcher in high school, a member of the National Honor Society, and was awarded a full four-year athletic scholarship to Louisiana State University in Baton Rouge, the school he graduated from. He married a fine young woman, and they produced adorable identical twin daughters. I could not have asked for a better family, and I would continue to thank God for them and ask Him to look out for them every day.

Once everyone received his or her own special robe, we smiled at one another as it was becoming clear we would soon arrive at our new destination.

As there is no timetable in heaven, no one is ever in a hurry. We were all enjoying the satisfaction of having made it here, and now we were going to see people we had all hoped and prayed to see again. It was heartwarming and more than a little exciting. I wondered how many people I had known in my life would be there to welcome me.

Other questions swirled in my head. *Would there be music? Would there be food to eat and something to drink?* I couldn't remember being hungry or thirsty even once since I had arrived in heaven, and I remembered Wisdom explaining how it worked.

Actually, you will experience many times of rejoicing in heaven and that will involve the human enjoyment factor of feasting, which is included in many of the celebrations. The food is always fresh and easily prepared and does not require the slaughtering of animals. Chicken and fish are the exception.

As you know, spiritual fasting on earth involves giving up the pleasures of eating those things you love in order to focus your energies on becoming a better Christian. Since heaven is filled with such joy and contentment, one does not find the need to eat unless it is a celebration. Spiritual fulfillment is already here.

Heaven is filled with gardens full of vegetables and fruit, fields of wheat, lakes stocked with fish, and yards abounding with chickens. As there is no need for bodily functions anymore, food and drink are consumed and savored, and then they disappear within your system. Rather than nourishment, it's more about fellowship and the "breaking of bread" with others.

The only two organs needed in your body right now are your brain and your heart. God allows you to have freedom to live your heavenly life as you wish. That includes giving you the power to think, to learn, and to improve your existence. The other is to give you the power to love others, to worship God, and to experience true peace.

You may recall that Lucifer was one of the most highly respected angels in the heavenly kingdom. His rebellion and that of his followers still amazes us but, again, God gives us all free will and that included Adam and Eve on earth and Lucifer in heaven. Rebellion in any color is still rebellion.

I was so happy to hear that food was consumed only in celebrations and that the calories would not stick as I had counted calories and attempted every diet in the world since I was about thirty years old. To be able to sustain my own existence without the benefit of lasagna, pizza, bread pudding, homemade biscuits and gravy, and thick slabs of bacon, gave me a moment of relief as I had always found food either comforting or extremely condemning.

All the pressures were being eliminated. The way I understood this bit of good news was that I could have the pleasure of eating to my heart's content without fear of the consequences. Heaven was getting better and better. How thankful I was to be a part of it!

Wisdom directed our attention to the approaching shore. "Look to the front of the boat, and you will begin to see many beautiful mansions. Once we dock at the pier, you will disembark and some of your family and friends will be at the shore to greet you. Have no fear as God has already prepared your mansion and greeters for your arrival. This is one of the happiest times you will experience in heaven. God has made special preparations for you in anticipation of this glorious event."

We all stood and stared in fascination at the amazing scene that unfolded in front of us. There were thousands of beautiful homes in multiple layers situated on a huge hill overlooking the Sea of Reconciliation. It reminded me of some of the homes that are layered and stretch high up hillsides in California; only these would never be the victim of a mudslide.

Every style known to mankind was represented. There were traditional and modern types: Tudor, castles, log houses, farmhouses, bungalows, domed houses, Colonial, beach houses, ranchstyle, haciendas, and various large and unique tree houses. No two were alike, and that alone was enough to impress anyone.

Had I been an architect on earth, I would have been deliriously happy with what my eyes were feasting on. The larger mansions were magnificently designed, some two to three stories high. Smaller but well-designed homes also were included, and both large and small ones brought a collective "Oohs" from all of us on the boat.

Was my heavenly home like one of these? What could I have possibly done on earth to rate something this incredible? I was suddenly overwhelmed by what was about to transpire, already imagining the strong arms of my husband around me and the unconditional love of my parents.

As if on cue, Wisdom said, "Okay, everyone, take a deep breath and remember that God never gives you more than you can handle."

I looked at him, smiled with love and appreciation, and replied, "You're right, Wisdom, I believe I can handle it."

I was only a few minutes away from seeing my loved ones and my new specially designed everlasting home. Needless to say, it was hard to stay calm as we had now reached the Other Side.

17

The Other Side

As our boat neared the solidly built wooden dock that extended way out into the water, we noticed that a multitude of people were waiting on the shore, dressed like us in their family's finery. Robes in varying shades of red, purple, green, orange, blue, brown, yellow, pink, and gray, and other bold prints painted a picture of regality, and I was thrilled to be a part of it.

Uniquely designed hats, some with huge plumage, adorned both men and women's heads. I also saw many brightly patterned turbans, sombreros, Indian headdresses, straw hats, stylish and unusual hats of different colors, and a huge array of period hats dating from the beginning of time to today.

I would later learn the significance of the "Wearing of the Hats," a tradition patterned after one dating back to 1875 when mostly Southern men and women started wearing stylish hats on "Derby Day" at the Kentucky Derby.

Huge queen and king palm trees, swaying coconut trees, and lemon and lime trees were abundant both near the seashore and throughout the yards of many mansions. A beach area with flawlessly white sand was located about two hundred feet from the dock and was packed with heavenly beings in their body suits enjoying the sand and the water.

Others were enjoying fishing and water sports in small watercraft, wave runners, and fishing boats of all sizes while elaborately designed kites flew from the hands of beachgoers and from decks of homes in the distance.

Heavenly beings of all backgrounds and ages were on boats of every type heading in the same direction as us, peering into the throngs of those waiting, just like we were. We were all anxious finally to know who had preceded us here.

I was thankful that stress and anxiety were no longer a part of my psyche or else I would have been blown to pieces with excitement at just the thought of seeing so many wonderful people again.

I knew we would have no problems reconnecting as they had been calling me since my arrival, and I knew they were somewhere out there looking for me as well. My heart was beating a little faster than usual, and I could feel the threat of tears forming in my eyes.

My arrival here on the Other Side is what we had always called a "homegoing" in our church. We never called the service of someone's passing a funeral, which to us always denoted something dreadfully sad or macabre. Rather, it was a celebration of their life, especially of those who had spent more time doing good for this world than bad.

Wisdom gently guided the boat to the dock with movements from his arms, and we settled against it quite easily. So many boats were arriving at once, and judging from the chatter, we could see that others were as excited as we were as we all realized that our new lives here were taking a drastic turn for the better. As we stood to leave, Wisdom spoke to us once more.

"I will be stopping in from time to time to visit with you and your families and friends. I will notify you when it is time to return to the garden of Tranquility where you will resume your journey through heaven. In the meantime, please enjoy your first time in your new surroundings and reminisce about your life with those who have patiently awaited your arrival. I have to leave now and help other newcomers. Remember, God will show Himself to you in many different forms throughout your heavenly journey. Keep your spirit open."

I remembered the huge watery face that had risen out of the lake on the way to the Pearly Gates and the outrageously artistic work God had painted in the sky over Disciples Walkway. The sudden appearance of Jesus Christ in all His glory had literally amazed me with its majesty. God had shown Himself in so many ways already, and Wisdom would have known that. I was anxious to see more.

We took turns hugging this marvelous creature and watched him walk away until he disappeared in the wink of an eye. I missed him already as he had been such a comfort to me. He was teaching me about the richness and fullness of heaven, which in turn would lead me to discover my place and destiny in the vastness of it.

Before we left the boat, the five of us held hands and prayed for one another and the unknown situations that we would soon encounter. There was a bond forming between us.

Rashid clasped his hands together, bowed to all of us and said, "Peace to you, my new and lovely friends."

Abbie looked at each one of us and said, "I cannot tell you how much it will mean to me to see my Andy and my son." We could feel the intensity with which she said it, and we took turns hugging this young and beautiful soul.

Tiny, whose name just didn't go with the frame, spread his

arms wide and gushed, "I cannot wait to feast on some rich, heavenly foods." He cracked us all up. Funny, I could remember few times I had laughed this much on earth.

Sophia, who was busy primping with her jeweled mirror, looked around at us, replaced the mirror in her pocket, and said, "Gee, I'm not quite sure whose gonna be waiting to party with me, you know? But maybe I could drop in on you guys sometimes?"

"Yes, yes! Please visit!" we all chimed in and agreed we would visit with one another later after spending time with those we had been eager to see. I prayed the other four would have as good an experience as I knew I would with those who had gone before me. It was time to go, and I could feel the excitement building.

I adjusted my sash, smoothed my robe, and fluffed my hair in anticipation of the next big step in my new existence. I called the mirror up once more, and it appeared in my hand. I was still trying to get used to that. I checked again, enjoyed the contented image staring back at me, placed the mirror in my deep pocket, and took a deep breath. As I briskly walked on the dock toward the shore, I heard a precious familiar voice calling my name even before I got to the end of it.

18

The Family

"*Po d'Amore! Po d'Amore!*" I heard my father yell with glee before he even saw me. He had always called me that because in Italian it means "little love." It was his pet name for me, and it had never sounded better than it did right now.

"Poppa! Momma!" I screamed, and I literally ran into my dad's arms as he ran to greet me. My mother, always the patient saint, stood waiting, and I could see she was anxious to welcome me as well. I picked her up, and she giggled as I swung her around, then I held her to me, thankful to be so near to her again. Joyful tears were running down all of our faces.

They looked full of youth and vitality, and neither had a sign of wrinkles, moles, scars, age lines, or illness. Both were in excellent health and happier than I had ever seen them. In my mind, my mother and father looked like they had just turned fifty as there was a strong vibrancy coming from both of them. I could smell the scent of Old Spice, my father's favorite cologne, and Chloe, the perfume I had always associated with my mother.

Each of my parents had full, short silver hair, combed straight back and my father wore a purple robe that was identical to mine and bore the same family crest that showed stately, full-maned male lions standing face-to-face in front of a bright yellow sun. The lions denoted strength, and the sun indicated powerful character.

My mother's silk robe was a deep emerald green with a crest

119

showing an eagle holding stalks of grain in its talons flying east around our world. The significance of this was that the eagle represented her family's courage and their love of distributing food to the needy. There was also a purple silk tasseled scarf with a smaller logo like mine around her shoulder which denoted her marriage to my father. She and my father both sported stylish hats.

For a moment we just stood looking at one another and holding each other's hands, then my mother looked at me and said, "Julie, we knew this day would come as you have always served the Lord, and we knew He was preparing a place here for you. We know you are a little overwhelmed right now, and we will do all we can to make this an easy transition. You have no idea, really, what is in store for you, but I can promise that you will love it. Welcome home, darling."

Those beautiful green eyes twinkled like they always had, and I kissed my mother on her forehead and leaned my head on my father's shoulder, thankful to be in their presence once more.

"I saw Jesus on Disciples Walkway," I shared. "He was more amazing than I had ever imagined. Those eyes. That voice. He's omnipotent, yet as real as the three of us standing here. It was, to date, the greatest moment of my life." My parents heartily agreed.

"Hello, Julie," I heard a familiar voice say, and I turned to see standing before me the love of my life—a newer, more improved edition. Bobby now looked healthy, with a full head of hair and flattering weight gain. Unfortunately, during the few months leading up to his death, I had seen this man I love go from two-hundred-forty-five pounds to one-hundred-sixty. This was the Bobby I had fallen in love with all those years ago.

We held one another for a very long time and then I looked

into his rock steady eyes and said, "Thank God you never suffered, Bobby. I don't think I could have handled it if you had."

He laughed, "I have to agree with you on that. Thanks to Him I am a new person, Julie, and I have embraced my new existence here. Heaven is a place that is paradise, utopia, and nirvana, all rolled into one. It is a place that is guilt-free, stress-free, and where praise and celebration to God are everyday occurrences, not just once a week on Sunday.

"We were a great couple together and made a difference on earth. We actually imagined the beauty and peace here, but we really had no inkling how much more there is to it. Don't doubt for once that God didn't take notice of you, girl. You have done an amazing amount of good works since you were a young teen and that probably earned you some big points."

Feeling Bobby's arms around me once more took me back to the circumstances so many years ago surrounding our meeting.

19

The Commune

I remember the terror I felt when I stood before my seated parents all those years ago, with my heart in my throat and an inability to even form spit to speak. I had said, "I have made the decision to postpone college for a year and pursue my dream of experiencing life inside a commune that follows the Jesus Movement. If it isn't the life for me, I will return home to my studies. I'll only do it with your blessing, though." There, I'd said it. I'm sure I didn't breathe for the next five minutes.

Instead of a lecture, my dad had said, "A year away will be a hands-on, eye-opening education, and anyway, it is high time for you to learn how to make it on your own. Since we should be in close proximity, I can assure you, you will be all right, and we're only a phone call away." My mother hadn't looked so sure.

"Momma, do you think Poppa can manage the restaurant without me?" I was worried about that, but my mother assured me one or two of the other kids would step in and take up the slack in the meantime.

I was at once afraid to fly, yet free!

A few days later, my 1960 Chevrolet Corvair was packed with two large suitcases containing clothing, shoes, and toiletries; boxes of dried food, canned items, spices, powdered milk; toilet paper, paper towels, and garbage bags; charcoal, and lighters; a kerosene lantern, candles, and matches; galoshes and a rain hat; linens, a pillow, and blanket; and enough medicine to take care of a small tribe, all compliments of my mother whom I could tell was already worried. My fellow believers and I would all later carve our thanks to her in a beautiful large oak tree in the commune as she had understood the harshness of "roughing it."

While staring at my car, which was now sitting perilously close to the ground, my father pressed five one-hundred-dollar bills into my hand.

"Use the money wisely, Julie. Hide it and don't tell anyone how much you have. I suggest you get one of the $100 bills broken down on the way so you'll have change. Although, Lord knows where you will spend it. I hope there's a town nearby. Call me collect at any time and for any reason."

"I don't know who's more nervous—you or me," I quietly said, while he placed his arm around my shoulder, hugged me, and kissed my head.

"We both are Po d'Amore."

My goodbyes with my younger sisters and brothers were painful.

"Are you ever coming back?" my baby sister asked me, tears pooling in her big, brown, frightened eyes.

"I promise I'm coming back, goofy!" I replied, and I held her close to me while she cried.

This started a rainstorm with two others now crying. I assured them I would call them as soon as I arrived at the commune and that I would come home soon to visit. I had a difficult time driving and must have cried for a solid hour after leaving the only security I had ever known.

Commune life was the most laid-back I had ever seen. Everyone wore jeans or shorts and tie-dye shirts, long skirts or dresses, and never-ending hair flowed down their backs. I wore my hair down to my waist, my locks intertwined with fresh flowers and naturally dried while I sat on a sundrenched rock in the middle of a meadow crowded with colorful flowers and located adjacent to our site. Colorful vines between my toes served as my footwear and I wore a variety of flowing cotton dresses without the hint of undergarments.

It was a time of total abandon, and I was madly in love with this long-haired, sandal-wearing rebel named Jesus, and I devoured His teachings.

Life was primitive. Forty of us lived in a dormitory-style wooden building with a thick wall separating the men's and women's living quarters, twenty individuals in each. The building had been designed to allow the north to south winds to blow through the huge, screened windows, giving us some respite from the summer heat. Large wooden shutters were kept open all the time and closed only in case of a hard-blowing storm. With no electricity, we were thankful we had chosen the Appalachian Mountains with their cooler temperatures as our haven.

We used gas lanterns to light our path at night and for reading. We hand-washed our clothes then hung them with clothespins on outdoor clotheslines to dry, just like our grandmothers had done before electricity. We even learned how to churn butter and bake biscuits and bread from scratch over a hot campfire, warm butter running down our chins as we devoured those thick and crunchy biscuits.

In our half-acre plot of land, we grew potatoes, okra, squash, peas, tomatoes, and corn. Most of us had become semi-vegetarians, knowing meat could be hard to come by. We raised egg-laying hens and chickens for eating, kept a couple of goats for milking, and we learned how to prepare dishes like soybean succotash and tofu meatloaf that were surprisingly quite delicious.

Freshly caught mountain trout we fried in an iron skillet over an open fire, spicing it with the wild rosemary we found growing in one of the meadows.

Water was hauled in from a creek nearby and heated for bathing in an old-fashioned stainless-steel tub, then afterwards used to wash clothes. On hot days, most of the men chose to bathe in the creek, but we women bathed in the privacy of the bath house located next to the dormitory. Two hastily built wooden outhouses, one marked for women, the other for men, were shared by the entire community and therefore, were my most unpleasant experience.

At night, we would sit around a well-built campfire, watching as the firelight cast strange shadows on the trees around us. The sounds of the night creatures that made the trail their home would buzz around us as we spoke in conspiratorial tones of how we were going to make our troubled world a better place for ourselves and for future generations. As an acoustic guitar played softly nearby, we would sing along, and then later pray for those in need of prayer.

Daily Bible study and prayer were the norm, and one didn't go even one day without experiencing the spiritual power of our community. That is what had drawn us here physically and tugged at our hearts to stay.

It was in the second month of my new free, blissful life while I was chasing down chickens for the evening meal that I was approached by a tall, attractive guy who was either lost or looking for the dormitories.

"Hi, I'm Julie," I said, while sizing him up.

"Bobby. Just got here from New Orleans."

"My hometown as well," I replied.

As we walked to the men's section, I learned that, like me, he was a recent convert to our mystical and magical journey into self-discovery.

Somehow, I knew the moment I laid eyes on him that this was the man God had chosen for me. A tall man at 6'3" and weighing around 220 pounds, he carried his large frame well, a result of many years of competitive football and a belief in exercise I would later learn. I also found out he had grown up in a lively and loving family. We both appreciated the belief our parents had instilled in us to not limit ourselves in our talents and capabilities.

Bobby fit into commune life very well and immediately started pulling his load by milking goats, working the garden, and clearing the land. He won the hearts of everyone when he built two more outhouses, placing them further from the other two. We women now had a little more privacy. He was a well-trained survivor through and through, having grown up in the swamps of the Atchafalaya before moving into the city. Generations of his family had tracked alligator, nutria, snakes, and turtles down in those swamps, not to mention crawfish, the area's staple revenue.

Showing great skill with his bow and arrow, Bobby, our new chef, created mouth-watering dishes from a wide variety of forest creatures: squirrel, grouse, turkey, and rabbit. He simmered his "kill" over the fire in a sauce he created with red wine vinegar, spices, and herbs he located nearby. The meat literally fell off the bone, and the sauce was delectable.

Suddenly I felt safer now than at any other time since I had arrived. I felt God was showing me that Bobby was the one for me. He was a survivor and had certainly become my protector.

Before we knew it, we desired the company of one another more than I was ready for.

"We need to back off a little before I break my Christian vows," I shared one night after we had spent some time in heavy petting. Man, that boy could kiss. "I made a promise to my parents and myself to remain pure for the man God chooses for me."

Bobby laughed, tousled my hair, and said, "That's okay, I'm around for the long haul."

I had already lost my heart to him, and that was all I was willing to give up for the time being. We enjoyed every minute together and laughed continually. I realized I had found my soul mate, and life was indeed good.

June in the commune passed with warm and bearable weather. July brought rain, mosquitoes, mud, and weird brown spiders with a violin image on their backs. I quickly learned that these are brown recluse spiders and very poisonous, which required that we check our clothing and beds constantly for them. With no air conditioning and unusually high humidity, tempers ran short, and we were all tired of washing our clothes three times over to try and get the red clay stains out.

I passed the time writing letters to my siblings and parents, trying to mask my weariness with forced cheerfulness. At times, I had to admit, I really missed the comfortable bed and ease of living I had left behind in a city churning with a revitalized spirit and a family that truly missed me. One positive thing about the rain was that it gave me more time to spend with Bobby, and we never ran out of things to talk about.

We moved into the fall and helped harvest our neighbor's crops, sold the balance of our produce, and managed to make it to a time when the trees were stripped of their lively colors and the first mountain winds of an early winter coldly blew through cracks in our shuttered windows. It was November, we were cold, and we had run out of money.

Just like that, it was over, and I was conflicted. Part of me had really loved the easygoing lifestyle, and I would miss that. The other part of me was relieved; the harsh pioneering life had begun to wear on me. As we broke down our camp and packed our vehicles, we all shared how meaningful the experience had been and promised to keep in touch. I wondered if we would.

I was very grateful for two things: One, I had learned to survive from the land and that had been exceptional for one who had not spent much time in the wild. Two, I had met the person I believed I would spend the rest of my life with, and I was looking forward to getting to know this gentle man even more. It was time to go home and back to the real world.

20

Life with Bobby

My family ecstatically welcomed me, and I returned to school after the winter break and resumed my classes, glad to be back in the land of real bathrooms, running water, air conditioning, and refrigeration. Not to mention, I needed some of my dad's pizza and lots of hugs.

I soon completed my studies at Tulane and received my degree, then I diligently went about pursuing my dream of helping repeat offenders. At the commune I had realized that the only way problems could be solved in this world would be to get involved directly and not just sit around talking about them. Laying low in the mountains was definitely not the solution.

Bobby and I continued to see one another, and he and Dad hit it off from the beginning. My crazy family embraced him, and my mother fussed over him as if he were one of her own, which meant feeding him at every opportunity.

"Bobby, Bobby, come here, I have ziti, piping hot out of the oven. Here's a plate full. Try it. You can't eat a meal without fresh hot bread. Save room for dessert. You're wasting away to nothing," she would go on and on. He couldn't believe I didn't weigh 300 pounds.

I also became closely acquainted with his parents, and we would sometimes have them join us at the pizza parlor and enjoy a meal together with my parents after closing time. They were a warm, gracious family and thrilled with our relationship. The stories they shared about Bobby and his two siblings growing up in the Atchafalaya Swamp would have us all in hysterics. His father occasionally brought his fiddle to play, and we would sometimes jump up and dance with late-staying customers.

We both fell deeply in love, and Bobby proposed to me one moonlit night on the top deck of the Natchez riverboat, with the mighty Mississippi River flowing beneath us and music from the orchestra playing inside as beautiful accompaniment. I wore a pink chiffon tea-length dress and white high heel shoes. Bobby was handsome in khaki pants, a blue blazer, and tie. We leaned over the railing, held hands, and gazed at both the stars and the lights of our beautiful city, breathing in the smells of the river.

Bobby turned, looked at me, and said, "Julie, from the second I set eyes on you in the Appalachian Mountains, I can't stop imagining having you in my life. That's only happened one other time. It was when I took up bow hunting. The moment I had that bow in my arms and fired that first arrow, I knew I was going to be doing it for as long as I could. It energized me, and so do you.' (Some women might have been confused by that; I chose to be pleased by it.)

He continued. "I was wondering how it would feel to be around you away from the commune. There we were far removed from normal pressures, and I didn't know if returning to the real world would affect our relationship. I have spent months with your family, and I feel like they are my own. Your mother has fed me every dish known to mankind, and I've gained only ten pounds. And your father? Well, this is what he said when I spoke with him. 'I'm a cook, right? I'm extremely good with a cleaver. Be good to my daughter and don't make me go Sicilian on you.' Then he roared with laughter, and I grew weak with relief. What I am saying is this, marry me, and let's fulfill all of those dreams we had in the mountains. Marry me, and let's fill our home with children and laughter. Marry me because I love you, and you're the one for me, Sha."

While a breeze lightly blew my dress and swirled my hair around my face, I replied, "Okay, you're not the only long-winded person here, mister. Before I say yes, and cry, and get mascara all over my face, I want to say this:

"Thank God for those days in the mountains. My family may have scared you away before I had time to properly prepare you." We both chuckled and I continued, "I thought I was running away from life up there until I met you. God had to get me removed from the demands in my life in order to hear and see His will for me. I knew you were the one, Bobby. You were from the beginning, and you will be 'til the end. It would be my honor to marry my best friend, and I love you too."

My brand-new fiancé then pulled a ring box out of his pocket, opened it up, and I just gawked at the beautiful, twinkling marquise-cut diamond. Bobby laughed at my expression, then placed it on my ring finger. It was a perfect fit!

My childhood priest married us in the side yard of Poppa's pizza parlor. My parents prepared enough food for the entire town to enjoy, and we all celebrated late into the night. Things got better with each year as Bobby and I built a life of peace and contentment together.

I looked at my husband and my parents, sharing in the joy we were feeling at actually seeing, hearing, and touching one another again. I prayed I wasn't dreaming it.

Bobby continued, "'Ever since I have known you, you have always worked hard to ease the burden for others. I marveled at your belief in those who had absolutely no one pulling for them in the legal system and how you went the extra mile to give them a shot at a normal upbringing.

"Believe me, Julie, you will find your heavenly home is more than just a house—it's a mansion," he finished. He hugged me once more, and it felt so good. How I had missed Bobby's hugs!

"Wow, Bobby, thanks" was all I could manage to say, another huge lump forming in my throat. Just hearing his voice brought a smile to my face, and I looked at this man who had played such a huge role in my life in a new and different way. No longer did I see him as my husband but as one who was still my best friend and close brother in Christ.

"Bobby, Wisdom told me there is only one marriage in heaven, and that is between Christ and the Church."

"That's right, Julie, we are all joined together as brothers and sisters in our faith, and the only thing that matters is to continue to pray for others, to worship our Savior, and to enjoy the heavenly smorgasbord God has prepared in His kingdom for His children."

I looked at him, smiled, and shook my head. Yes, we had been married and had a son together. We had built a beautiful life on earth, but here that didn't matter. We all have our own unique personalities and gifts that God has given us, yet we are the same. We all belong to the family of God. I was happy to be able to love freely, with no pressure from anyone, at anytime, anywhere.

It was such a relief now to have no worries about satisfying someone else's ego or going against your will to make a partner happy or doing twelve things all at once like juggling school, a spouse, children, a home, church, and a full-time job. Oh yes, and making sure your siblings stayed out of trouble and received their education.

In this calm and gentle place, there is no criticism or unmet expectations. No jealousy, suspicious nature, tirades, or harsh words said in anger and later regretted. I had seen what a harsh life can do to people who have no hope and how it turns them into empty and bitter street survivors without a conscience. I had seen it all during my many years of social work, and, over time, it had torn at me, worn on me, and pulled me down.

Here, you feel unconditionally accepted by every single person you encounter. After rejection during my gawky and awkward years of being naturally clumsy and the heckling and snide remarks I received, I embrace this totally loving and non-judgmental environment that goes beyond anything I perceived heaven to be.

Wisdom was right about taking it in over a period of time. This process is so much better as God's plan is always to have order and to make our metamorphosis totally painless and memorable.

Flanked on both sides by both parents and Bobby, I was led up a path bordered on both sides by small hills completely covered in bougainvillea, orchids, and other exotically perfumed flowers. Butterfly types like skippers, gossamer wings, brush footed, swallowtails, parnassians, whites, and sulphurs were in abundance and quite beautiful.

With a big grin on his face, my father shared with me, "A celebration is being prepared in your honor, Julie, and you will have a chance to see all of your relatives and friends who have come here before you. You will be greatly pleased with the mansion Jesus has already prepared for you. A feast with every type of Italian food that you have loved over your lifetime will be represented, and several of your favorite musicians will perform at your concert."

"Does that mean we will all dance?" I eagerly asked him, cherishing that rugged and handsome face once again.

"Yes, my daughter, and I ask you to please reserve the first dance for me," he finished, while taking off his hat and bowing from his waist, bringing out a girlish giggle in me.

Naturally, I curtsied and replied, "Oh, Poppa, I have dreamed so many times of dancing with you again. How many times I bragged about you and Momma and wanted to see you dance again. And, here we all are—together once more. So, I bet you dance even better now, huh?"

"You better believe it!" dad bragged, picking up my mother as if she were weightless, and she squealed with laughter. "Wait until you see the two of us dance like we did in the '40s."

Now I wondered if I'd be able to keep up. What a great time we all would have, and I would just have to learn how to get in the swing of it!

The road we were walking on was comprised of golden bricks, carefully fitted to make a smooth surface. Their temperature was just perfect on my feet. The sky overhead was streaked with turquoise, coral, baby blue, and peach colors like a swirl of sherbet ice cream. Jaybirds and blackbirds flew overhead and filled the sky with their happy chattering.

I could hardly believe it. After years of being without the two most important people in my life, here they were beside me, ready to help me face this transition with ease, just like they had at my original birth. Actually, with the pain my mother suffered during several childbirths, she might have laughed at the term "ease."

"Mother, what's with the hats?" I asked curiously.

"I told your father you would ask about the hats," she laughed.

"This tradition started in heaven long ago when a famous lady racehorse owner died and came here. The concept was introduced through her guardian angel, it went up the ranks of the angels, then it was approved by God. "Hats are custom designed by milliners in the City of God and are worn for homecomings, festivals, concerts, and special events in the Temple of Praise and Worship. It will be my pleasure to take you to my milliner when the time is right."

"I'm ready when you are," I replied.

"You got it. Anyway, that's how it works here. They are always thinking of new ways to make heaven even more glorious than it already is. Believe me, there is always something interesting going on in heaven. Just wait."

"Just wait," I mimicked. "I've been waiting sixty-seven years, I guess I can just wait a bit more," I chuckled.

The closer I got to my homecoming, the more I was filled with newfound joy and knew I was about to experience something unlike anything I had before.

21

My Heavenly Mansion

"Take a deep breath, daughter. We're here," my father announced. We had arrived at a tree-lined and heavily scented, winding, cobblestone walkway bordered on the left by a large meadow filled with more flowers than I could ever name and on the right by the glittering and endless, clear, blue sea.

This dazzling garden contained decorative statues, exotically carved birdbaths, bubbling fountains, and brick walkways. One area featured a huge collection of day lilies, my favorite flower to garden. A curving vine-covered trellis led down a worn grassy path to a white wrought iron seating area comfortably arranged around a fire pit for intimate conversation.

Pecan and walnut trees, apple, pear, and fig trees, along with muscadine and scuppernong grape vines grew in abundance. These, I was pretty sure, would be used in the near future to make some great homemade wine.

"Uh, Poppa," I asked, "is homemade wine allowed in heaven?"

"Of course, Po d'amore, it is allowed at celebrations or any time you wish to drink it. Anyway, no one ever gets inebriated, acts crazy, or falls down now. The food and drink are enjoyable to taste and nothing more. It's a time of celebration when we can relax, have a good time, and savor life, plus everything is free!" *My father, ever the frugal man,* I thought.

I could see this place had worked wonders on him, and I was

really looking forward to making my own white and red wine, cooking good old-fashioned family recipes, and entertaining.

"There's a small lake on the back of the property stocked with sac au lait, blue gill, catfish, largemouth bass, and a few nice-sized turtles. It has a strong pier for fishing and a nice area for gutting and cleaning," I was delighted to hear my father tell me.

"Great, Dad!" I exclaimed, "Suppose you'll have some free time coming up to give it a try?"

"I'll have to check my calendar, of course, and remember that I'm in much better shape than I used to be. I can really give you a run for your money now."

"Bring it, mister!" I challenged, while hugging him tightly. Thankfully, he had not lost his sense of humor.

As I took a close look at my parents, I noticed that the stress lines on both their faces were gone. I knew what a toll the pizza business had taken on the health of this giant of a man, but he had loved it. I also had seen what my dad's death had done to my mother. She had never recovered as they had been true soul mates, and grief had overtaken her in the end. Together, they had raised six children, lived through the Great Depression and several wars, learned how to survive and thrive in a foreign country with all its hurdles, and given more to their community than most people could ever remember.

I had chosen to not date or remarry after Bobby's death as I had found in him the one and only one for me. It had been a good decision for I had poured the time and effort into my son, helping him to recover from the loss of his dad.

It had seemed unfair at the time to lose my husband at such a young age, but I never questioned God, I just suffered in silence.

Now I had left my siblings, my son, daughter-in-law, and precious grandchildren behind. Yet, I knew God was watching over them and they too would become stronger and feel my prayers for them from here in heaven, just as I had felt my parents' and husband's prayers over those years.

I abruptly stopped as I saw what dominated the other side of the meadow.

"Wow!" I exclaimed as I took in what I knew to be my heavenly mansion—a stately two-story antebellum mansion. I would later find that it was complete with four fireplaces, two of which had smoke curling up from them. An impressive columned portico contained a hanging swing on both ends, several wooden rocking chairs facing the water, and potted plants and hanging plants of many types.

The beautifully crafted Civil War-era home was placed at an angle to take in both the exquisite beauty of the multiple-shaded blue sea and the meadow bursting with fragrant flowers that more than filled the air with their exotic aromas.

A second story balcony was located to one side of the entrance, and I assumed it was just off my master bedroom. I saw more beautiful furniture spaced around the balcony as well as plants, flowers, and a couple of hand-tied hammocks—*no doubt made in Mexico*, I laughingly thought. I was sure it would be a favorite space of mine.

"I am beyond amazed," I blurted out, swept up in the magic of the moment, gazing at a dream that had manifested itself right before my eyes. It was designed in a similar style to the antebellum mansion "Tara" from *Gone with the Wind*, minus the extra wing.

I looked at my parents and my mother said, "God knew how

much you loved the book and movie, especially Scarlett's family home. It's very beautiful."

"You know, at one time I wanted to be Scarlett O'Hara, except I would have loved Rhett Butler and treated him well and not just because he was such a beautiful man, but because he was kind and loving."

"Julie, I agree with you on that one."

Our eyes met, and I was struck by how real this was all becoming to me. I was waking up to the fact that heaven is indeed created just for you as a reward for how you lived your life.

I looked over at Bobby and smiled. "You were right when you said God had given me a mansion. I'm ready to see the rest!"

We stopped and took in the unobstructed water view from my hilltop vantage point, watching new arrivals to "our side" and the entertaining boat activity that extended as far as my eyes could see. I couldn't wait to get out there and enjoy the water like the rest of the heavenly beings.

Dad began to enumerate all the wonderful things set before us. "At any time, you can look out and see sailing regattas, pleasure cruises, dinner boats, fishing boats, speed boats, pontoons, cruisers, kayaks, canoes, and an old-fashioned riverboat paddle-wheel that is always packed because of the live music and dancing it provides on all three levels. You know your mother and I have tried that out on more than one occasion," my dad finished.

"Why Poppa, I'm shocked. You and Momma dancing? I can't wait to see it again!" My eyes filled with tears as I realized I would see my parents glide around the dance floor once more, their timing and execution so well-coordinated. They were such a joy to watch.

"Julie, this is an excellent location God chose for your home," my mother said while putting her arm around me. "He knew how much you love your southern roots and being near water. He knew you before you were even formed in my womb. Do you remember that scripture?"

"Jeremiah 1:5. But, if He knew me before I was formed in your womb, why didn't He make me born rich?" I laughed. "Of course, now, that doesn't really matter. I'm certainly rich here."

"You have no idea," Bobby added.

Not only had I always loved being near the water, but I cherished the strength of trees. I was happy to see the house surrounded by tall, thick magnolia trees whose branches draped the house, as if protecting her. A scattering of Southern oak trees stretched out their majestic limbs like giant, muscled arms trying to embrace other arms. Some of the massive limbs even touched the ground. Many were heavy laden with Spanish moss, reminiscent of my New Orleans upbringing, and I could almost smell the salt and muskiness of the bayous from here.

The happy sound of squawking seagulls hovering in the distance, combined with glittering sparkles dancing on the turquoise and aqua water below, created a feeling of permanence inside me, and I knew I was truly and finally home.

I stopped for a moment, took a deep breath, and said with sincere thankfulness, "Mom, Dad, thank you so much for raising me to be a Christian. I strayed a few times, but just seeing your faces while I was praying would help get me back on the path."

"Bobby, thank you for always being a faithful and loving husband, and for giving me the world's most beautiful son and grandchildren. I am so glad to see the three of you again, and I appreciate you staying near me today as this is all so new, and I've already been through one wild ride." This brought a knowing laugh from everyone.

After passing through the fragrant meadow, I was welcomed by colorful purple balloons (my favorite color) tied to shrubbery, and calligraphy signs that read, "Welcome home, Julie." These were attached to trees and columns at the front of my new glorious home.

A huge sycamore with two long ropes supported a large wooden swing, and a young child was already pumping her legs to go as high as she could go. That certainly brought back more childhood memories.

I stood and took in every square inch of the home Jesus had prepared for me, the one I had designed inside my head for most of my adult life. I was extremely excited to see what everything else looked like and what awaited me inside.

As I got closer to the front yard, I heard loud barking in the distance, and I have to admit, I was shocked pets were in heaven.

"Mom, is that a dog I'm hearing? Really?"

"Why not, Julie? God created animals as well as He created us, His children. If He liked them enough to create them, why wouldn't He want them here to delight everyone, including Himself? I mean, He did save two of each animal kingdom species on Noah's Ark. One of the best things is that their bodies function like ours now, so hey, no messy cleanups!"

Just as I was thinking how cool that was, I saw a little white furry body running toward me, ears flying sideways like wings and short legs churning as fast as they could go. It was Buffy, the peekapoo I had owned and loved long before Bobby Jr. was born.

This adorable mixed breed of Pekingese and poodle had

gotten hit by a car in front of my parents' house the day before Christmas, then dragged herself to the front door, and within minutes, died in my arms. I had been only twenty and mourned her passing as a mother would her child. I buried her collar, toys, and dishes with her in her backyard grave, and swore I would never have another pet as long as I lived. Naturally, that changed when my son was old enough to have a dog of his own.

Buffy still had on the pink hair bow I had tied in her hair the morning she died. I fell to my knees, and she jumped into my arms, licking my face in a frenzy. I was almost overcome with happiness.

Then there was Woody, my beautiful and crazy cocker spaniel, who at the age of nine, met his fate after accidentally eating a neighbor's rat poison. He was the next pet that jumped in my lap. I scratched him under his ears like he had always loved, and he licked my face as well.

Rocky, the coolest calico cat in the world, began purring his familiar welcome, while rubbing himself against my legs, eager for attention. I picked him up and held him close while stroking his furry coat, and I could feel his little heart strongly beating.

I sat down on the wooden swing on the front porch and played with my furry children, basking in our joy at my home-coming. It seemed like just yesterday I had been with them, and my new life was just getting better and better. I now had all three in my lap, and my parents and Bobby were smiling with pleasure at such a sight.

"They can go inside with us, right?" I asked.

My father laughed his booming laugh and said, "Well, Julie, this is your home and your belongings. I suppose your pets have as much right here as we do. Are you ready for this?"

"Let's do it!" I cheered, and all of us, including my adorable furry family, marched through the open doors to my heavenly mansion, and I was soon overwhelmed by the huge number of familiar faces grinning at me throughout my living room area. No one spoke. No one moved. They just smiled and waited in anticipation.

There was no rush, no stress, just a totally comfortable feeling. A sense of respect hung in the air as everyone here had been through a similar experience. This, however, was all brand new to me, almost a sensory overload, and it took some getting used to.

I looked around, taking everything in. The living room was very large, with ten-foot-tall ceilings, Tiffany floor lamps, and built-in bookshelves overflowing with many familiar titles and some I had yet to explore. Soft jazz was playing somewhere in the background.

There was a soothing calm in the sea foam green color that graced my walls and the three-tiered white crown molding that gave it just enough elegance. Peach and aqua pastel patterns created a feeling of comfort on oversized and tastefully decorated sofas, complete with colorful pillows and crocheted blankets my *nonna* had painstakingly and lovingly made for me over the years.

Ceiling-to-floor windows were softly draped in polished cotton in the same print as the furniture and tied back with peach tasseled drapery ties. A spectacular view awaited anyone who looked out those open windows toward the sea, and I could almost taste the westerly breezes.

Original artwork that I had yearned for over the years hung on the walls around the living room. "The Key," a four-foot by five-foot oil-on-canvas by abstract expressionist Jackson Pollock dominated the room and had always been one of my favorite paintings.

"The Mona Lisa," one of Leonardo da Vinci's most famous works, held a place of honor over the fieldstone fireplace, and I remembered often wondering what was behind that mysterious smile. Maybe I would now have a chance to ask the great artist.

Dutch post-impressionist artist Vincent van Gogh's 1889 oil on canvas, "The Starry Night," was featured on the fourth wall, surrounded by other paintings I had long admired by lesser known, but extremely talented artists.

Photos of my family and close friends here and still on earth stood on a long highly polished mahogany library table against the wall where the steps led to the upstairs section of the house. Thankfully, all I had right now were the fondest remembrances of time with them, and I would look forward with great antici-pation to their arrival here as well.

I looked again at the beautiful faces staring back at me, grinned my hello, and asked, "Where do I put my luggage?" Everyone laughed heartily and crowded around me.

The first ones I hugged were my grandparents, one set imported from Italy, the other born in America, and all four a major influence in my life. I thanked them for their sacrifice and hard work and assured them that I knew without a doubt they would be here waiting for me. They, in turn, kept hugging me and my *nonna* and *nona* kept planting kisses on both sides of my face as I laughed hysterically.

I then spent some time with my mother's two sisters and two of my dad's three brothers, and they said there was still a big crowd of friends waiting for me outside around the swimming pool. Other older family members I didn't know all that well introduced themselves and welcomed me to my new heavenly home. A good number of them were from my father's side of the family so I had never met them as they had died in the "old country."

"Poppa, I would never have understood a word they said had we been on earth. Language barriers, racial bias, and status—it's all gone. It's wonderful that we all speak the same language and communicate without a problem. This was how the garden of Eden was set up, and it was a shame Adam and Eve had to mess it up, you know?" I stated more than asked.

"It's what it is now, my pet. No sense of thinking of things that are already gone. Want to see the rest of the house first or go out and catch up with some good old friends? You know your mother; she is getting things ready in your kitchen."

I have to admit, at first, I was torn, but then I exclaimed, "Friends, of course," and I proudly went through the large, open French doors arm-in-arm with my father. I squeezed my dad's arm and said, "Thanks, Poppa, for being here. You've always been there for me, and I love you.'

"I love you, too, Po d'Amore! I'm so happy you're here."

22

Friends in Heaven

I was again allowed some time to stop and take everything in before I mingled and embraced those I had not seen for some time. I scanned the crowd and was thankful to see many I had thought about over the years and whose presence I had missed in my life. It was a large crowd, waiting patiently to hear me speak.

I stood there taking it all in. The sparkling clean and inviting Olympic-size pool was the largest residential pool I had ever seen. I could already envision the parties, celebrations, and competitions that would soon happen around it, not to mention the laps I would swim, enjoying the feel of the water on my skin and keeping myself energized.

That thought made me smile as I realized I would live forever and never again fear death. I was free of disease, both mental and physical. I would never have another pain or need of a doctor's assistance. No headache, backache, menstrual cramps, arthritis, high blood pressure, strains, breaks, depression, or allergies.

My eyes continued to roam, and I was warmed to see the famous sculpture of Michelangelo, *David*, beautifully positioned on a marble stand keeping watch over one entrance to a private cabana styled like an Arabian King's desert tent while the armless *Venus de Milo*, graced the other entrance. At 6'8" tall, she was exactly like the one I had seen in Paris on our last trip the summer before Bobby died, and a classic example of Greek sculpture. "Oh yes, I am so sure, Miss de Milo, that you are the original," I said to no one in particular.

The entire area around the pool was made of teakwood planks and groupings of friends visited around teak tables, chairs, and comfortable recliners. Forty-foot-tall queen palms ringed the pool and gently swayed in the pleasant, continuous breeze.

I cleared my throat, overcome with emotion, and spoke. "I want to thank you all for being here to welcome me home. I know we all have traveled the same road just to get to this point, and you all know what I am experiencing. I am definitely in overload and elated to see all of you again.

"I am happier than I ever thought I could possibly be. Heaven is bigger and better and greater than anything those on earth could ever imagine.

"On earth, it seemed that as Christians, we were always in the minority and at times it was hard to stand for our faith in the face of adversity. Having the faith to believe in someone or something you can't touch, see, or feel is the reason we all are here. We believe God and Jesus and the Holy Spirit are real, and that His Word is true and everlasting. It's what kept us going in the harshest of times. I am so proud to be a part of the incredible family of God.

"To God be the glory!" I yelled with such enthusiasm that everyone at the party started saying it in unison, and we could feel the rush of the Holy Spirit enveloping our beings. At the same time, beautiful fireworks began lighting up a darkened sky above us, enchanting us with the magnificence that rendered even the best Chinese fireworks lackluster. We all stood rooted in amazement.

As I watched with my father, I remembered all the firework

displays we had attended as a family over the years. The Fourth of July and New Year's were celebrated with sizzling and beautifully crafted explosions of light over the Mississippi River. We would bring folding lawn chairs, soft drinks, and popcorn, and share family time together. We were the family saying the most "oohs" and "aahs" and I was fascinated by the light of the pyrotechnics reflecting off the lenses of Poppa's horn-rimmed glasses.

I started moving through the crowd, greeting old friends I had shared time with in Catholic school and church. Still others were there whom I had met while at the Christian commune so many years ago as well as students I had befriended in college.

I saw a few male and female friends holding babies or the hands of small children. When I looked questioningly at my father, he replied, "These are the children who come to heaven prematurely and need parenting. They are cared for by all of us until their mothers hopefully arrive, but for now, women who were never able to birth a child are given the chance. It's another prayer answered for them."

"And fetuses that are aborted?" I inquired.

"Yes, they develop into newborns as they pass through the tunnel."

"Poppa, that is the most beautiful thing I have heard yet in heaven. I'm curious, do babies and children grow up on the same timetable as we did on earth? Oh, and another question, when do we stop aging? Do we have a say-so in it? I kind of like the age I am now."

My father again boomed his laugh and answered. "You haven't changed since you were a little girl. You and the questions! Here's the answer: Children grow in the same timetable as on earth. When they reach an age where their brains are more fully developed, they can elect to continue aging or they may stop and live their current age for an eternity. You can also decide at what age you wish to stop. You can't go back in time and recapture your youth, but you have to remember, you will always be healthy and happy here, so age doesn't matter anyway."

"Isn't it wonderful that these children will never be exposed to some of the horrors we were exposed to throughout our lives?" I noted. "Now, that's an amazing blessing." I was enjoying this new life more and more.

Standing and admiring the sculpture of *David* was Mr. Adams, a shut-in neighbor I used to deliver a pecan pie to each Christmas. He smiled and waved at me.

Then, I looked over at another familiar face. Looking at me and grinning from ear to ear was none other than Ray Devereaux, the young man I had counseled for years and who had died by my side at the pizza parlor. I grabbed him and held onto him, grateful that he was now out of harm's way.

"Miss Julie, I owe my existence here to you. If you hadn't believed in me, I would have already been dead and gone straight to hell," he said with as much relief on his face as there was on mine.

"Oh, Ray, I thank God you are here and safe now. And just maybe you're overstating that "hell" thing a little bit. You always had a good heart; you just had a lot of bad breaks."

"Thank you, Miss Julie, but you're the one with the big heart." He looked quite handsome and at peace like I had never seen him. I wondered how many more repeat offenders I had counseled and prayed with that would be here to greet me. *Dear God, let there be more*, I silently prayed.

Raymond Devereaux had grown up in the Lower Ninth Ward of New Orleans among derelicts and drug addicts—streets littered with broken down automobiles, and walls covered with offensive graffiti. It would be many years before he would go to sleep without the stench of urine in his nostrils. His was a life of desperate means. By the time Ray was thirteen years old, he had been in trouble with the law for three years and already bore the scars of a life lived without parental love as his father was in prison for life for murder and his mother was a street prostitute and heroin addict.

Ray had been placed in detention so many times the system identified him as a repeat offender, and many had long ago given up hope for any type of a successful future for him. Petty thievery, running numbers for the Mafia, "boosting" cars, and breaking, entering, and robbing expensive homes was already a way of life for him. For some reason, though, he had never committed a violent crime and had not yet become hardened.

I met Ray at the Orleans Parish Prison, the one and only time he visited his father. I had been visiting and counseling Ray Sr. for a few weeks, and he had expressed concern about his son, knowing the boy's mother would be gone for days at a time, trying to earn money however she could to support their only child and her out-of-control drug habit.

He was already aware of Ray's illegal activities, and he intended to help him choose a better course for his life. I had arranged for the meeting with the warden and prayed things would go as planned.

I remembered the six-foot-tall, thin, and very mean-looking fourteen-year-old teenager leaning against the wall with his arms folded and forearm muscles bulging, either as a means of shutting me out or an attempt at intimidation. A toothpick dangled from his lips and the beginnings of a sneer played around the corners of his mouth.

"Hey, Ray," I had begun all those years ago, my clipboard held against my chest, perhaps as a defense maneuver. "How are things going?"

"Hmmm, let me think, I was thinking of flying out to Los Angeles later today, catching a movie premier, then jetting on up to New York for an interview on *The Tonight Show*. How you think I'm doing?' he asked while rolling the toothpick around in his mouth.

"Well, truthfully, your life sounds much more interesting than mine." This actually brought the small start of a smile to his face. At least he had a sense of humor.

He stayed sullen, suspicious, and uncommunicative until I asked, "Watched any Saints football lately?"

His brown eyes lit up and somehow his mouth started working overtime. He started sharing stats, and his feelings about recruiting. That was when we established the bond that would help us in future counseling efforts. Luckily, I was a huge college and professional football fan and found that to be great common ground for easy conversation.

After the awkwardness disappeared, Ray agreed to hang out with me and Bobby every Saturday and hopefully that would help him feel like part of a family. We planned picnics, baseball outings, and strolls through the French Quarter and around busy Jackson Square, with the St. Louis Cathedral looming in the background.

The three of us attended Saints' football games and ate peanuts and hot dogs and drank ice cold soft drinks. We all cracked up when we put paper bags over our head one season with the eyes cut out, and Ray commented, "I cannot believe I haven't been arrested for this yet," and we all laughed. One of the local radio celebrities had dubbed that year's team the "'Aints" after placing a paper bag over his head in protest over the dismal one-win season, and we got caught up in the fun of it.

We introduced Ray to a gentler part of the Big Easy, a way of life that now seemed within reach for this desperate child-man who had known only a vortex of despair. We also insisted he attend church with us on the weekends he visited, and after an initial reluctance, he started enjoying it.

Our pastor pulled some strings, and with my help as well, Ray got placed with a foster family in our church who could provide him with a stable environment. He started feeling the new sensation of a solid foundation under his feet when two people were willing to give him a shot at life. He had a safety net for the first time in his life and would be the first of his family to graduate high school.

My father, ever the champion for the underdog, quickly took to Ray and hired him to work at the pizza shop. Under his tutelage, Ray learned how to build the 800-degree fire, to work tables for tips, and help clean up at closing before returning home. We were all thrilled to see him finally gain some weight as he had been frightfully thin when we first met him. He was certainly enjoying trying everything on the menu, and we couldn't imagine where he was putting it all. It was, unfortunately, his passion for gambling and his inability to repay his debt to the Mafia that caused both our lives to end. I hugged him once more, amazed at how good he looked.

I almost gasped out loud as I saw Jimmy, my teenage boy-friend who had taught me how to drag race and speed shift walking toward me. I remembered he had died in a bad car accident trying to outrun a train two years after we graduated from high school. He had retained his twenty-year-old looks and quick smile.

I was a senior in high school when, thanks to Jimmy and my Uncle George, a stock car racer, I developed my love for drag racing. My uncle had raced in the very first NASCAR race, placing fifth, and he and Jimmy had become fast friends.

"You ought to try it, girl," I remember that my uncle had said, balancing a cigarette between his lips, while tightening something under the hood with a wrench. He was working on another race car in his large backyard garage. "You've certainly got the guts for it. Your dad told me you actually went up against the priest, asking him if you could be an altar girl. Hot dang! A priest! I figure you'll either get a crown of glory for that one, or a short trip to hell. I'd bet on the crown, myself." I reminded Jimmy of that episode, and we both laughed aloud at the remembrance.

Jimmy taught me how to drive fast and speed shift in his bronze-colored, souped-up Pontiac GTO with leather bucket seats. When I drove, he would give me pointers with great patience. He was quite proud of me because of my desire to drive fast.

"You should see her speed shift," he bragged to just about everyone. "She uses this oversized black gear shifter with a white skull painted on it."

The two of us spent most weekends racing down a few of the far back, empty streets outside of New Orleans, and we had the routine down pat. One person would mark off a quarter mile with chalk, and then he remained there with a black and white checkered bandana, waiting to flag the first one to cross the finish line. Another remained at the start line with a white handkerchief to start the race.

Racers dressed in black leather jackets, white tee shirts, and tight jeans; cigarettes dangling from their lips, lined up Mustangs, GTOs, Corvettes, Chargers, Camaros, and other muscle cars of that era, their .327s and .409s thrumming with sounds of the hooves of hundreds of horses. Once that white flag came down, the thrill of the fast ride for even that short a distance was probably like crack cocaine today. The high was powerful.

Jimmy grabbed my hands in his and continued, "Julie, you turned out so good, but then I always knew you would. You were one of the few in school that shot straight with people, and I always admired your work ethic. After I passed through, I always kept up with you, praying for you and your great family. You went through a lot, but it made you stronger. You always were special to me."

"You know, you were one of the few guys who didn't try to violate my purity in high school," I replied, placing my hand over my heart. "Thanks again for that. How has it been here for you? Silly question, right?"

"Julie, you have no idea what's in store for you. Words cannot describe it. Period. I'll put it this way: If you put all of the superlatives in the dictionary on top of one another, and they stretched upward for thousands of miles in the sky, it wouldn't come close to describing it.

"There is purpose in everything here. Life as you knew it on earth will become dimmer over time as the splendor of heaven eclipses every planet ever formed. You will still remember the positive aspects of your life there, and you will continue to pray for those you love, whether it's for salvation, healing, victory over life's challenges, or anything else they need you to pray for. Your prayers here in heaven are the most powerful as you have the direct power of God, Jesus, the Holy Spirit, the angels, and the heavenly saints to back you up."

My thoughts then went to my son, Bobby Jr., his wife, Deanna, and my precious grandchildren, Annabelle and Alana. How were they holding up after the murder? I was again appreciative that no sorrow was associated with that memory. I did know that I would need to continue praying for all of those who had been affected by my untimely death.

My son had a good, strong heart, and he would pull his family together and help soothe the grieving process. Being his mother had been my proudest achievement.

Others from our high school started crowding around us, and I was extremely comfortable to be around so many who had grown up in the same era as I had and whom I could relate to so well.

There was Alicia who had died of muscular dystrophy at four-teen—my friend Belinda and I had sung at her memorial; Tommy, who had been crushed two days before graduation when his car shifted off the jack while he was changing a flat tire; and Samantha, a close friend who choked to death right in front of me while eating a sirloin steak at Delmonico's Steak House on her forty-fifth birthday. Even the Heimlich maneuver didn't work that night.

As I weaved among others who had come to celebrate my arrival, I heard *Revelation,* beautifully created spiritual music by Kitaro, the famous Japanese musician whose haunting and inspiring pieces stirred my soul, soothing and calming me over the years. This particular rendering seemed appropriate for tonight's event.

My thoughts were interrupted when one of my dearest friends from high school came up and grabbed me with a bear hug. Robby had been a letterman in high school football, baseball, and basketball and one of the best-looking guys in our school. I felt my eyes misting when I realized that he was here in heaven after having committed suicide a few years after graduation.

"Robby, it's you. Oh, thank God, you're here!" I happily exclaimed while hugging him fiercely.

"Julie, Julie, Julie," he said in that mocking voice of Cary Grant's. "And why wouldn't I be here? Do you think God's forgiveness doesn't extend to those who choose to end their lives, after having asked for it?"

I remembered how pleasantly surprised I had been when Wisdom had shared the story of Judas' appeal for God's forgiveness before taking his own life.

"I'm just thankful it does, Robby. Wow, you look great!"

"As do you, Julie."

Mr. Harding, one of my father's best friends who had died from throat cancer in the '70s, joined us and talked about how great it was to see everyone in such great shape. I said "Mr. Harding, you look excellent yourself. Mrs. Harding hasn't arrived yet, I see."

"Nope, she's still taking care of the family on earth. I'm sure ready to see her, though, but it's just not her time yet. Hey, I have tennis courts at my place. You guys stop in anytime, and we'll play a few sets."

"You're on," my father replied, and I looked forward to spending time with such a wonderful man who had always treated me like a daughter.

Heaven was filled with beautiful people, one-of-a-kind mansions, swimming pools, tennis courts, boating, celebrations, and so many more things I had yet to experience. Happy people were filling time with everything they ever wanted in their lives and all of it granted by God Himself. I was no longer dreaming of heaven; I was living it.

I closed my eyes and thanked God for my new home. It was at that moment that I felt the urging of the Holy Spirit pulling me toward the sea.

"Excuse me, everyone," I said, as I moved away from the pool area. With my dogs running happily at my side, I then walked to the highest point of my property and looked out over the water. There I saw Jesus walking on the water from one side of the sea to the other. The incandescent glow that illuminated from Him made Him a breathtaking sight. It was as if He were on fire. Friends from the party began forming around me, captivated as well. Others in various watercraft had also stopped their activities to watch.

"Jesus! Jesus! Come to the party!" I yelled, while wildly waving my arms. Everyone around me began repeating those words and before you knew it, our Savior was standing right before us, and I was just as enchanted this time as I had been on Disciples Walkway earlier. We all bowed in wonder to Him.

I could gaze at those crystal blue eyes nonstop for an eternity, and the best thing is that I knew I would. The aura surrounding Jesus was always a wonder to see as no one else so far in heaven could come close to it. I knew Jesus embodied both God the

Father and the Holy Spirit, representing the fulfillment of God's promises throughout His Word.

Once I surrendered myself to God's leadership and guidance at the age of twenty, I started studying the Bible, "from maps to Revelation," I always said. I learned that there are almost four thousand promises given to us by God in the Bible and that if we ever truly grasped the significance of that fact alone, how much easier our existence could be.

I realized the Bible's importance as a positive tool in raising my son, being a supportive wife, and counseling desperate young men and women with compassion and professionalism. I learned that Jehovah doesn't expect us to be perfect. I mean, after all, He selected ordinary people to achieve extraordinary things. He just wants us to trust Him and to love others, no matter what.

"Julie, you know I couldn't stay away from your homecoming celebration," said Jesus. "Come, let's go to the feast, and I will turn the water into wine for your special occasion." I loved the twinkle in his eye at that moment. It was endearing to me.

"Now, that's a great idea. Does this mean I finally get to see the rest of my magnificent house?"

"Of course," Jesus replied, while bending down and petting Buffy and Woody who were jumping up and down at the sight of Him. Were you surprised to see them?" He asked.

"In a way, yes. That was one of the things I wondered about after I lost them. I truly hoped it to be so, but I could find no scripture to support it. I guess you see which of my pets is missing."

"Cats!" we both exclaimed at the same time and started laughing. As usual, I had no idea where Rocky was.

"Well, let's all go and enjoy a true Italian family feast!" Jesus exhorted as He led the way to my new southern plantation, my arm comfortably hooked through His. Ahead of us in the distance, homecoming festivities were lighting up the multi-colored sky, and I felt a joy that truly passed all understanding. It was great finally to be home.

23

Checking Out the Mansion

My mother was waiting at the pool entrance to the house, and my pets ran to greet her.

"Jesus, we are so honored to have you at Julie's homecoming," she exclaimed while bending her knees to the ground in adoration. Everyone else followed her lead, and we were all on our knees worshipping Him. I was still amazed that Jesus Christ was here in front of me and had made a point of coming to my homecoming party.

"Please, get up my friends, let us go break bread together and enjoy the party that Alejandra has prepared for her daughter," Jesus said, coming into the house with my mother, and immediately being surrounded by a throng of people.

I was left alone to wander and enjoy the beauty of the dining room—one of my favorite rooms in a home and what I considered to be the "heart" of the home when large family functions were held. I was not disappointed.

The lofty ceiling was frescoed with many of Michelangelo's famous Sistine Chapel figures, including *The Creation*, which shows God reaching out His finger to touch the finger of Adam. I remembered the first time I saw this particular work by Michelangelo and how it made me consider the reality of God. I realized He is always reaching out to us, patiently waiting for us to reach up to Him.

As I was considering that, I reached my hand up and immediately felt God's hand inside mine. The heat from His touch sent a jolt through me. I felt as if I had put my finger into a light socket, but without experiencing the pain. It was truly unbelievable, and I lovingly caressed where His hand had been.

The ceiling also showcased the nine paintings showing *God's Creation of the World*, *God's Relationship with Mankind*, and *Mankind's Fall from God's Grace*. I would gaze on their magnificence forever.

About thirty round tables with white linen, gold-embroidered tablecloths were located in the oversized room. Placed in the center of every table were elaborate golden candelabras intertwined with ivy and rich, red roses. The finest bone china, crystal, and silverware graced each place setting. Ten high-backed chairs at each table were covered with the same embroidered cloth as the tables, and sweet roses perfumed the air.

I was beginning to feel the enormity of it all, and I rejoiced at the significance of a life lived well. I walked around the room with a few of my other guests, admiring the oils—many that had been inspired by God and entrusted to those who would do His will.

Picasso, Dali, Degas, Monet, Rembrandt, and Van Gogh masterpieces that I had always admired were hung around the room. I was pleased to see brightly colored flowers, mixed in with other roses, overflowing from urns and baskets spaced comfortably around. Lighting was provided by large windows that looked out over a sculptured garden, a greenhouse, and an area in the distance already set up for musical entertainment. I wondered who would be performing for me,and the thought brought a giggle from my mouth.

"Gee, all this fuss, just for me," I said to my mother who had just walked up to me.

"More to come, my dear. How do you like everything so far?" she asked.

"It's almost surreal, Mom, it's all so new. I'm really in heaven, right? This isn't just a long, drawn out dream, is it? Because if it is, I am going to be extremely disappointed when I wake up."

She hugged me and laughed. "No, honey, it's real. Come with me and check out your kitchen. You're gonna love it!"

In my earthly life, I had always dreamed of having a commercially outfitted kitchen that would contain the best cookware and gadgets to enhance my love of cooking. I also wanted to maintain the tradition of having a large, round table in the kitchen area for everyone to sit around and keep me company while I cooked. That table was a place to share recipes, gossip, and stories about the family.

Once I reached the entrance to my kitchen, I stopped and gazed at a sight that was a true blessing to me. The kitchen walls were painted a bright white while the kitchen floor was comprised of carefully laid white bricks. A large kitchen island topped with gold-flecked granite occupied the middle of the room and included a sink, faucet, and large cutting board. A dazzling display of the finest stainless-steel pots and pans hung over it.

A large oak table with six chairs and huge claw feet with legs to support it, sat at one end of the large room. I could see my manicured lawn through the bay windows. It was an exact replica of the kitchen table my family, friends, and I had shared for many years in my New Orleans home.

As I gazed around the room, I admired several thick, white flokati rugs that adorned my brick floor and Rudi Carsten's oil painting *Esther's Sacrifice* hanging on the largest wall near the French doors that opened onto another garden area. I was especially glad to have this one in my new collection as I had admired this woman's courage in facing her husband, the king, with the threat of death on behalf of her Israeli people.

The large, stainless steel stove was literally covered with huge pots of sauce and pasta boiling, and the delicious scent of baking bread filled my nostrils. Though Wisdom had suggested food was for pleasure and not sustenance, I could swear I was beginning to develop quite the appetite as I continued to check out my new kitchen.

Several of my mother's friends and other family members were busy preparing other dishes like antipasto, salad, and a huge array of desserts that would make even a French pastry chef envious: apple, cherry, lemon-ice box; and pecan pies, brownies, and fudge; tiramisu; German chocolate and red velvet cake; and ice cream and cookies. Coffee, iced tea, and homemade wine completed the evening's menu.

"This is a feast indeed!" I exclaimed, and everyone was pleased at my appreciation.

I checked out the walk-in pantry of my kitchen and found it filled with staple items like flour, sugar, corn meal, cornstarch, vinegar, seasonings, and, naturally, lots of olive oil. There are no canned items in heaven as everything is freshly picked when cooked; however, there were several varieties of dried beans and peas.

Large glass containers were stocked with several different types of cereal that I enjoy eating. Three large containers were also packed with oatmeal, grits, and popcorn kernels, comfort foods I had cherished over the years. Shelled pecans, macadamia nuts, cashews, almonds, and peanuts were also displayed on a shelf, and there was a large box of yellow, white, and purple onions, a box of white and red potatoes, and fresh garlic. It was as if I had given God a shopping list to complete, and He had done it quite well.

My pasta-making machine was already in use on the center aisle, and I knew lasagna (my favorite Italian dish), spaghetti, and fettuccine were on the menu. I could eat to my heart's content and not gain a pound. I had hit the culinary jackpot!

I exited the kitchen and stopped at the garden I had seen from the kitchen. It was packed with fresh herbs like basil, thyme, oregano, dill, chives, mint, and tarragon. Rosemary grew in abundance not only in the garden, but around the house as well as rich soil with nutrients encouraged a bountiful harvest everywhere in heaven. I couldn't wait to inhale the phenomenal aromas of herbs I had always grown in my own garden on earth, and I knew cooking here was going to surpass anything I had done in my former life.

I followed a flagstone pathway to the stage area that had been assembled under two massive magnolia trees with thick branches creating a huge canopy over the seated area. It was already set up with a full drum set, keyboards, and various guitars and brass instruments resting on their stands. I saw no hint of microphones or a sound system, as I fully understood that the concert would be performed without a need for the towers of speakers, mixing boards, and a sound crew.

I began tingling with excitement, knowing this would be like nothing I had known yet. *Who was going to perform for me? What would they sing?* I was delighted beyond belief that all this work had been done just to welcome me home. I couldn't wait to see what happened next.

Farther down the pathway, I watched as a twirling wind blew

fragrant honeysuckle petals across the path, and they tumbled all over the yard. I stopped, closed my eyes, and felt the wind blow my hair. It brought back memories of unbridled bike riding as a young girl and the thrill of the wind blowing in my face the faster I pedaled my Schwinn bicycle. My poor poppa had patched that bike up so many times, but it ended up lasting several years.

I was happy that wind, rain, clouds, rainbows, and stars existed here in heaven. Wisdom had explained that those elements of life on earth that we enjoyed, such as certain types of weather, are incorporated into our lives in heaven. However, there are no floods, hurricanes, tornadoes, earthquakes, tsunamis, fires, mudslides, or any other calamities. Life is perfect.

After passing by the concert area, I could sense the lake had always rejuvenated me and had been a large part of my life. I guessed it to be a couple of acres, and it was crystal clear and brimming with fish just as my father had said.

Dad and I are going to do some serious fishing here, I commented to myself.

While circling the lake, I walked out on the sturdy pier and studied the water below. I could actually see to the bottom of the lake, and I was amazed at the huge number of fish just waiting to be caught. Now I understood what my father had meant earlier in the day.

"God, again, I thank You for the abundance you have blessed me with," I prayed aloud. It was beginning to dawn on me that this was really and truly all mine. There would be no mortgage payment, insurance requirements, taxes, or maintenance. Everything was already paid for and would be this way for eternity.

Suddenly, I saw the same movement in the water I had seen before on my walk to the garden of Tranquility. I was mesmerized again by the watery face that rose up and appeared to me from the lake. Although formed from water, I could see the love inside that face, and I could feel it radiating from Him.

"Holy Spirit," I said as I dropped to my knees. "I am so humbled by Your generosity and love for me. I cannot thank You enough."

"He knows that Julie," I heard a familiar voice say from behind me. Turning, I saw my favorite heavenly angel. Wisdom's countenance shone even brighter as he gazed at the Holy Spirit, also kneeling in His presence. A feeling of extreme calm came over me, and I breathed in the energy of the Holy Spirit. As soon as I opened my eyes, He was gone.

Once I recovered from my second encounter with the third part of the Trinity, I ran over to Wisdom, embracing him with extreme joy.

"You came to my party! I mean, you did come to my party, didn't you? Please tell me you're not leaving. You're not leaving, are you?"

"Whoa, Julie! Slow down! I wouldn't miss your party for anything. I am still your guardian angel. Ready to go fishing?"

"You bet. I can't wait to get Poppa out here and out fish him!"

We both laughed and started back to the party. I was so happy, I felt I would burst.

24

The Feast

As we were walking back to the house, I asked Wisdom, "Have you already met everyone at my party?"

"Well," he chuckled, "you have kept me pretty busy these past sixty-seven years, not to mention the others I have under my guardianship as well. However, to answer your question, yes, I know your parents and Bobby quite well, and maybe a few others who will be at your party, but I am certainly looking forward to meeting them all."

The party was in full swing when we returned, and dishes were being placed on the tables, piled high with all types of Italian food delights. I offered to help serve but my mother quickly told me that, as the guest of honor, I would be doing nothing of the sort, so I found my way to my chair.

My seat at the front of the room was marked by colorful balloons and the table was to include the closest members of my family, with Bobby seated next to me. Jesus was seated between my parents and across from me while I remained in awe of the fact that He was at my party. The King of Kings and Lord of Lords was sitting right here in front of me, ready to eat spaghetti no less.

Within a few minutes, Jesus was surrounded by children of all ages, begging Him to tell them another story. It was just as I had pictured it throughout my life. He had always loved the children, the true innocents.

Wisdom, as usual, was standing against the wall and was enjoying the festivities the way only angels do, I suppose. He was surrounded by several of my friends and family, and I wondered if he was their guardian angel as well. *They couldn't do any better,* was all I could think.

Eventually everyone found their seats, and I remained standing. I wasn't about to pray in front of this crowd, especially with Jesus here, so I asked Him if He wouldn't mind giving the blessing, and to my relief, He was more than happy to oblige. Jesus came and stood beside me, and I could feel His incredible aura; His magnetic personality was almost overwhelming. This is what He said:

"My friends, we are here today to honor the homecoming of Julie, one of God's cherished children. Julie's life has been one of unselfish sacrifice and service to others, and she will now reap the benefits of a life lived in devotion to God and His purpose for her life. Welcome home, Julie."

Everyone then stood, lifted their wine glasses to me, and said in unison, "Welcome home, Julie." I was greatly touched by it all, and I have to say, the wine was quite delicious.

We then bowed our heads, and Jesus thanked God the Father for my arrival, the celebration, and for all who were attending. He gave thanks for the bountiful harvest we would all enjoy and for those who had lovingly prepared it. He also pointed out the joy I had shown continually since my arrival here. I couldn't believe I was actually hearing Jesus talk about me. All I could think about was how incredible my Savior is. For the second time that day, I was close to tears.

The meal was like no Italian meal I had ever eaten. The sauces were richer and tastier, the pasta was perfectly cooked, and the bread was crispy on the outside and flaky on the inside, just like the famous Leidenheimer bread we used to make "po-boy" sandwiches in New Orleans. Delicious, freshly grated *parmiggiano* topped the sauce. The meal was so good, I practically inhaled it.

"Mom," was all I could say, while shaking my head and beaming at her with sheer joy. I couldn't find the words to describe exactly what I tasted. This was my very first heavenly meal, and I was ecstatic.

"I know, honey, our sauces were always very good and our entire menu as well; however, this surpasses anything we ever created on our own."

"Well, it's probably a good thing, Mom, because we would have had some seriously overweight people in our town. Truly, this is a savory explosion inside my mouth," I remarked, and the entire table laughed.

As is the Italian custom, our next course was the salad, and, again, it was the best lettuce, tomatoes, radishes, onions, carrots, and croutons I had ever put in my mouth, and just as tasty as the pasta dishes. A light sprinkling of olive oil and vinegar perfectly enhanced the salad.

My parents were in a lively conversation with Jesus. As Italians do, my father was expressing himself with his hands, and so was Jesus. I wondered once more if I wasn't dreaming this. If so, they could have made a feature film out of it. I hoped I would never wake up.

I could only imagine what my other four heavenly friends were eating right now, and I wished they could have been at the party. However, they were surely enjoying their own homecoming as much as I was. I could see there are no downsides to heaven. *What a glorious place*, was all I could think.

I realized that I hadn't even seen the rest of the house yet, but it could wait as, again, there is no timetable in heaven. I was still clothed in the silk robe Wisdom had given me, and I noticed everyone else was wearing their own particular design. It was so comfortable I could hardly even tell I had on clothing. I also liked the fact that, with it, I could continue to be stylish.

Equally stylish were the variety of hats being worn at the party and I realized most people wear them to set themselves apart. Being a hat person myself, I was looking forward to wearing some of my own designs, and I couldn't wait to go to the milliner with my mother.

Wisdom was still leaning against the wall, his arms crossed, taking in everything in the dining hall. I was thankful he was here, and I could feel the intensity of his presence envelop me as I approached him.

"You know, Wisdom, I am so thankful no animals are slaughtered here in heaven. I never once considered becoming a vegetarian, but to think animals may have suffered in order for me to satisfy my appetite did occur to me at times, and I almost felt guilty about eating meat. I am curious, though, do chicken and fish suffer here when you kill them?"

Wisdom chuckled his answer, "You know, Julie, I have never been asked that question by anyone. I'm not surprised it was you to ask it, though. No, neither the chickens nor the fish suffer.

"Actually, God allows the sport of fishing, but guns are obviously not in existence here. Peace and joy reign. Animals have their own place in heaven and were created to worship Him as well."

"Well, I always said that when I get to heaven, I am going to ask God this: 'Platypus? Anteater? Aardvark? Really?'"

This brought another laugh from Wisdom, and he replied, "Funny, I've actually heard that one more than once."

As a young child with an unquenchable thirst for knowledge, I had read that the long-snouted anteater can eat over 35,000 ants in a day, from just one ant mound. This impressed me, and I asked my dad, "Wow, if there are that many ants in just one mound, how many zillions of ants are there on this earth? I mean, if they were much bigger, couldn't they just take over?" He had reminded me to go do my homework and not worry about an ant invasion. I have to admit, I often wondered who counted those ants.

I smiled at the memory, anxious to bring it up to him, and I continued weaving my way around the tables, loving the buzz in the room, while greeting and catching up with other's new lives.

The story was always the same. Heaven is indescribably delicious! Everything good you ever experienced in your life is found here, only it's hundreds of times better. People don't just "talk the talk, they walk the walk."

Respect has a new meaning—I could see that. Everyone from every type of background you can imagine gets along, and we all speak the same heavenly language, eliminating conversational barriers.

I felt as if I were the star of a huge epic production, and everything had been planned in perfection, down to the very last detail. I looked again at the magnificent ceiling God had painted just for me, and I bowed my head in gratitude, then I heard my mother's voice calling for me from across the room.

All I could think of at that moment was how many times over the years, after her passing, I had wished to hear her little sing-song voice just once more.

I saw the reason for her summons. A huge German chocolate cake (my favorite) was waiting on the table for me, and it was lettered with "Welcome Home, Julie. We love you." The lump in my throat was real, and I looked out at the faces of those who had gathered around to honor me.

"For the first time in my life, I am almost speechless," I began. "However, we all know that's not going to last long. I must tell you all that this is an experience I am looking forward to sharing with the rest of my family when they arrive in this blessed place.

"Want to know the coolest thing about this? I can actually look right at Jesus and say, 'Thank You, Jesus.' Wow! I can touch the faces of my father and mother, my wonderful Bobby, and others I have loved once again. I can embrace my pets, and laugh, and live, and shamelessly praise my Father God.

"Thank You, God, thank you my parents, for raising me to love God, and for leading by example. Thank you, Bobby, for being the husband I prayed for all my life. And, to everyone else, thanks for being here to celebrate this auspicious occasion. Now, let's eat us some dessert!"

We all devoured the tantalizing desserts and were thankful we didn't have to worry about the calories. My fresh, ice cold milk was a perfect accompaniment for dessert.

"By the way, Julie, the milk is fresh from your own jersey cows, grazing down in the lower pasture," Bobby told me. "I milked two of them earlier."

"Thank you so much, Bobby. You know how much I love milk. I bet that was your first time to milk cows, right?" I asked.

"Yep," he replied, "but I did milk goats in the commune. I didn't do too badly, did I?"

Man, he was so handsome, and I would look at him as long as I wanted to, I thought.

"Any hints about who is performing for me later?" I asked no one in particular between bites while glancing around the table.

"It's a surprise. Sorry," my father commented. "Remember, daughter, patience is a virtue." He then looked at me and winked that old familiar wink. We were back!

25

Touring the Upstairs

Once I finished the best Italian meal I had ever eaten, I said to everyone at the table, "You guys carry on without me as I must satisfy my curiosity and see the rest of my home."

"Well, it took you long enough," my mother kidded me.

"Hey, kiddo, don't be gone too long. We've got a whole lot more celebrating to do!" Dad enthusiastically added, while helping himself to seconds. He always had a big appetite.

I excused myself and started up the stairs to see what God had prepared for me in the upper level of the house. I made a beeline for the master bedroom, pleased to see that it ran across the entire front of the house, with huge windows that opened out to the sea.

A queen-sized poster bed was located against the back wall with an expansive view. Frankly, it looked good enough to nap in right now, considering I was still reeling from everything I had seen and done so far.

My timeworn leather NIV Bible was right next to the bed on a matching night table. Missing next to it, however, were my reading glasses, something I could shout "Hallelujah!" about now. My eyesight was perfect for the first time.

I opened my Bible to the first page and again read the inscription: "My darling Po d'Amore, always be true to God's Word. I love you, Poppa." This brought a smile to my face as this had been my father's special gift to me at my Confirmation.

On a matching dresser was an elaborate gold tray with every perfume I enjoyed wearing. Next to it was my wooden jewelry/music box that played, "Somewhere over the Rainbow," the song Judy Garland had sung, and my mother had loved from *The Wizard of Oz*. I smiled when I realized I was definitely somewhere way over the rainbow up here. Opening up the little drawers to the jewelry box that special day, I had been thrilled to see a strand of real pearls and the earrings to match that my mother had picked out just for me for my Confirmation as well.

A beautiful ivory-handled brush and comb set were also on the tray, and I picked up the brush and ran it through my hair. Memories came swirling back about nights as a young girl, when I lay in my mother's lap, eventually falling asleep while she sang Italian love songs and lovingly combed my long, silken hair.

Framed photographs of my parents and grandparents, Bobby, Bobby Jr., and his family, and other family members and friends were scattered throughout the room, lending a feeling of connection to the past for me. A framed fleur-de-lis hung on the wall, and, next to it, a 16" x 24" copy of the *Times-Picayune's* article entitled "AMEN!"which reflected the spirit of New Orleans' citizens when our beloved Saints brought the Super Bowl trophy home in 2009 for the very first time in franchise history.

"God thinks of everything, down to the smallest, minute detail," Wisdom had told me upon my arrival. Now I could see it.

The walk-in closet contained several robes like the one I was wearing, and replicas of a couple of stylish hats that I had proudly worn to church on many occasions. Although shoes were not necessary in heaven, I saw a couple of pairs of brown leather sandals, similar to the ones Jesus wears. I imagined they were available if I needed them, which was most likely for special occasions.

One of my favorite paintings, *The Tastes of New Orleans*, hung over my bed and had been painted and signed by the famous New Orleans artist Terrance Osborne. I was elated to have this particular painting because it had retailed for $20,000, an astronomical amount of money for a poor pizza storeowner. I thanked God right on the spot for giving me that one, as it had certainly been on my wish list.

On another wall hung a second painting by Osborne. It was a depiction of a New Orleanian playing a tuba with the words *Rebirth* on the instrument. It was painted following Katrina. My son bought it for me in 2006 as a celebration of the fact that we survived the worst hurricane in our city's history, and my business was still alive, when so many others had perished. I had chosen to ride the storm out, safe in the attic of my home, which was located on higher ground, unlike so many others in New Orleans.

The wind's fury had torn part of my roof off, and one of the large oak trees in the backyard had found its way on top of it, falling uncomfortably close to me. This opened up a huge hole, bringing rain into the living room. It had been a terrifying experience, and my prayers had brought me through it.

Thanks to FEMA, I was supplied with a temporary trailer while repairs were made to the house and pizza parlor.

French doors opened onto the balcony off my room, and I could already smell the roses that were growing in abundance on my property. I walked outside, taking in the incredible view of which I would never tire. I saw myself reading my Bible here in any one of the three comfortable recliners or hammocks spaced around, encompassed in a safe world that had been created just for me. I could only imagine how even more real the pages of His Word would be to me once I had experienced all that heaven has to offer.

The balcony was tastefully decorated. "Thanks again, God," I mentally noted. Numerous plants and flowers were scattered about on the tile floor in brightly colored ceramic containers, which added a certain coziness to the area.

I could hear musicians tuning a variety of instruments in the distance, and I realized I would soon have to return to the party in my honor. I could hardly wait for the concert!

But first, I was going to try that magnificent bed out and I can honestly say, it was the most comfortable bed I had ever lain on. It was only a matter of minutes before my menagerie of pets scampered into the room and jumped up on the bed, just like they had on earth. I gathered them to me, more content with the after-life than I could have imagined, and this was just the beginning.

Before the four of us headed back downstairs, I checked out the second room, which was beautifully decorated in whites and pastels and had one door leading out to its own balcony with a panoramic view of the gardens.

A day bed, with a solid brass headboard and footboard, a solid oak dresser, and high-backed oak chair completed the furniture ensemble. I was looking forward to hosting visitors in the near future.

An art easel was located in front of one of the floor-to-ceiling windows, and a sketchpad, an art palette, and brushes were lying on a table next to it. I immediately opened the door to the balcony, placing the easel outside. Sketching and painting had always been one of my favorite hobbies and I knew I would now take it to a new level.

I was aware that there are no toilets in heaven as bodily functions don't exist anymore; however, I was happy to see a silver-toed, claw-foot, white porcelain bathtub in a bathing room next to my huge bedroom. A variety of soaps, bubble baths, thick towels, and candles were situated around the tub, and I couldn't wait to try it out. A silk purple dressing robe was hanging on a hook next to the tub. How thoughtful of my Father God.

"You and me…later," was all I could think while gazing longingly at that huge tub.

"Okay, kids, let's go on down to the party," I told Buffy, Woody, and Rocky, and we all headed back down the stairs, their joy swirling all around me.

"Well?" my mother asked from the kitchen as I walked in. "What did you think?"

"Everything okay, princess?" my father quipped, going for his second (or third?) helping of carrot cake, while my mother swatted his hand away.

"Since you've all obviously already seen the entire place, you should know how much I love it, right?"

My mother sheepishly grinned and replied, "Yep, wanted to check it out for you first to make sure everything was okay."

"Right, uh huh, I just bet you did," I kidded. "And just what would you have said to God if you didn't like it?"

"I don't know," she replied, "I never got that far."

We all laughed heartily. Man, it was so awesome to be with my parents and Bobby again.

"Is Jesus still here?" I asked, and everyone responded that He had gone ahead to visit with the musicians.

"Come on, girl, let's go hear some great music," Bobby said, putting my arm through his, and we headed out to the concert, my parents and pets alongside us.

26

The Concert

Someone had reserved the central area in the first row of seats for me, Bobby, my parents, and my grandparents. My seat was dead center, with a perfect view of the stage. I was very excited and ready to hear some of my favorite performers, and I knew I would be far from disappointed. I certainly hadn't been so far.

I noticed that two beautiful ivory baby grand pianos were facing one another, much like dueling pianos. "Hmm, wonder who will be playing those?" I asked out loud.

"Well, it won't be long, you'll get to know, Miss Fiddlesticks," my dear mother said. I laughed. This had been her pet name for me my entire life since I had never been able to sit still as a child.

Music had always been one of my passions. I always enjoyed listening to the local bands that would play occasionally for a complimentary dinner at our restaurant, and I felt the freedom and joy music can bring to those who take the time to really listen to it.

The lightly perfumed garden quickly filled with guests who had come to enjoy the concert and to celebrate this event with me. Much to my amazement, there were several hundred people here, and once the seating area was filled, they spilled over into the surrounding gardens. People were talking and visiting with one another everywhere I looked.

Heaven is such a friendly place, I thought. Though everyone seemed excited to be here, no one was pushing or angling for a better position. Everything was so civilized. This was different from the few rock concerts I had attended with friends during my college years, when we would all rush the stage at once to get a better view, and my feet would get stomped every time.

As I stood and looked around, I waved at many I recognized, mouthing my thanks at them for coming. I have to say, I kind of felt like one of those rock stars at this point.

Again, as if my mother could read my mind (and she almost always had), she said, "A homecoming is a very special celebration that is open to others who wish to rejoice in your arrival. News spreads very quickly in heaven, you will see. Since there is no bad news here, everyone knows how incredible these parties are, and they come to welcome you as well. The special dinner is by invitation only; however, the musical celebration is open to everyone. We are all one in the family of God; the only agendas here are His," she finished.

Everyone here regards one another with pure, unconditional, uncluttered love. It is total acceptance on every level. And I would never feel the stress of trying to combine a busy life with a spiritual one. I was free to grow spiritually as much as I wanted to now.

The tools I had used on earth: prayer, church attendance and involvement, Bible study, and serving the needs of the community, would now be my way of life, rather than something I had to fit into an already busy existence.

We all had been rewarded with our own special "heaven" and yet so little had been required on our part. All He had unselfishly asked was for us to accept, love, and worship Him, to turn from sin, and to love and not judge others.

In return, He would provide us with the hopes, dreams, and

aspirations we had always yearned for—and been made for— forever. I was never a betting person, but I would say right now that these are one-million-to-zip odds in favor of those who believe.

While waiting for the music to begin and feeling the crowd's growing excitement, I thought back to music's evolution over the centuries and how much it had changed in just my short lifetime. I had lived long enough to experience a lot of it, and unfortunately much of it had changed for the worse.

My poppa leaned over, squeezed my shoulder, and said he'd be right back. I wasn't the least bit surprised when he walked up onto the stage and greeted everyone. He had always been fearless, and I was happy that the same magnanimous personality of his was still present when I got here. I was beginning to wonder where Jesus had wandered off to.

"Hello, dear friends," Dad started. "As you know, our beautiful daughter, Julie, is now home with us. We all thank God for that, amen? Not that we ever doubted it."

There was an exuberant round of applause and other "amens."

"In a few moments several of Julie's favorite musicians and singers will perform for her, and you can bet it will be a musical concert like she has never heard before. I, for one, cannot wait for the festivities to begin. With that said, let's welcome to the stage two of God's talented songwriters and performers—Keith and Rich.

I jumped to my feet, screaming along with everyone else. Here were two of my favorite Christian artists, performing at my party. I was elated!

I couldn't help but think back to that awful day in 1982. I

remembered that I had pulled my car off the highway when I heard the news on the radio that Keith Green and two of his small children had died when the Last Day's Ministries' Cessna 414 they were riding in was flying over the weight limit and crashed, killing all eleven passengers and the pilot. Keith was only twenty-six and his children were three and two years old, respectively. We had all been shocked and devastated by the news.

The day Rich Mullins died in 1997 was also burned into everyone's memory. Rich and a friend were traveling to a benefit concert when he lost control and his Jeep rolled over. Neither man was wearing a seat belt, and they were thrown from the car. Unfortunately, a passing semi-trailer truck swerved to miss the Jeep, hitting Rich, and killing him instantly. The Christian world had deeply mourned his passing.

Neither man looks a bit worse for the wear today was all I could think.

Keith stepped up to the front of his piano and said, "Hey everybody! Welcome to Julie's homecoming party! Julie, welcome home. Are you ready to praise and worship our Lord and Savior, Jesus Christ?"

"Yes! Yes! I'm ready!" I exclaimed, while pumping my fist into the air.

"How about you guys, are you ready to worship the Lord of Lords and the King of Kings?" Rich shouted out to the crowd.

We were all on our feet, screaming at the top of our lungs, "Yes! Yes! We're ready!"

Rich then chimed in with, "I can't hear you!"

We started laughing and shouting even louder. It was then that both men went to their respective pianos, launching into

"Sing Your Praise to the Lord," one of Rich's most beautiful songs, and perfect for our opening praise song. We all sang along, with our arms raised in adoration.

We then sang "Shout to the Lord!" and "Open the Eyes to My Heart, Lord." Many of the guests were dancing in the aisles when we swung into "Jehovah Jireh," a song that made me feel as if I were dancing around a huge fire in the wilderness alongside the Hebrew men and women who had fled Egypt with Moses.

It was when we started singing one of Keith's best worship songs, "Oh, Lord, You're Beautiful" that Jesus not so much walked but glided out on the stage to a rousing and thunderous ovation.

Here He was, available in person to receive all of our praises.

Will I ever get used to this? I wondered, doubting I would, hoping it would always feel this way, and not knowing it would get so much better.

As we watched, Jesus walked over to Rich's piano, pointed to the bench, and asked, "Do you mind if I join you?"

"Do I mind?" Rich replied, "I would be honored, Jesus."

Jesus joined him on the bench, and he launched into "Piano Concerto No. 3" by Rachmaninoff. Without missing a beat, Keith joined in, then Rich, and the three were playing one of the most difficult piano concertos in the world as if it were "Chopsticks." Their fingers were flying over the keys, and we were all on our feet applauding and cheering. This was another gift to me as Jesus knew how much I love that piece.

When they were finished, Jesus thanked Rich, stood up from the bench, lifted His arms and face upward, brilliant light emanating from Him. We began singing praise and worship songs like "Praise the Name of Jesus," "Love Like No Other,"

"Jesus, Name Above All Names," and "How Great Thou Art," with Keith and Rich leading.

When we began singing the great worship song, "Awesome God," and we increasingly lifted our praises, the aura surrounding Jesus became even brighter, almost blinding. His countenance was effervescent now, and we all shouted "Hallelujah!" and "Praise You, Jesus!" as he started ascending into the sky. As he stretched His arms out, fireworks began crackling against a newly darkened sky, and it appeared as if the stars were colliding with one another.

Jesus then disappeared in a moment, and I really hated to see Him go. "Bye," I said, while looking up and kind of half-heartedly waving. *This really is going to take some getting used to*, I thought.

The sky was literally bursting with fireworks. It was purely spectacular! Each explosion would produce hundreds of shapes, designs, sparkles, and colors I couldn't even describe, sometimes overlapping. Even the phenomenal fireworks display at America's bicentennial celebration in 1976 couldn't come close to duplicating this.

The grand finale was topped with all of the existing fireworks' explosions coalescing to form a huge, brilliantly glowing cross. It started out large but then grew to an enormous size, almost taking up the entire sky. We were all clapping, cheering, and whistling. Then it all disappeared.

As our attention had been diverted, the stage had been transformed into a small replica of the French Quarter (minus the strip clubs, bars, transvestites, and staggering drunks). I was pleased to see The Court of Two Sisters, The Preservation Jazz Hall, Brennan's, Pat O'Brien's, Café DuMonde, Felix's, and so many other well-known New Orleans places serving as a new artistic backdrop.

Also situated on the stage were an old vintage upright piano, a stand-up bass, several trumpets, a trombone, saxophone, and clarinet, propped and waiting to be played. Gone were Keith and Rich, and the fireworks had also ended.

Again, my father bounced onto the stage and announced, "Hey folks, we're going to take a short break. For our guests, we have homemade white and red wine under the gazebo, as well as fruit, crackers, cheese, and apple and orange juice. I have also baked my best pizza yet in celebration of my daughter's home-coming," he finished.

"Knowing my poppa," I whispered to Bobby, "there will be enough of everything under that gazebo to feed all of heaven."

"Wait until you eat some of his new pizza," Bobby answered. "He has a replica of the pizza oven from the old restaurant and has been trying out new recipes without meat. I can't even describe how delicious it is."

"You know, I could never make a pizza like he does," I said. "I think I just might have time to learn now. Come on, let's go to the gazebo, I'm thirsty."

Later, after greeting what seemed like almost everyone at the party, we returned to our seats and the next phase of the concert. The pizza had indeed been as delicious as Bobby had described, and I was still licking my lips from the excellent red wine from my very own vineyards.

"Oh, my goodness, this is going to be so good," I said to Bobby, anxious for the music to start back. "Any idea..." I started asking, but then interrupted myself by saying, "Oh, never mind, I'll wait."

Bobby laughed and said, "Let me guess, somebody called you Miss Fiddlesticks again."

"Gee, what makes you think that?" I asked.

"Let's just say, I know you pretty well."

I looked deep into Bobby's big green eyes, and thanked God for the life we had led together. It had been rich, and full, and gratifying. Now, we would celebrate eternity together, serving Christ, and that felt mighty good. I remembered when we had commented to those who were not yet Christians that, even though we were married and best friends, we still considered ourselves a brother and sister in the Lord. Some folks never quite understood that.

As I watched my father bound up the stairs to the stage once more, I realized I was going to have my hands full with our fishing excursions. He had the energy of a teenager, and way too much enthusiasm. He was in control and loving it.

"You folks know that Julie loves the music of her New Orleans' roots. She learned to dance to the unique sounds of Zydeco as a young child and grew up watching and listening to the music of the great New Orleans and Louisiana artists that will now be performing for her.

"Ladies and gentlemen, please welcome to the stage none other than "Satchmo," Al Hirt, "Jelly Roll," "Kid," Miles Davis, Professor Longhair, and Sidney Bouchet."

When I heard the crowd roar, I realized I had not been the only person in history to appreciate these talented performers.

These music greats waved to the crowd, then picked up their instruments and immediately launched into "When the Saints go Marching In," one of the songs that defines New Orleans. I noticed the lyrics had been changed to "Oh, Lord, I'm glad to be in that number." *Crafty*, I thought.

My mother grabbed me and started a conga line, and before you knew it, we were snaking around the garden, plucking more and more heavenly beings from the crowd, and singing at the top of our lungs. This was definitely a New Orleans tradition in our family, and I loved it!

Thinking of New Orleans traditions, I realized with relief I would never witness another New Orleans jazz funeral, and I thought back to the very first one I had attended. It was in 1980 for the famous blues singer and pianist, Professor Longhair. Some friends and I joined in around Bourbon Street in "the second line," waving white lace-embroidered handkerchiefs, while twirling little parasols. At the very end, the brass band broke into any number of lively songs, symbolizing the "everlasting joy" the deceased was now experiencing. I was curiously refreshed by it all.

As the conga line wound down and we returned to our seats, someone in the audience yelled, "Hey, throw me something, mister." Next thing you know, Louis reached down into a box behind one of his trumpets, picked up a handful of Mardi Gras beads and started throwing them into the crowd. Other musicians grabbed beads, and we were all reaching, catching, and then throwing the beads around our necks, sharing extras with those around us. It almost reminded me of a pillow fight, and I laughed hard from my belly.

Once all the Mardi Gras beads had been tossed, and we calmed down a little, Satchmo came to the front of the stage, looked straight down at me, and said, "Miss Julie, we have a surprise for you. Antonio and Alejandra, come on up here."

I jumped up and clapped while they went to the stage to perform. I couldn't believe it: my parents were going to perform again! It had been so many years since I had seen them glide around the dance floor. They had always had that "magic," and I was sure they had only gotten better.

27

The Dance

The band started playing and Satchmo began singing, "It Had To Be You," my parents' song to one another. They had lost neither their style, nor their ease together. We were all spellbound as they moved with grace around the stage. It was beautiful, and tears again spilled over. Bobby placed his arm around me and hugged me. I truly was in heaven.

"People love seeing them dance, you know," Bobby told me. "They are always dancing on those riverboat cruises where people never tire of watching them."

"I know, and neither have I nor will I. I am so blessed."

Once my parents finished their dance to wild applause, my father came for me and led me onto the stage. My heart was pounding as the crowd went wild in anticipation.

"I'm sorry, I know I promised you the first dance, but Satchmo sprung that one on me," he said apologetically.

"Dad, that was so beautiful. You have no idea how much I have missed seeing you and Mother dance. It was magnificent."

Comfortable in his strong arms and with a huge grin on my face, the band then launched into "String of Pearls" by Glenn Miller while my fantastic father and I jitterbugged around the stage, full of enthusiasm and joy to be dancing once more. We didn't miss a beat, familiarity driving our steps.

After we finished to great applause and returned to our seats, the great band that had come to honor me began playing one familiar New Orleans favorite after another, and everyone started dancing all over the property.

After playing a multitude of numbers, Al Hirt, one of my absolute favorite jazz trumpeters, walked up to the front and said, "Julie, come back up here, it's about time we got a good look at you!"

The crowd started chanting, "Julie! Julie! Julie! Julie!" and then the thunderous applause began. I was giggling all the way up to the stage, and I stood on tiptoes to give Al a huge hug.

"You know, Al," I said, "I spent a lot of time over the years watching you perform in your club."

"I know, Julie. I remember you and your friends from your college days. It's great to see you again. In fact, if I recall, I sang happy birthday to you on your twenty-first birthday when you and your family stopped in that night. It's good to see you made it, kiddo."

"You too," I laughingly replied.

Al then stepped back and suddenly I was standing at center stage and there were hundreds of eyes looking expectantly at me, and the audience had grown quiet. I knew it was time to speak, and since I now had no fear, I was ready.

"You know I would sing, but unfortunately that wasn't one of God's talents He bestowed upon me," I commented to the crowd's chuckles. "Remind me to ask Him about that. However, I am deeply grateful for all these incredible musicians who came to pay tribute to me. Wow, what can I say?

"I also thank each and every one of you for being a part of this momentous event. Right now, I would like for my parents, my grandparents, and Bobby, to come up here on stage with me." Once they were all on stage, my pets ran up and joined them, and everyone howled with laughter.

"You just can't keep these three out of the limelight," I responded.

I turned to look at my family and said, "You guys are the reason I am here. Had it not been for your continuous prayers, your deep faith, and your unwavering belief in my salvation, I would probably not have made the cut. For that, I am grateful to you. To others out there in the garden who prayed for me, my thanks as well. Enjoy this evening and especially that delicious pizza my dad made."

The enthusiastic applause that followed that was soon followed by Al's return to the front of the stage.

"Okay, folks, for Julie's grand finale, we welcome Rich and Keith back to the stage. Julie, you guys just stay here."

I was overjoyed to see that Keith's children had come in with him as well. They looked to be in their early teens, and I remembered that one can grow at one's own pace here.

Al continued, "Let's also welcome to this illustrious event one of the finest voices I have ever heard on both earth and in heaven—Miss Ella Fitzgerald."

I was delighted. This woman with a powerful voice was here to honor me.

"We're gonna walk down memory lane for a moment," Ella began, while walking to the front of the stage. "Folks, let's put on our worship faces and honor the One who made it possible for all of us to be here, our Lord and Savior, Jesus Christ."

She then looked at me and said, "Welcome home, Jules."

I was flabbergasted that Ella used a nickname I had always wanted others to use, but it had just never caught on. When she winked at me, I realized this was something special between us girls.

Ella led us in old worship hymns like "Holy, Holy, Holy," "Blessed be the Tide," "Just a Closer Walk with Thee," and "Just as I Am." I felt myself going back to those first days after fully surrendering to Christ.

"Please join us as we close Julie's celebration with 'Amazing Grace,'" Ella stated, while kneeling.

We all fell to our knees immediately, worshipping our Father God. The time-honored lyrics poured from our lips with the most deeply felt pure gratitude backing them up. We all knew it was God's grace that had brought us to this magnificent place.

We stayed on our knees in prayer and thankfulness after the song ended. Finally, when I could, I stood and went to greet everyone who had performed. I hugged famous artists I had only seen from a distance over the years, thanking them over and over for making my celebration so fantastic. They seemed to be just as happy to be speaking with me, as many of us reminisced about wonderful memories of the Big Easy.

At one time, I would have referred to this experience as being among greatness. However, the only greatness one finds here is in the form of the Godhead—God the Father; Jesus Christ the Son; and the Holy Spirit. How refreshing I found that to be. There was no need for ego building or overindulgence. We were most assuredly all one in the family of God as my mother had mentioned.

As my guests were leaving, I had so many invitations to visit that I couldn't imagine how I would remember them all. My mom smiled at me and said, "Don't worry, daughter, everything works out without any concerns on your part. Everything will fall into place. It is God's way."

"Well, that's certainly a relief," I replied.

"Come, let's go," she said while steering me away from the garden and linking her arm through mine.

"I'll catch up with you two in a little while," Bobby said. He wished to stay with my father and visit with the New Orleans' musicians.

"What did you think of the concert?" she asked.

"It was truly beyond my expectations. Seeing you and Poppa dance again was almost surreal. I had dreamed of it over the years, and wished for it hundreds of times, and then I got to see it again. I would like to know, Mom, did you have a similar homecoming party? What was yours like?"

"Good question. Mine was a little more subdued, yet entirely enjoyable. A famous string quartet from my hometown of Palermo played, and Caruso, the great Italian opera singer, performed "Vesti la Giubba," my favorite of his.

"There was much dancing, laughing, wine, food, and happiness. Just like yours, it was a grand celebration of my homecoming, and there were many family members and friends from my island and from New Orleans to welcome me home."

"How wonderful, Mom. You know, I could have never even dreamed how heaven would be. It's impossible, and you know how vivid my imagination can be."

We both laughed and continued walking down the flagstone pathway on the way back to my antebellum delight.

Once I arrived home, I marveled at the fact that everything had been so quickly put back in order while I attended the concert. I couldn't wait to explore my mansion, my property, and the homes of others as well.

A short time later, Bobby and my father arrived, and the two were still talking about how good my homecoming party had been.

"Well, Alejandra, I guess we need to head on out of here and give these two some time alone," my poppa said.

It was heartwarming to realize I would see them both for an eternity.

"We'll see you as soon as Wisdom finishes his job," my mother responded. "We await your visit with great expectation and joy."

"Speaking of Wisdom, where in the world is he?" I asked, and then chuckled at my slip of the tongue remark. "I mean, where in heaven is he?" We all laughed.

"Comes and goes, just like Jesus and the rest of the heavenly hosts. One never knows. Just comes and goes. Yet, they are always there when you need them," Poppa said.

"Hmm, I am finding that out already," I replied.

After my parents kissed and hugged us both, Bobby and I went upstairs and out onto my bedroom balcony. My two crazy canines and one crazy feline had gone ahead of us and immediately hopped onto the bed.

I looked at them, shook my head, and commented: "Some

things just never change," and Bobby laughingly agreed.

It was just fantastic to be with this man again. He had been my rock, and to lose him to such a vicious disease had been the most difficult thing I had ever faced. However, I had never doubted I would see him again, for I knew heaven was as real as the Bible says it is.

We breathed in the salt air and the familiar scents from the bougainvillea that graced my balcony. As Bobby wrapped his arms around me, I could hear the tinkling sound of water cascading from a myriad of fountains, and an owl hooted from one of my huge sycamore trees.

I could feel Bobby's heart beating, and I looked up at him with an even stronger love now. The sadness surrounding his disease, the extreme weight loss, and then his death, had taken a tremendous toll on both me and our son. Now he was completely healthy, robust, and full of life again.

"I love you, Bobby," I said, while hugging him fiercely.

"I love you too, Julie. I am so thankful you are now here, and we are together again. One day Bobby Jr. and the family will join us."

I hoped it wouldn't be premature, though.

"Hey everybody, I made it!" I hollered. "I'm in heaven!"

Bobby also screamed out, "And thank God, she did!"

We could hear music and laughter off in the distance; no doubt someone else enjoying a homecoming party like mine. As I beheld the beauty before my eyes, I prayed aloud, "Thank you, God, for everything You have already provided for me. Thank You for the blessing of seeing those that I have loved and missed so much. Thank You for this perfect home. I cannot wait to see what else You have planned for me. Now, I respectfully request a little bit of darkness so that I may close my eyes for a little while and sleep."

"Want to stay?" I asked Bobby.

"What do you think?" he replied, and we moved into the bedroom.

I added my family coat to the others in the closet then settled in with Bobby and my furry friends on my extremely comfortable bed. Before I knew it, the room had darkened and the only sound I could hear was that of cicadas rubbing their legs together in observance of their nightly musical ritual.

Before we could drift off to sleep, I remembered how wonderful it had been to go to sleep to the sounds of thunder and rain. A gentle breeze blew through my windows, and there it was: the sound of faint thunder in the distance. Soon the night was lit up by the brilliance of lightning and we got up and went back onto the balcony to watch.

The sky was ablaze with crackling lightning that seemed to shatter its way across the sky, sometimes looking like a giant spider web or cracked glass. A few strong, powerful bolts zigzagged to the ground. It was a magnificent show, and I hoped others saw it as well. Before long, a light rain began to fall, mingling with tears of happiness running down my face, and I silently thanked Him again for His love.

We quickly returned to the bed, snuggled under the down comforter, then "spooned" like we always had, falling into a deep and uninterrupted sleep. I was in my sweetheart's arms again. Content. Happy. Thankful. That was me at this very moment.

28

A Heavenly Visit

I didn't know how long we had slept but, when I opened my eyes, Wisdom was standing by the door leading out to the balcony, waiting for us to awaken.

"Now, that's a happy sight," he commented, taking in Bobby, me, two dogs, and a cat all piled on top of my bed.

"Wisdom, how long have you been here?" I inquired, really happy to see him again.

"How's my favorite angel in heaven?" Bobby asked, while climbing out of the bed.

"I only just arrived, Julie, and I am quite well, Bobby. Obviously, you two are doing pretty well yourself. It's good to see you together again. So, Julie, has everything sunk in yet?"

"I'd say. I was really exhausted for some strange reason after the concert."

"To be expected, Julie. A lot to absorb in a short time. However, we have only just begun. Do you have thirst or hunger? Wish to bathe?"

"Actually, I am still full from the feast in my honor. That was an awesome Italian meal, and the concert, wow! Come to think of it, I need to get some water."

After Bobby and I got dressed, we all headed down the stairs to the kitchen, and Wisdom commented, "By the way, I have a surprise for you."

"Oh, really? Well, it's about time, considering I haven't had ANY surprises since I got here," I kidded. "Man, there is something new with you all the time."

This time Wisdom laughed. "That's my job. When you're ready to leave, we'll go. The pets will be fine here while you're gone. No harm will ever come to them."

At the sound of that, both dogs barked and wagged their tails, and my cat meowed as if they all understood. I looked at Wisdom questioningly.

"They do understand what I'm saying, Julie, they just can't speak."

Again, this magnificent angel had read my thoughts. It then dawned on me that I didn't have to worry about locking my doors to protect my belongings, or rushing around looking for lost keys, or paying the neighbor to feed the animals in my absence. My goodness, this was just getting better.

After we downed a cool glass of refreshing water, Bobby looked at me and said, "You know I don't want to leave you. But I know what you're about to experience, and it's far greater than anything you've ever experienced before. Can't wait to see you when you get to the City of God." He then hugged me tightly and reluctantly walked away.

My crazy pets ran off to the garden, and Wisdom and I set off again. I marveled at every beautiful aspect of my property, eager to finish exploring it. The greenhouse held particular interest for me as I could vaguely see some new, interesting tall plant groupings through the windows. What else could possibly be in there? I wondered.

Wisdom stopped at the meadow and took my hand in his.

"Close your eyes, Julie, we are going to transport ourselves to a place you haven't seen yet."

"Transport?" I asked bewildered. "Does that mean what I think it does? Are we gonna....."

I seriously had no time to think and within seconds we were standing in front of a two-story, white Cape Cod clapboard-style house with smoke drifting out of the large centrally located chimney. Deep burgundy shutters bordered large windows that faced a huge lake covering the majority of the property.

After I cast a questioning glance at Wisdom, he replied, "Tiny's dream was to live as close to water as he possibly could. Spending countless hours enjoying both the beach and water sports on Lake Michigan created a lifelong desire, much like yours, to gaze always upon the beautiful, changing faces of water."

"I understand how he feels. This looks like a man's home already. I cannot wait to see the rest."

The front door opened, and I could see him smiling and waving, beckoning us inside.

"Wisdom!" I exclaimed. "This is fantastic. The first heavenly mansion I will have been in besides mine."

"Tiny's home is well-appointed, you will see," Wisdom replied.

Once inside, I was delighted to see Tiny, Sophia, Rashid, and Abbie sitting before a comfortable fire on oversized leather furniture in a walnut wood-paneled den. Tasteful artwork graced the walls, and I walked over to a library table containing family photos, including one that had to be Tiny's wife and three children.

"Nice family, Tiny. Hey guys," I said in welcome. "How is

everybody?" Tiny then walked over to me, enveloping me in those oversized arms. We all started talking at once and took turns hugging one another. We were mostly comparing notes about our homecoming parties, and complimenting Tiny on his beautiful home.

After a while Wisdom interrupted our revelry. "Okay, here's the drill. After you guys catch up with one another, we will hear Tiny's story. After that, during a nice, long cruise back to the Garden of Tranquility, we will hear Sophia's and Julie's life stories, then it's on to Mount Transfiguration."

"Mount Transfiguration?" I exclaimed. "Seriously? The place where Jesus was transformed?"

"Yes, the very same. You guys ready for Tiny's story?"

"Let's hear it!" we all exclaimed and, as I settled myself on a deep burgundy leather divan for the duration, a large, solid white Cheshire cat jumped into my lap, looked into my eyes, licked me, then purred its demand for attention.

I pointed at it, looked at Tiny, and he said, "Meet Princess Leah. I call her that because she absolutely thinks she is one."

We all laughed, and I started petting "her majesty" while Tiny poured out his story.

29

Cecil and Alma

We were all excited to hear Tiny's story, hopefully getting a little insight into where his huge appetite comes from. Tiny took a deep breath and began:

My life began forty-six years ago in 1963 inside Mercy Hospital on a bitter cold winter night in the Southside of Chicago. I was one of the largest newborns the staff had ever seen, weighing in at 12 pounds, 2 ounces and measuring 22" long.

My uncle Frank had commented, "Man, he's a hoss. Let's call him "Tiny." Everyone in the room laughed and the name stuck.

Cecil, my father, was a Baptist preacher, having gotten the call to preach at a fiery Holy Ghost tent revival on a mosquito-infested summer night in the Heights, the allocated "colored section" in a small, segregated Alabama town just east of Birmingham.

He said, "When the power of the Holy Spirit set upon me, it felt like electricity running through my body, like it was on fire. It changed everything inside of me in a beat of my heart." Without hesitation, he then made the leap of faith to be a preacher man and went about the business of healing the sick and saving the lost, although he had no formal training.

Cecil was a young man of little means, barely educated, and only nineteen when he started hitchhiking around the

Southeast. He preached at black tent revivals packed to the brim with an endless sea of various shades of dark skin on the upraised faces of hopeful men and women.

He asked for no pay, just a special offering at the end of the night, and God always gave him just what he needed. His sharecropper parents, the offspring of a hard-working bunch, had encouraged him to follow God's call.

"Son," his father told him, "Don't fall over your ego lest it get in your way."

He found that church people are some of the most kind-hearted people you will ever meet. The young and vibrant preacher man was never lacking for an invitation to stay with any one of the locals who had an extra bedroom now that the kids were all grown and on their own. They would invariably feed him a meal fit for a king.

Cecil always offered to pay for his room and board, but those sweet souls wouldn't hear of it. "You go and do God's will," they would say, while stuffing additional cookie jar money in his pocket for his next small-town adventure. "You're welcome to stay here anytime you're in the area."

The thrill of going to new places and meeting different, interesting people fueled him, which, in turn fueled those who witnessed the fervor with which he called upon the Lord to save His poor children, to set them free from their ancient bondages, and to give them the courage to change their ways.

His altar call was both unique and compelling as he stated in a loud voice, "The Lord God and His Son, Jesus, are right down here at the altar, waiting with me for those who wish to change from the inside out and become a new person. Bring your troubles to the altar and let the King of Kings and the Lord of Lords change your life!" He never begged, only commanded in a silken voice that was hard to ignore.

As a small, local choir sang "Just as I Am," Cecil stood, his head pouring sweat, his hands out, pleading and welcoming, and a wide smile filled with perfect white teeth shining in the brightness. At times he would direct his eyes and arms up to heaven and some swore it looked like a halo rested over his head. Miracles of healing and marriage restorations abounded, and word quickly spread from church to church about the newest and youngest Holy Ghost preacher in the Deep South.

Over that first summer, they said my daddy led hundreds to Christ, and they began putting up circus-sized tents whenever he was coming to town. I considered that quite an accomplishment for one so young.

Cecil eventually hooked up with a well-bred, traveling medicine man that went by the name of Chief Nosakahaki, a full-blooded Cherokee Indian who welcomed him to ride with him in his well-painted step van to small towns with names like Andalusia, Biloxi, Jackson, Bessemer, and Cullman, and which were sometimes hard to find on a map.

His long, salt-and-pepper braided hair fell down his back from under a rumpled, black cowboy hat with an eagle feather stuck in the band and a couple of fishing lures affixed to the side of it. No matter what the temperature was inside or outside the step van, Nosakahaki always wore a cotton striped Mexican-style poncho over a cotton shirt, jeans, and polished cowboy boots. Dark sunglasses hid time-worn and wrinkled eyes and the world of hurt he had tried to escape but which could not escape him.

Cecil appreciated the safe ride, and Nosakahaki enjoyed the conversation, and the two hit it off from the very beginning. They were an odd match; the Chief had the preacher man by thirty years and almost as many years working the road. The preacher man brought nothing but desire and a fire burning deep inside his spirit to win as many to Christ as possible. They were two men who were different yet very much the same. One had come to feed the flock; the other had come to fleece it.

When Cecil asked the Chief what his business was, he replied, "I'm selling Angelica Root, a sixteen-ounce Indian herbal medicine which, for only three bucks, helps cure coughs, depression, childbirth pains, menstrual cramps, digestive disorders, delayed menstruation, autism, high blood pressure, and heart problems," the Chief read off one of his labels. Cecil was flabbergasted. He was also amazed that the Chief spoke like a real Indian but with a Southern accent.

"Are you telling me that concoction you're selling can cure everything you just mentioned?"

"Why, sure. We've actually been using it in our tribe for years. The roots, stems, leaves, and seeds are removed and either eaten in salads or can be roasted or boiled. My operation also helps out older tribal women on the reservation in Madison County, Alabama, to locate the root and package the medicine. Although they're considered cheap labor by most area's standards, this is the only income some of them have."

He felt he was helping those without families to survive. Once the laborers loaded enough cardboard boxes with the product to completely fill up the step van, the Chief would pay them for the load and head out until he sold it all and had to return again.

After a while, Cecil ascertained that the Chief must be receiving some type of mystical powers from the "Big Spirit in the Sky" because he was making a killing with that medicine. The step van was outfitted with a sliding glass window on the side and in the center, which made it easy for customers to walk up and purchase his wonder medicine. Sometimes the line stretched way down the road.

The step van was now half-filled with boxes of root medicine. Cecil figured the Chief knew what he was doing since he always carried a large bankroll in a special pouch in his poncho and insisted on staying in nice, secure places with safes.

"A comfortable bed plays a necessary role in a traveling man's destiny; it's good for his psyche," the Chief persuaded him, and it was something he later thanked him for.

It was in fact the Chief who suggested to Cecil that he purchase some fireworks and shoot them off at the end of his revival as a way of creating additional excitement for the event. The idea was novel and brought even more seekers to the tent meetings and Holy Ghost revivals. By now, Cecil figured that maybe the Chief was sampling more than just his life-altering elixir.

It was in a small mining town outside Knoxville, Tennessee, where Cecil met the woman with whom he would spend the next sixty years. After a rather lengthy altar call had ended, and he was feeling the humid night's heat saturate every pore of his body, a scrappy young local girl boldly walked up to him, held her hand up to shake his, and said, "Hi, preacher man, my name is Alma June."

Standing only as tall as his shoulder, she had to crane her neck back just to look up at him. She had the cutest dimples and ringed short hair he had ever seen, and he found himself grinning like a long-tailed Cheshire cat, the night's fireworks long forgotten.

"What's the matter with you? Cat got your tongue? I just heard you talking like a jaybird," she taunted him. Cecil had indeed gotten tongue-tied for the first time in his life.

"Excuse me, Miss Alma June, I just never had anyone flirt with me before, but I believe I like it."

Not being one prone to shyness, Alma decided she liked what she saw as well and then set about captivating him with her throaty laugh, funny jokes, and oversized personality. He too captivated her, and she surrendered her heart as well to the Lord the next night and was baptized by the young fiery preacher in the Tennessee River the following Sunday after church.

Cecil was hooked the first time he laid eyes on her, and after wrapping him around her little finger with her delicious Southern-style cooking, it didn't take long before her well-crafted plan to make him her husband worked. They were joined together in holy matrimony by her Southern Baptist minister within a few short weeks, and a small select group of friends and family was in attendance.

With job opportunities almost nonexistent in their part of the country, Alma's sharecropper parents had given their approval and profound blessings on the union, feeling this may be the best opportunity for happiness their daughter would probably have. They also deeply appreciated the love offering of $100 Cecil pressed into their hands before leaving, a mighty sum at that time that would help buy seed and fertilizer for their land.

Cecil continued his tent revival circuit, traveling again with the Chief with his young and nervous eighteen-year-old bride now sitting between them on a crate in the middle area between the seats. He and Alma were compatible in the only way two people who believe they are ordained to be together are. They finished one another's thoughts and sentences, enjoyed an easy compatibility, and filled the empty spaces with earnest looks of endearment.

As Cecil's reputation grew, the money really began to pour in, and Alma kept it safe in a locked box she kept in her possession. Crowds were drawn to her husband's fiery passion (she could certainly vouch for it) and the compassion he had for helping his own.

"Turn your life over to God, and He will turn your life around," he called out to the crowds. "There is a man who walks among us, and He is our friend. His name is Jesus. All you have to do is have the faith to believe."

Cecil was now preaching to huge crowds and a few white folks were also peeking under the tent. He soon received invitations to be a guest preacher at some of the largest and most staid Baptist churches in the South.

The two had already saved enough money to buy a decent car, and Alma was thrilled. It was the first one either had ever owned, but first Cecil had to pass a state driving test in order to drive it. After some mentoring by the Chief, he did so with flying colors, and they were ready to go out on their own.

Parting with the Chief was hard. "Chief, we sure would like to keep in touch. We'll try to make it a point to get up to your reservation in the future and try to catch you there. Do we need to send up smoke signals?" Cecil asked.

The Chief laughed and replied, "I never know when I'm going up there. Let's just say our fate is in the hands of God. I will never forget you two, and I'll be praying for you." When Alma cried, Cecil wondered if it was because of the fact that she would miss the Chief or if she was thankful for their much-needed privacy.

The young bride was never jealous of her husband's popularity; rather, she reveled in it. At his insistence she was now standing with him during his altar call, holding his hand and reaching out to the flock with the other one. Together they were unbeatable, and the crowds clearly respected them and rewarded them with life-changing decisions.

Within a year, Cecil received a request to become the youth pastor at a medium sized church in the poorest section of Chicago called Southside. It didn't matter that Cecil had no formal training Pastor Roberts had told him; it appeared he didn't need it.

The Pastor leaned back in his swivel rocker and said, "Our church membership is slowly dwindling because of our aging church population. Add to that the fact that there are a number of new churches that have started up within a few miles of us. The new competition is certainly hurting our attendance. Also, as you know, we are located in one of the most crime-ridden areas of Chicago. It was built here over one hundred years ago to serve as a beacon in a sea of darkness and to help bring much needed change to the neighborhood."

Pastor Roberts was fighting to save the Southside landmark while trying to build it into a strong church again. He needed their youthful strength and unbridled enthusiasm to make this happen.

A starting salary was offered, and though it was less money than Cecil was accustomed to, its consistency would allow them the chance for a normal life off the road as newlyweds. Plus, they both welcomed the challenge of helping turn an almost hopeless situation around. They had survived life on the road; they could certainly handle this.

A small but well-furnished one-bedroom apartment just off the property was included in the job, and the lovers were thrilled finally to have a place to call their own. The kitchen was compact but well stocked, with up-to-date appliances. The double bed was quite comfortable, and the bathroom contained a tub and shower and a new toilet and sink. The combination of the living and dining area was only large enough to entertain about four people but that wasn't important to them at the moment.

The church also included a small wringer washing machine and there was a clothesline located behind the apartment.

"This is heaven for a sharecropper's daughter," Alma said later, while lying in Cecil's arms in a divinely comfortable bed.

"Tell me about it. Let me ask you something, when would you like to start a family?" he asked.

Alma snuggled even closer to him and replied, "There's no time like the present."

Both felt they were smack dab in the middle of God's will for them and quickly adjusted to life off the road. The commitment required them to try and save a quickly sinking ministry.

Alma was the most organized of the two, so she put together a plan of attack, which involved sectioning off certain gang related and high crime neighborhoods that would not be canvassed. In other safer neighborhoods, they would spend Saturdays handing out colorful pamphlets to families who were hanging out on their front porch or in the yard and not expecting someone from a Baptist church to stop by and invite them to visit.

If no one was home, the invitations were rolled up and put through the front door handle. They invited everyone they could find.

"Y'all come on down to 'Sunday Morning with Cecil and Alma.' Enjoy two hours of fun, games, music, puppets, snacks, Bible stories, and free transportation," both proclaimed, while handing out pamphlets on separate sides of the street.

Included in the pamphlet was a promise that if you attended "Sunday Morning with Cecil and Alma," ten times in a row, you would receive points entering you into a drawing every ten weeks that involved giving away a brand new bicycle.

Gold medallions with your name handwritten on them with a black marker were deposited in a large drawing box. The more you earned, the better chance you had of winning that bicycle. You also received a bonus medallion for every new visitor you brought on Sunday. A poster was kept in the front of the room with gold stars glued under classmates' names so you could see the ones who loved coming and bringing their friends as well. It was a little like multi-level marketing, utilizing child labor, and it worked quite successfully.

Things started happening, and they were soon educating over one hundred kids for two hours every Sunday in the basement of the church. Membership classes were full once again, the pastor found a replacement couple as youth pastors, and Cecil and Alma were promoted to associate pastors.

Alma had proven to be so good with kids and organizing such entertaining and educational Sunday morning celebrations for the youth that Cecil, the Pastor, and his wife, agreed she should become a teacher.

"Alma, we've had a little meeting and wish to offer you the chance to become a bona fide teacher. We have enrolled you at the local teaching college for women and paid for your course in advance."

"I don't know what to say, Pastor." Alma was overcome with emotion. "I guess 'thank you' would be appropriate." She then hugged the three who made it happen, giggling the entire time. Alma chose English as her Major and received her teaching certificate in record time.

She was moving up in the world and so was her masterful husband who, after three years, became senior pastor of Southside Baptist Church, stepping in after Pastor and Mrs. Roberts decided it was time to retire and turn the reins over to a much younger leader. The church doubled its membership in a couple of years, and I was born soon after.

30

Growing up on the Southside

Tiny's cat jumped up in Sophia's lap, she squealed with joy, and we all laughed as Tiny continued his fascinating tale.

After graduating from teaching college, Miss Alma, now affectionately known as "Big Momma," started teaching English and Literature at one of the worst public high schools in the entire country. This worn out place was known as "The Hood," a school filled with punks, thugs, rival gangs, and young girls who already had the used up look of their mothers.

A new ten-foot chain link fence with razor wire around the top completely surrounded the property; it was not to keep the enemy out but most definitely to keep him in. Crushed soft drink cans and beer bottles, used condoms, and "roaches" from hastily smoked joints littered the area around the fence.

There were no bright flowers planted at the front entrance or potted plants swinging from the eaves. No marquee boasted of school plays, dances, or sports events. It was stark and unfriendly and had the cold look and smell of a small prison.

An armed guard was stationed at the entrance, checking students and visitors for weapons and paraphernalia. We always thought he must have been a retired Marine, with his razor cut hairdo and tough stance, facing the world with such a fierce expression. Two younger security guards roamed the hallways during the day, armed and quite serious. This broken dream piece of land was my mother's battlefield and the one on which her cry for reform sounded.

This scrappy woman used to kiddingly say, "I know I grew up inside a shoebox. I'm almost as wide as I am tall." She held our attention with her thickly fringed, sparkling brown eyes and dimples as deep as pennies.

Her homemade brownies were famous and were often used to keep rival gangs from fighting. She figured it was hard to fight when you were eating. Big Momma was an icon on the Southside, had indeed made a difference in many lives, and, with those brownies, most probably contributed to the spread of obesity. She was one tough lady; she ran her classroom and our house like a prison warden, and I dearly loved her.

Daddy was a positive preaching man and truly lived like a man of God. He was quite strict with us children and brought new meaning to the term "spare the rod, spoil the child." Not one of us was spoiled.

All around our large brick home, crime was the rule, not the exception. A six-foot tall symmetrically placed brick wall surrounded the property, and Dad had cemented sharp, jagged, and broken pieces of bottle along the top to discourage anyone's entry. A state-of-the art alarm system was installed, and motion-detector lights were placed in many directions. We were probably better armed than Fort Knox, I imagined. Lord, help the person who tried to penetrate those walls!

Many clear and warm nights we would stand out on the large second-story balcony located on the kids' side of the house, which is perched high upon a hill overlooking a busy intersection. From this clear vantage point, we received a world of education from the area that was once referred to as the "Levee," one of the country's most notorious sex districts.

Many ethnic gangs ruled and roamed the streets, clothed in their colors, and with power-fueled evil their intentions. Names like the Blackstone Ranger Nation, the Conservative Vice Lords, the Latin Kings, and Latin Counts identified the gang, and each member wore their group's name and colors with pride.

For hours we would watch as drugs of every kind were switched between furtive hands on poorly lit street corners and glassy-eyed druggies staggered down sidewalks, drunk and totally wasted. Hailing down cars were prostitutes (or "women of the night" as my father kindly suggested) with their thigh-high patent leather boots, tight, low-cut dresses, and cigarettes dangling from their lips as if busy hands couldn't hold them.

My soul saving father told me late one afternoon before darkness filled the sky, "Son, I want you to go down to the street and invite those poor lost girls to visit our church." Now, mind you, I was only sixteen years old. The look on my face brought a snicker from my mother.

"You want me to do what?" I asked in disbelief. He was kidding, right?

He armed me with some flyers about church services and times and what our mission as a church was, patted me on the back, and said, "You're going to face them in your life at one time or another. I'd rather be the one to see you through it." This was a task I was not looking forward to and strenuously objected to. I had forgotten he has selective hearing.

With a huge lump in my throat and a tight feeling in my gut, I walked down to no man's land, more scared of these women than I was of my momma.

"Hey, sonny, you here for a little fun?" I heard a tall brunette with stockings up to her thighs ask. I was having a difficult time keeping my gaze on her eyes.

I gulped and replied as fast as I could get the words out of my mouth, "Uh, no, ma'am, I'm here because my daddy told me to come here. He wants you ladies to come to our church. Here's the flyers, I gotta go." I had never seen so much of a woman's skin up close, and it was very unsettling.

"Wait a minute, preacher boy," a redhead commanded me, and I turned around. I was getting a little queasy from the smell of cigarettes and cheap perfume, two things that were strangers to me. "We might consider popping into your church if your old man will come down and invite us himself."

"Got it," I replied, and relieved, I hurried back to the house, listening to their mocking laughs until I was out of sight. I then instructed my father about the request from the women of the night. With an affirmative nod of my mother's head and a smile playing on her lips, my father was out the door like a rabbit running from a pack of wolves.

Less than an hour later, Johnny Appleseed was safely back in the house, grinning from ear to ear.

"I talked to them a little and listened to them a lot, and they want to start coming to our AA meetings on Wednesday nights." I could hear the pride in his voice, and I was happy to be a part of that. "This will be a great start for women who deserve to have the best in life, and like the rest of us, they just need help. You're a part of this, son. That took a lot of guts." It also showed me that fervency for your beliefs has to come out on the winning side more times than not.

The people we were exposed to in the Levee were among the dregs of society, and we had been raised among them. Our parents made sure we were safe from them, yet, in a way, we were prisoners because of them. I was hoping maybe our family might get some extra "God points" just by being willing to suffer a little more for Him. When I casually mentioned that to my father, he simply clucked his tongue, shook his head, and walked away from me. I simply could not understand where my father's sense of humor had gone.

I asked my parents one Sunday over lunch, "Why didn't God, in His infinite wisdom, lead our family to a safer mission field?"

My dear mother looked at me as if I were a two-headed alien that had joined the family for dinner and replied, "Whom should He send to replace us if we are to leave? Would it be someone less important than our family? Perhaps their lives aren't as worthy as ours. Let me ask you this, since when did you start to question God? Lord, help me, Jesus."

That woman had a mouth on her, and it appeared I might have inherited it.

My father stifled a laugh and patiently explained, "God called us to plant ourselves in an area where we could do the most good. We became associated with our Baptist Church in the Southside area of Chicago right after we married.

"It was a struggle at first. As Southerners, we were overwhelmed with the huge differences in our cultures. We dealt with drastic changes in our lives—changes in weather, food styles, and a fast paced way of life rather than our laid back style. It was culture shock. However, crime was growing in this area every year and the need for home missionaries increased as well. We knew what we were up against but were willing to answer the call.

"Once we adjusted to this new way of life, we began the process of bringing you kids into the world, trusting God for protection every step of the way."

As we grew older and began asking them about the violence in the neighborhood, they would often quote scripture to us from the book of Exodus.

My mother reminded us, "Moses had to put up with a whole lot worse when he and an entire nation wandered around totally lost in the wilderness for forty years before reaching the land of milk and honey. Not to mention, they were running for their lives from the wicked Egyptians before, thanks be to Jesus, they crossed the river on dry land. Hallelujah!" she exclaimed.

I stupidly pointed out, "Well, okay, I'd have to say that was pretty good but, again, he was not dodging bullets." Then I got the look from my mother and almost peed down my leg.

Ours was the largest Baptist church on the Southside with around 400 members. It had survived two small fires in the kitchen, several robberies, and the constant problems of having too little funds for such large needs. Families gave what they could, and somehow we always found a way to make frail ends meet.

So many of our century-old stained glass windows had been broken by vandals hurling bricks through these magnificent works of art that we eventually had to replace them with Plexiglas windows that proved much harder to break and came with a lifetime guarantee. It almost killed my mother to see those beautiful windows hauled off and lifeless ones put in their place.

"One hundred years of church history, gone," she quietly said. I understood how she felt for I too had loved their splendor.

Daddy gently reminded her, "God's people are the church, and it's not about a bunch of windows." My mother had her opinions, but my father had his style. That man could always get her to smile.

Over the years, and after many hours of preaching, burying the dead, marrying the innocent, visiting the sick, counseling the troubled, and helping everyone in our congregation, our father had built a contingency of devoted followers and, as a family, we stood together and withstood all that was thrown our way.

As far back as I can remember, I began learning the ways of Christianity under my father's tutelage, and I clung to him like a fresh born cub to its mother. I both feared and admired my parents, and one thing I can say about them is that they were consistent in their discipline. No amount of whining, pleading, or cajoling would alter their decisions. After years of trying, I just gave up and gave in. These people were hard-headed and never changing.

I enjoyed Vacation Bible School so much, my mother later trained me to be one of the teachers. You would have thought I was a missionary in the Amazon, I planned my classes with such fervor and dedication. I taught other young people in my class arts and crafts, and we would make things like a large-scale Noah's Ark out of Popsicle sticks and weave colorful potholders for our mothers.

Afterwards, lukewarm, orange-flavored Kool-Aid, potato chips, and wedding cookies were served. It was almost a feast to us. Before leaving, we would all sit in a circle on the floor and sing comfortable songs like "Every Day with Jesus is Sweeter than the Day Before" and "I Have Decided to Follow Jesus" and pat ourselves on the back for being the greatest VBS class ever.

I gave my heart to Jesus at a Billy Graham revival at Wrigley Field when I was only twelve years of age, blubbering like a baby when I walked down that long aisle toward the platform. I know my father was probably disappointed that he had not been the one to take me through the sinner's prayer, but somehow, I just had to let Billy do it.

I was quietly thankful I hadn't gotten "the calling" as no electricity feeling had gone through me like it had my father, but I did feel a whole lot better. I knew I would look at the Bible a little differently now that a stirring had occurred inside my soul.

High school was one of the favorite times of my life as I truly enjoyed the academic part of it. Thank heavens my father was not a huge fan of football or basketball as I had absolutely no desire even to try out for either team.

"Come on, Tiny, as big and tough as you are, you should play football. You'd make a great linebacker," the coaches constantly said. I knew that this was a position that would require tackling or blocking and causing great pain to others. They even tried to lure me with comments like, "You could win a scholarship for both academics and athletics."

"No, thanks," I replied, "I have witnessed enough pain in

my own neighborhood to last a lifetime. I have no use for more of it."

I was, however, a fan of our baseball team and served as the team equipment manager, a position that allowed me to enjoy all the games and hang out with my buddies. I also kept stats for them every season when I could.

Frankly, I had more of a love for chess, a game that required strategy and strong advance planning, at which I found myself incredibly talented and adept. I was a member of my school's chess team, the Illinois Chess Association, and the United States Chess Federation. I also won the Illinois K-12 All-Grade Chess Championship for six years in my category and the National K-12 All Grade Chess Championship my senior year. I was never defeated in my entire four years at my high school.

Girls were another matter. They fascinated me. I loved looking at them, enjoyed dating them, and I had quite the reputation for being a great kisser. I decided to make it my hobby.

Having demonstrated a keen knack for numbers from a young age and having maintained a straight-A grade average throughout school, my parents were encouraged to apply for a full scholastic scholarship for me at Robert Morris University in the heart of downtown Chicago during the summer before my junior year.

They had saved as much as they could over the years and had only enough for the first two years of my education. We were hopeful that at least a partial scholarship could be offered. With my excellent scholastic track record, my success with chess, and the other volunteer work I had performed through my church, I was later granted a full scholastic scholarship upon graduation, and the money that my parents had saved for me was now returned to the newly locked, brown and old, boxy suitcase under their bed. It was a new and welcome chapter in my life.

31

College and Career

We were all looking at Tiny with even more respect for what he had accomplished in spite of such adverse conditions.

While enrolled at college, I found the freedom I had been searching for to help me escape my violent neighborhood. Just a few hours a day spent around "normal people" was like an awakening.

When I was walking into class one day with Elliott, a fellow chess player, I commented, "You know, I didn't know there are people out there who don't have to worry about checking around for danger before entering their home or watching for a stray bullet while watering their garden."

"Seriously, man? That's not good. You from the hood?"

"Levee area," I replied.

"Man, you need to get out of there," Elliott earnestly said.

"Hence, the reason I'm in college. First step. I'm on my way." I could already feel a difference in my life.

Needless to say, my parents were constantly concerned about my safety as I rode the "L" train near our neighborhood to South State Street to and from classes. Considering my short and stout mother was known to reduce most big thug's brave threats to ridiculous rhetoric, not too many in our part of the war would take the time to provoke her. Most people clearly didn't want to fool with me, which would mean fooling with her. Had my mother had the desire and money, she would have made a formidable, yet sincere, politician.

I found a part-time job at a Dairy Queen close to our home in the evenings and also received payment from several of the parishioners for helping them with their business books. This enabled me to study more, and I began keeping my father's church books, a fact that greatly pleased him.

I thoroughly enjoyed my studies, maintaining a 4.0 grade point average throughout college. I also joined any association that would help open doors for me in my profession and fatten my portfolio and marketability.

Now I only played chess occasionally for fun as I was enthralled with the newness of being a college student and absorbing an entirely unique lifestyle.

I actually dated one or two downtown girls a few times but due to having a packed school schedule, working a part-time job, and providing accounting services on the side, not to mention hours of study, I was pretty much out of the serious relationship market, a fact my mother loudly applauded.

After graduating with honors and earning a BA degree, I was hired by Alexander Grant and Company of Chicago, one of the largest accounting firms in the world and founded in 1924 by Chicagoan Alexander Richardson Grant.

I quickly earned the respect of my bosses as I was usually the first to arrive at the office in the morning and the last to leave at the end of the day. I found that, rather than resent the extra work they piled upon me, I enjoyed it.

One day I was called into the office of Jack, one of the partners, and told to sit down. "You've been with us for three months now and have proven yourself to be a dedicated employee and one of the best recruits we've had in a long time. We've decided to finance classes for you to earn your master's degree. We see a great future for you here, Tiny."

"That's wonderful, sir. I accept your kind offer," I replied. "I'm looking forward to being here for a very long time. This is like home." He didn't realize I was just relieved to be outside my neighborhood.

Within two years, I completed my studies at night and received my MBA with my proud family and business associates looking on. I was not only the first in my family to earn a bachelor's degree, I had raised the bar and earned the first master's degree.

I absorbed everything as quickly as possible and began climbing up the corporate ladder at a rapid rate.

In no time at all, I bought a decent used Cadillac Eldorado and located a small furnished studio apartment close to the office. Being the worrywart she was, my mother insisted, "You call me as often as you can and let me know you're all right." This from a woman who heard gunshots at night. I could see she still worried about me like she had when I was a young child.

In two years, I earned enough to buy a one-bedroom condominium in the downtown area, and I furnished it with a leather "pit group," a king-sized bedroom suite, and a walnut dining room suite. My bachelor pad was complete when I added Cerwin-Vega speakers with a Marantz amplifier and receiver that literally shook the walls when I played my music.

I became quite the entertainer, and I took cooking classes to impress my dates with my culinary skills. As I had been told that I was a good-looking man and a snappy dresser, I behaved like quite the ladies' man and flaunted my newfound success unabashedly. I was quickly getting full of myself and pulled away from my family for some time. I wouldn't know how I had hurt them until much later.

One of the few things I would take time to do solo was to watch the Cubs play baseball at Wrigley Field, a legendary Chicago landmark which fascinated me with its rich and storied history. I sang "Take Me Out to the Ballgame" along with all the other fans at the seventh inning stretch with sports announcer Harry Caray, and I was present when the Cubs won the National League East Division Title in 1984. Although the team continuously lost more games than it won, I was a Cubbie fan through and through.

When I reached the quarter-century mark, I figured it was time to settle down, and I earnestly began looking for the right woman to complete my life's picture. Unfortunately, I looked for this perfect woman in all the wrong places—local bars, then later disco clubs where compelling music and psychedelic lights filled the dance floor and a lot of carefree singles hung out.

Mind you, there were some spectacular looking women roaming those fertile grounds, but where the looks were quite appealing, the intelligence was sorely lacking.

During that time, I experimented with many types of liquor, beer, and wine, and kept my condo bar stocked with plenty of everything I liked. I never even once thought of playing with drugs as I had seen the devastation suffered by those who fell into their death grip in our neighborhood, and I drew the line at that.

Then there was another empty Saturday night spent with a complete stranger. I awakened early the next morning staring at the serene, sleeping face of somebody named Tiffany, or maybe it was Bambi. Anyway, she was a design consultant who had been highly recommended by one of my firm's partners. A nice enough girl, but not destined to be my girl.

"Excuse me, madam." Uh oh, not a good start. "Excuse me, lady," I said, giving her shoulder a shake. "You need to leave. I'm going to church." I got the distinct impression she was mad when she slammed out of my condo.

I was tired of my unfulfilling life, and I felt that going back to church could turn out to be one of the best decisions I ever made.

32

First Love

Tiny walked over and picked up a framed photograph of his wife Juanita. While lovingly looking at the photo, he said, "Let me tell you, this was an angel God put into my life, and she is one of the reasons I'm here. I owe a lot to her." We were all moved by his gesture as he continued sharing.

I found a large Baptist Church located within my area and sat way in the back of the church. I was approached right away by one of the greeters whose name tag read "Juanita."

"Welcome to our church. I'm Juanita," she said, while offering her hand. I noticed her smile was dazzling. I was immediately smitten by her huge, dark brown eyes, rimmed with the most incredible long eyelashes I had ever seen. Her skin was almost velvety and the color of caramel. She was smartly dressed and confident. She reminded me a little of my mother.

"Hello, Juanita. I'm Tiny, and I like your church already." This was said with much sincerity. I just hoped she wasn't married. It didn't take long before I found out.

"So, Tiny, you're definitely new here because, believe me, I would have taken notice of you if you'd walked through those doors before." There was that dazzling smile again. "So, single or married?" she asked.

"Single. Why?" I asked.

"Would you like to join me and a group of single adults for lunch after church at a nearby barbecue restaurant? It's something we do regularly."

I quickly answered yes for two reasons: One, I love barbecue, and two, I didn't want Juanita out of my sight.

When I asked if she would ride with me, as I wasn't sure where the place was, she quickly accepted. I was quite bowled over by her personality.

I remember other enthusiastic people in my age group being at the three tables we pulled together, but I couldn't tell you a word they were saying. In Sicily, there is a saying that when a young man falls in love for the very first time, he is struck by "the thunderbolt." The bolt had definitely struck.

During the course of our meal, Juanita told me a little about herself and that she had left Rochester, New York, two years earlier to accept a job with the Consumer Affairs Department of the City of Chicago.

"I love my job," Juanita said. "The benefits are great, the hours are good, and I learn a good deal about the workings of government. The good thing is that I take no work home and that leaves me with a lot of free evenings."

I was planning on changing that and definitely happy she had no other man in her life. After paying for our meals, I offered to take Juanita home if she wanted me to, or we could go to an afternoon movie matinee.

We chose an action flick with Sylvester Stallone, and the comfort level we experienced told me that this might be the one for me. Over a period of time, we could not get enough of each other, but I never broached sex with her as I felt this was something that neither one of us needed to get involved with at this point. Juanita was special to me, and I treated her that way.

Over the next couple of weeks, we found common interests in many things, especially food. We both loved Chicago-style deep dish pizza and the city's famous Vienna Beef hot dogs loaded with an array of fixings that included yellow mustard, neon green pickle relish, pickled sport peppers, a dill pickle spear, and tomato wedges, then topped off with celery salt, and wedged into a poppy seed bun. I liked them so much, I could have eaten half a dozen.

We wandered the streets of Chinatown and occasionally stopped in to enjoy a full Chinese buffet and chat with the fascinating Asian transplants who had taken the time to learn our language and culture.

Juanita was a source of continuous joy and amazement to me and truly the first woman outside of my family I had ever cultivated a genuine relationship with.

It was less than a month before I took my girl to meet Cecil and Big Momma, and they fell in love with her on the first visit to our humble home.

"Welcome to our world," my spry mother had commented. "I'm sure my son has told you all the war stories."

"Yes, ma'am," she replied. "I wore my protective vest, and I brought my helmet." This elicited a hearty laugh from my family and an approving nod of my mother's head. Juanita had captivated them just like I knew she would.

I could almost hear the wedding wheels turning in my calculating mother's mind as her son had never once brought a woman to her home. I'm sure she was already mentally making space on the mantle for her grandchildren's pictures.

One year later, I nervously proposed to Juanita on bended knee at our favorite Italian restaurant on Valentine's Day, presenting her with a 2.0 carat diamond ring.

"You're the light of my life, and the treasure of my heart. Will you marry me, Juanita?" I asked with a trembling voice.

With tears in her eyes, she replied, "I can't see my life without you, Tiny. Yes, I'll marry you." At that very moment, both my mother's and my dreams came true.

We were married by my father at our church, and the ceremony was attended by several hundred well-wishers. One of my younger sisters caught the bridal bouquet. We honeymooned in an all-inclusive resort in Mexico, and I knew I had picked my soul mate. I had never expected love could be like this, although my parents were one of the happiest married couples I had ever known.

Exactly nine months later, our son Devonte was born. Two more daughters, Tamika and Danielle, followed over the next six years. Obviously, I had given up my bachelor pad a long time ago, and we now lived on the North side on the outskirts of Chicago in a four-bedroom home with a white picket fence in a typical, quiet, middle-class neighborhood. It was a far cry from the dangerous ghetto area my family lived in.

After eight years with Alexander Grant and Company, I was again called into Jack's office for a private meeting. After we both sat down, he said, "This is starting to become a habit with us two, right?"

"I don't know, it's been, what, eight years?" I asked. "Some habit, huh?" We both laughed, and I started relaxing.

He leaned forward in his executive chair, steepled his fingers and said, "I'm speaking for myself and on behalf of the other two partners of this firm. We wish to offer you a full partnership. You have most certainly earned it. Take some time to talk it over with Juanita and let us know if you accept. Here's a package with information on an attractive compensation plan that we worked out for the partners, and it includes rewards and incentives for surpassing goals. We hope you say yes."

"I appreciate your trust, Jack. I'll let you know tomorrow." My head was swimming.

I reviewed the partners' package with Juanita, and after doing calculations in my head, I looked at her and said, "This is truly a gift from God."

"I was thinking the same thing," she agreed, while letting me envelop her in my arms. I had dreamed of this for a long time, and I felt like I was on top of the world. Little did I know what effect it would have on our future.

Juanita was a fantastic mother and soon quit her job with the city. She now had the time to ferry our children to private school, dance lessons, baseball practice, and church. As a family, prayer was a vital part of our lives, and our children grew in the knowledge of the Lord.

Now that I was a full-fledged partner, I found my workload stayed basically the same, but my stress level increased exponentially. We were the largest accounting firm in the city, and I found myself staying later and later during the week, eventually renting another furnished studio apartment so that I would not have to commute so late every night. The strain started to show on our marriage as I spent more time at work than I did at home.

Trouble was brewing.

33

Trouble in Paradise

Tiny cleared his throat and began what would prove to be a very difficult part of his story.

My downfall began after a particularly stressful day at the office with my first venture into a neighborhood bar located in the same block as my apartment. Feeling the emptiness one feels at being away from the warmth and familiarity of family, the music and laughter beckoned to me like a siren to a sailor.

I stopped in to have "just one" scotch and water, and the camaraderie I felt there with others who were filling the same empty niche as I was eventually led to my consumption of several more "just one more" drinks. I found myself laughing at crude, drink-induced jokes that, at the time, probably weren't all that funny, but in my state were hilarious to me. How I later made it back to my apartment in one piece amazed me. It had been years since I had even tasted liquor, and I found it strangely satisfying for a time.

There were several frantic calls from Juanita on my message machine, and my guilt produced small chest pains which alarmed me a little. Once I had satisfied her concern by fibbing about the evening's activities, I quickly fell asleep and awoke the next morning with a huge hangover. I made it through the next day, although, how, I don't know. Unfortunately, even that didn't stop me from a daily routine of drinking and now smoking cigarettes, which only exacerbated my health situation.

Sober weekends at home would temporarily help me put things in perspective as I proudly cheered from the stands while my son excelled as a pitcher in high school. He had become taller, filled out a little more, and reminded me of myself a little.

"Look, Daddy, we're ballerinas," my daughters would say, pretending they were Sugar Plum Fairies while twirling around in their fluffy pink tutus, sparkly tiaras, and pink ballerina shoes. I would feel my chest puff out with pride. These beautiful angels were mine.

Juanita had always been a fantastic cook, and she plied me with meals of fried chicken, fried steak, meatloaf, fried okra and squash, tomatoes, and huge homemade biscuits. My weight ballooned over time as I also ate mostly fast food during the week.

Eventually, as I became more addicted, I could no longer hide my nicotine habit from the family, and my wife and children did not hide their displeasure.

"Well, there goes your 'Father of the Year' award," Juanita said, with the sound of ice in her voice after finding me sneaking a smoke out in our backyard.

"Ewwww," my daughters said, clamping their noses with their fingers while running back into the house.

"Okay, I'll not smoke in front of you guys," I responded to the attacks and harsh looks.

Juanita and I always planned a date night one weekend a month and, like eager teenagers, we would take the train into the city for dinner and a movie or other entertainment. We would hungrily make long and satisfying love afterwards in my apartment, and we both knew that continued intimacy was important to keeping us close while living apart.

Little did she know what crazy things I was doing to myself during the week until she found two bottles of Glenlivet scotch—one open and one unopened—that I had not attempted to hide in my pantry.

"So, things don't look like they're going so well after all," she stated, while holding a bottle in each hand, her head cocked to the side. I'm sure her hands would have been on her hips had she not been holding my scotch.

"Juanita, baby, I drink very little during the week. Sometimes I need it just to sleep. You know I miss you and the kids," I feebly said.

"Well, buy some sleep aids then. Anything else you've forgotten to tell me?" she testily asked.

"Nope, just working myself half to death. We've got kids going to college very soon, Juanita. Sometimes a man needs a little relaxation."

"First, cigarettes, and now liquor. You need to stop this madness, husband. You have to be there for us."

"I will, sweetheart, I promise." My assurances didn't work on my strong-as-battery-acid wife. The door to distrust was opened, and the nagging and questioning began.

My wife and I had always been extremely close, and I had created a wedge in the relationship, now adding guilt to my plethora of problems. I was on a downward spiral, and I became even more frustrated. I was living two lives, and I hated myself for it. I couldn't even imagine what I was doing to Juanita, and I didn't want to know.

One Thursday evening after dropping in at the bar, I shared drinks with an interesting and beautiful young woman named Cynthia. She had just been hired at our firm and had stopped in on my recommendation. This newly divorced, tanned, thirty-year-old leggy blonde was looking for some companionship. After several nights alone, being estranged from my wife and feeling such despair, I was ready for it.

"You are a very handsome man, you know that?" she purred, while slowly stirring her vodka Collins.

Careful, Tiny, this is like walking on hot coals with bare feet, was all I could think.

"You're a beautiful woman as well," I replied, careful to not look directly at her for too long a period of time. She had been the one to approach me in the office, asking where to get a good drink after work. I naturally had offered my services as a tour guide since she was new to the city.

"Why don't we move to the back corner table over there?" she asked. It had seemed like an eternity since a woman had looked at me with such interest and sensuality. I knew I was somehow crossing over a line that I didn't want to bring myself back from. Once the fire was raging, there was no turning back.

Gone from my memory were the vows I had so seriously taken, and now all I wanted was to be with someone who would hold me, care for me, and not judge me. Maybe I just didn't want to stop talking.

The intimacy we shared was for less than a month, but

those pale, blue eyes would haunt me for a long time as would the guilt I was feeling. Eventually, either guilt or good sense prevailed, and we stopped the affair, feeling we would most probably lose our jobs over it, and I was finding it harder to live with my transgressions. Life went on and the secret thankfully stayed between us.

The week after I turned forty-five, I complained about shortness of breath, dry mouth, and tingling in my feet to Frank, one of the firm's senior partners and one of my drinking buddies.

"Tiny, we are going to schedule an appointment with the firm's physician for a complete physical for you. This will include a stress test, EKG, angiogram, blood work, and chest x-ray. We will also schedule a future colonoscopy. We sure don't want anything serious to happen to you."

The grim results later that week certainly got my attention. I found I was suffering from extremely high blood pressure, high cholesterol, full-blown diabetes, and a heart that had become damaged from smoking, drinking, and carrying around too many pounds.

I was emphatically told by my doctor, "Begin an exercise program, quit smoking and drinking, and lose some weight. You are a heart attack looking for a place to happen." That certainly rang some important bells. I was prescribed several different types of medicine, and I reported the doctor's findings to the partners at the firm who expressed their alarm.

I kept telling myself I would start the plan the next week, but "next week" never came as I deluded myself that it would all go away. I did stop smoking and started eating healthier, but drinks after work had become more or less a routine and

I wasn't ready to let that go yet. Also, long hours at work were necessary to me as I was the sole breadwinner of my family, and my kids would soon be going to college.

After being threatened by Frank, I finally told Juanita about the test results. She became frantic, as I knew she would.

"I insist you cut back on your time at work, and you definitely must give up the downtown apartment. It's time you came home, Tiny," she said, while holding me so tight I thought I might die right then of oxygen deprivation.

I changed to four-day workweeks, giving me time to work on my health, which included abandoning the stress of downtown living.

My little busy bee wife took over, setting up an office, a treadmill, and Nautilus exercise equipment in the basement. My friends at the firm were all in favor of the new plan, and I was able to handle quite a lot of work from my new virtual office.

I was happy to move out of my city apartment and back into the master bedroom with my loving wife. We rekindled our romance, filling deep needs within one another in new and profound ways.

One day while walking around a lake at the local city park, she stopped and put her arms around me and said, "I am so happy to have you back here again, Tiny. The children are thrilled, and Devonte loves the hours you spend helping him with baseball. You know, he wants you to teach him how to become a statistician."

"I didn't know that, but it would be my pleasure," I proudly replied.

We became best friends again and spent hours together doing fun and senseless things. I was able to attend more sporting events with my son and enjoy time with my adorable daughters. I was home now, and it felt just right.

I also shared with my wife how I had strayed. There was a flood of tears, then she told me that she had her suspicions. Thank God she forgave me but it took some time. Juanita quoted Matthew 18:21-22 that says, *"Lord how often will my brother sin against me, and I forgive him? As many as seven times?" Jesus said to him, "I do not say to you seven times, but seventy times seven."* I knew then without a doubt that I had married an angel.

I also kicked up my spiritual life a notch by joining a weekly men's prayer group and becoming more involved in our church as the spiritual head of our family. The fact that I had emotionally and spiritually abandoned my family for quite some time was foremost in my mind, and I vowed to make things up to them.

My children were growing up quickly, and I was grateful that I was now more a part of their lives. It didn't take me long to realize how easy it had been to turn from God and live my life selfishly without thoughts of what Juanita was going through.

My son graduated from high school three months later, and I was thrilled he had been selected Valedictorian of his class. I realized how much I had missed out on over the years, and I was ashamed of the life I had chosen for so long to live. Thanks to the devotion and hard work of my wife, my children scored above average marks in their schoolwork.

I was blown away when Devonte regaled the crowd with

his Valedictorian speech which emphasized the need for graduates to begin volunteering their services both in our country and abroad. He spoke of the sacrifice his grandparents had made to help make a difference in their Southside Chicago neighborhood. He emphasized how his father had looked beyond that Southside neighborhood, graduating college, receiving his master's degree, and, as the first man of color, becoming a partner in a well-known accounting firm. He stressed how proud he was to come from such great lineage.

As I watched him receive his diploma, then throw his graduation cap into the air, I made the commitment to step up my plan for better health the very next week so that I could spend more quality time with him, Juanita, and most definitely my daughters, who were changing right before my eyes.

Friends and family were invited to our home for an after graduation cookout, and I was elated to see my aging parents make the long trip from south of the city. My once powerfully strong father was now stooped from osteoarthritis and walked with a cane, and my mother suffered from severe diabetes, a disease she unwittingly passed on to me.

I could hear her sharing a familiar story with our neighbors at one of the tables nearby. "You know those doctors warned me on two occasions that I was about to lose my leg to the sugar diabetes. Well, won't you just look at this, my leg is still here. Let me tell you something, if you pray hard enough, you will scare the hell out of the devil. I did it twice!" she exclaimed. I'm telling you, that evil eye was perfected.

Dad still preached occasionally on Sundays while perched

on a stool, but Mom had retired years back from her crusade in teaching and saving the Southside with home-baked brownies, a fact that greatly saddened the young people in our community. "Big Momma," though feared, was sorely missed.

My three sisters had survived war on the Southside and gone their own ways after graduation, one becoming a missionary in China and the other two, in attendance, were married with children of their own. It was a family reunion of sorts, and the contentment I felt at that very moment was indescribable. I reveled in it.

One of the last thoughts I had on earth was how blessed I had been throughout my life. I cherished my wife and children and couldn't wait to see what the future would hold for us all. I had almost lost the greatest treasure on earth—the unconditional love of the people whom God had blessed me with.

As I was flipping the last batch of hamburgers on the grill and gazing over at my children playing kickball with their cousins, I began to feel light-headed, short of breath, and experiencing double vision. I thought that maybe it had to do with the heat from the coals.

My right arm then became numb, and I dropped the spatula, stumbling backwards. My entire chest burned like it was on fire. I could not breathe.

"No!" I screamed, "Not now! Not when I've finally got it together!" The pain was so severe I clutched my chest and fell to the ground.

Juanita saw me fall, and screamed, "Someone call 911! Now!"

As my family crowded around to try and help me, my dear wife immediately cradled my head in her lap, stroked my hair, and fervently asked God for His help. She even bent to kiss my lips, an act to which I could no longer respond. I believe she knew it was over.

The last thing I saw before passing from there to here was the loving and terrified look on my wife and children's tear-stained faces. I could hear the prayers they were sending that were far too late. I was later pronounced dead on the way to the hospital, the victim of a massive heart attack.

I look forward to seeing my grandparents and other friends and relatives who have blazed the heavenly trail for me. I know without a doubt that one day I will see my beloved Juanita and my children again.

34

Back to the Garden

We all gathered around Tiny, hugging him and thanking him for being in our group. We all thought his life's story was outstanding, and his father's just as interesting.

"Thanks for sharing such a beautiful story, Tiny," Wisdom stated. "It's a true example of redemption. We are now going back to the Sea of Reconciliation. When we return here in the future, you will be entirely different heavenly beings."

"How is that?" I asked Wisdom. "Will we have wings?"

"Will we be able to fly?" Sophia eagerly added.

"Girls, you and your imaginations," Wisdom replied, closing his eyes and shaking his head from side to side.

"Unfortunately, right now there are things in heaven that cannot be explained, only experienced. In due time, you will understand this. In the meantime, let us go to the Sea of Reconciliation, board our boat, and return to the garden. There, we will proceed to another part of heaven that will literally blow your mind."

"Gee, Wisdom, you are always one step ahead of us," I said, looking at the others who were nodding their heads in agreement.

"Actually, Julie, it's more like eons ahead of you," he replied. and we all knew that was true.

Since time is not marked in heaven, and one doesn't know how many minutes, hours, days, weeks, months, or years have gone by, one just simply enjoys "being," without a schedule, time clock, or critical eyes monitoring every movement. For a neatnik and time freak like me, this was truly a new experience and not an unwelcome one.

"Close your eyes and hold hands, all of you, and we will quickly transport to the Sea," Wisdom commanded. Within what seemed like seconds, we were back on the Chinese junk and seated exactly as we had been on the trip over to the Other Side.

It was wonderful to be back on the water, and I leaned over the boat, splashing my hands. Minnows and small fish were swimming around them, and I tried to catch a few, bringing chuckles from the others.

"Hungry, Julie?" Tiny asked. "Hey, if you catch a red snapper, can I have it?"

"How about a whole school of them?" I asked in jest.

"Not a bad idea," he replied.

That boy has some appetite was all I could think.

I recalled several long weekends spent as a child with my family in Panama City Beach, Florida, a great vacation spot on the Gulf of Mexico. We always rented a room or cabin on the water as my mother stated she did not drive for hours to stay across the street and not be able to wake up with the surf in our ears. It certainly made sense to me.

Many mornings, as dawn was breaking, she and I would awaken to collect seashells along the waters of the beach. We would fill buckets with conch shells, sand dollars, starfish, and shells of all shapes, sizes, and colors, careful to watch out for jellyfish that might have washed ashore.

Sometimes we didn't talk; we just soaked in the world around us. The time spent with her was magical and special to me, and I was happy to have her all to myself for any length of time.

Later in the evening, armed with flashlights, our family would all grab our buckets and go hermit crab digging, waiting for the little crustaceans to poke their heads out of their warm holes in the sand. We would nab them and place them in our buckets. It was always a competition between my mother and father as to who would get the most loot.

When we returned, we would have crab racing by the pool, then later return the little boogers to their habitat. It was great fun though.

Wisdom woke me out of my flash to the past with his next words.

"Sophia, we have yet to hear your and Julie's stories. We will start with yours and end with Julie's. We are going to take the long, scenic route back to the Garden, so you will have plenty of time to enjoy the cruise."

With that said he lifted his arms, and the ancient craft easily left the dock and headed slowly out to sea.

35

Solomon and Estelle

We were all excited to hear Sophia's story, and we made ourselves comfortable and ready to listen. I was already feasting on looking at the stately and magnificent homes that we slowly and leisurely passed by.

I was born in Miami on September 9, 1956, the night Elvis Presley, my mother's idol, first performed on "The Ed Sullivan Show." This strange woman was more upset at missing Elvis' gyrations than elated at my birth I later found out.

My entrance was characterized by my thrashing and screaming at the top of my lungs, an early trait that unfortunately continues to this day. The doctor told my father he wasn't sure who was screaming the loudest—the newborn or its mother.

Poor Estelle suffered so much during her pregnancy and my birth that she told the doctor, "Get rid of the baby making equipment. I am done!" And, of course, the obstetrician followed her demands, much to the dismay of my father, Solomon who pleaded, "Estelle, I am forty years old. I have waited twenty years."

Due to their advanced age in child rearing, many friends teased him, calling him Abraham and my forty-one-year-old mother, Sarah, which greatly annoyed her.

"Let me tell you something," she replied, "Isaac was born when the Old Testament matriarch was over eighty years of age and look how he turned out. I'm pretty sure she was worn out, though."

My parents were descendants of King David of biblical times and swore that lineage must have something to do with the fact that my father owned the largest and most successful Cadillac dealership in Ft. Lauderdale and was considered by other Jews to be a wealthy man, a fact that greatly pleased him.

Success had not come easy for them as they had both endured and survived the Nazi death trap known as Auschwitz. They arrived at Ellis Island in New York City financially ruined and in ill health in the spring of 1945 after the camp's liberation by Allied forces on January 27 of that year.

With the help of family members who had immigrated to America before them, they moved into a tiny and cheap, third-floor, walk-up apartment in the poorest of sections in New York City called "Hell's Kitchen." It was a twenty-five block, rundown area located on the riverfront that stretched from West 29th Street to West 55th and had been settled by wild and burly Irish immigrants in the mid-19th century.

My parents were hired to work for my father's uncle and their benefactor, Isaiah, in his clothing factory. It was a two-story, red brick building located in Manhattan's famous Garment District, which housed about eighty-five employees, mostly European Jews who had fled Nazi persecution and systematic annihilation in the 1940s.

Uncle Isaiah had worked in the one-hundred-year-old building for twenty years, serving as the maintenance man for all the machines, and a part-time seamstress before buying it in 1939 from the previous Jewish owners.

Never marrying, he had lived like a pauper in a tiny, dark and dank studio basement apartment while secretly stashing his weekly cash earnings in a locked box, hidden under a plank beneath the floor. A survivor, he had learned to consume only one meal a day, usually Vienna sausages or Spam sandwiched between day-old bread slices and a can of any variety of beans or peas, heated over a hotplate. Rarely did he splurge on a real meal, knowing that the pain of frugalness now would be forgotten in the pleasure of ownership later.

In 1919, Isaiah had fled Buenos Aires, Argentina, seeking sanctuary in New York City after witnessing the brutal murders of his mother and father, Russian Ashkenazi Jews who were both tenured university professors. They were pulled from their bed in the middle of the night by the Argentine Patriotic League during the pogroms in January of that year.

These fanatics screamed at his parents, "We know you both are behind several Communist conspiracies, and you will be shot. Don't lie to us!"

"Please believe us, we are not doing what you are saying," they said in defense. "We are only professors. Nothing more." Isaiah knew this to be true.

It didn't matter. They were shot point-blank in the head before their son's very eyes and thrown aside like rubbish. He was only eighteen.

He remembered the words of his father once the pogroms began: "In a metal box under our bed you will find American currency and your legal papers. Should anything happen to us, take it and go to America. I have included information for contacting trusted friends in New York City. You will be okay, my son. *Yeshua* will guide you."

Isaiah had never dreamed that day would come. His two older brothers had left Buenos Aires years before, returning to their Russian roots, and now he would be alone in a new country with no knowledge of the language, the people, or their customs.

The tall and thin scholarly looking teenager immediately booked passage on a northbound freighter to the United States, providing his services as a deckhand to help supplement the costs. Although seasick and heartsick most of the time, he survived the two-week trip unscathed, landing at Ellis Island on a bitterly cold February day and witnessing a snowfall for the first time in his life.

Having been severely traumatized, he was enveloped in a network of love and care provided by others who had experienced more than their share of heartache. The tight-knit Jewish community provided more than hugs and home-made chicken soup to help begin his recovery process; they also provided employment at the garment factory and a small, cheap place to live. He chose not to mingle with others for quite some time as the grieving process totally consumed him and, respectful of this, they kept their distance.

Isaiah had chosen two treasured items of his parents to bring with him: One was the *tallis* (Jewish prayer shawl) that his father had worn daily while saying his prayers; the other was the pearl-handled brush and mirror set his mother had used every day of her life, brushing the long, lustrous hair she kept pinned up most of the time. It was all he had left of eighteen short years with them, and the emptiness he felt was pronounced.

When visited by his brothers later that year, he vowed,

"One day I will own my own factory in our parents' memory. I will treat employees the way I have always wished for myself and our fellow Jews to be treated. I will respect the rights of all and provide a place that isn't just about work, but one that will include an atmosphere of comfort, safety, trust, and healing."

Life's cruelties had tried to eradicate his entire race more than once and the efforts only served to strengthen and mobilize them.

His two brothers' resounding encouragement was all he needed. "Isaiah, we will stay in touch with you," they said before boarding their plane. Both pressed several hundred U.S. dollars into the hands of their overwhelmed and grateful brother who was thankful to have spent time with them.

When the owners decided to retire, the factory was offered to Isaiah at a fair price but one that was much less than he had saved. He moved into a small but fully furnished one-bedroom apartment with a kitchen and bath. It was quite a leap from his previous place and took some getting used to for the pauper-turned-factory owner. He also now felt comfortable entertaining friends in his new place and developing cooking skills.

The new entrepreneur immediately improved the conditions for the workers by providing easier jobs for the youngest and oldest women, introducing swing shifts, and installing a better ventilation system. Classical music was played on old RCA Victrola phonographs in the two large sewing rooms, soothing those whose days could easily be classified as mundane. Isaiah also introduced ten-minute breaks every two hours and a full hour for lunch. The changes had an immediate effect on the workers, and morale soared.

One of the most viable benefits he provided to workers was introducing English classes at the factory. These were held on Sundays and were paid for by Isaiah. Solomon and Estelle, though exhausted from the week's work, diligently attended these classes, eager to learn the language of their new country. By studying and practicing together, they quickly mastered it.

One of the daily traditions that began after Israel became a nation and that would continue until Isaiah's death was the playing of Israel's national anthem, "Hatikva –The Hope. "At exactly five minutes before quitting time, Orthodox and non-Orthodox Jews throughout the building would gather together, united as one, and sing the words that had been passed down through generations for over one hundred years:

As long as deep in the heart, the soul of a Jew yearns, and forward to the East to Zion, an eye looks, our hope will not be lost, the hope of two thousand years, to be a free nation in our land, the land of Zion and Jerusalem.

The words were written by Naftali Herz Imber with the desire that the Jewish people would someday return to the land of their forefathers, as prophesied in the Hebrew Bible. They had been exiled from Israel in 70 C.E. by the Roman army led by Titus who destroyed the Temple in Jerusalem.

He felt the song rekindled hope in them and enabled them to remember those whose absences were keenly felt and experience pride in their race and its chronicled history.

Over the years and before stepping up to ownership, Isaiah had learned to sew and made himself available as a backup seamstress, feeling that would provide even better job security, and it had.

The event that would make him become an activist had occurred on March 25, 1911, before his arrival in the States, when one hundred and forty-six shirtwaist makers of the Triangle Shirtwaist Factory tragically died after owners purposely locked the doors on the eighth floor to prevent theft or unauthorized bathroom breaks. Those who didn't die in the fire jumped to their deaths to escape the inferno. New York's citizens had been outraged.

Once he learned of this atrocity, Isaiah joined the ILGWU (The International Ladies' Garment Workers' Union), which was organized to protect its workers. The organization was mostly comprised of women, but membership was open to men as well. It was formed in the early 1900s and was also a pivotal player in the labor history of the 1920s and 1930s.

Isaiah was later active in the Jewish Labor Committee, which was established in 1934 in response to Hitler's rise to power and to defend European Jewry's rights. Others who joined the ILGWU were the Amalgamated Clothing Workers, the Workmen's Circle, and other like-minded groups. The ILGWU and other JLC groups also helped arrange adoptions of orphaned children who were survivors of the war.

Without Uncle Isaiah's help and compassion, many of the traumatized concentration camp survivors (if they could be called survivors) would have had a much harder time finding steady employment on the harsh streets of Manhattan. Everyone called him "uncle" because he acted like one, and he was considered a godsend in every way. He would kid with other factory owners that he was running a hospital, not a garment factory, a statement that brought great respect from those not quite as willing to take such a huge risk.

Solomon was chosen to keep an eye on the employees for him and to help with packing and loading the multitude of short and long-sleeved cotton dress shirts that were shipped daily to local department stores and others all around the country. Uncle Isaiah had found no shortage of labor, but he was satisfied now to have another set of family eyes he could trust to protect his investment.

Estelle was hired to work as a seamstress and was content with her new role, having made her own clothing since the age of twelve. She would occasionally have flashbacks of painful incidents she had suffered as a prisoner in the camp and would find her hands trembling and unable to sew. Thankfully others nearby were empathetic and provided a support system that she would later credit with helping her process and better handle the horrible memories.

The couple worked ten to twelve hours a day for minimal but decent wages, thankful to have any income at all. America seemed millions of miles away from Auschwitz, and they would do whatever it took to build a secure future in a safe place with unlimited opportunities. They were always the first to arrive at work and the last to leave, and their commitment was not lost on Isaiah.

"Solomon," Uncle Isaiah said one day, "come into my office." Once he cleared a space on a very cluttered chair, Isaiah sat down and said, "Four years you have been with me. Since the day you arrived, you have worked extremely hard. You have earned my trust in ways you don't even know. I would like to make you general manager of the operation, and that includes a large raise and bonus. I will continue in an ownership capacity. Talk to Estelle and get back to me tomorrow."

Solomon and Estelle discussed this new promotion, feeling that perhaps Uncle Isaiah was grooming him to take over the business upon his retirement. Though grateful, this unsettled my mother as she did not wish to live in the overcrowded city with such harsh winters longer than necessary. She also wished to escape those who unfortunately reminded her on a daily basis of the Holocaust's atrocities. A fresh start was what she wanted. He would, however, accept the job for now.

Three years later her dream came true as they were able to save enough money to move to Miami, a place she had dreamed about since coming to America and whose cut-out photos were posted on the refrigerator and walls throughout the small apartment. To Estelle, Miami was "heaven on earth," a comment heard regularly by my father.

Although saddened to hear of their decision to leave New York, Uncle Isaiah was understanding and appreciative of their seven years of hard work and loyalty. "*Yeshua* provides," he said while thanking them again for their loyalty and commitment.

Tearful goodbyes were later exchanged in the factory, and he presented my father with a parting gift of one thousand dollars in cash, a sum that would be equal to nine thousand dollars today. Needless to say, it was much needed and appreciated seed money to begin a new life in South Miami, and they would never forget his kind gesture.

The first thing Solomon eagerly bought was a nice 1950 Ford Tudor sedan for only fifteen hundred dollars over my mother's loud protestations. "Fifteen hundred dollars?" she gasped. "Solly, have you lost your mind?"

My father, who could truly charm the stripes off a zebra,

explained, "The long trip south will require a dependable car. The alternative," he argued, "is that we could just stay in New York." That would be one of the few arguments my father ever won with her, and it was the beginning of his lifelong love affair with automobiles.

As a first-time automobile owner, my father was impressed with the car's roominess and 95-hp flathead inline six-cylinder engine. With no power steering or brakes, he quickly developed larger muscles to help rein in his new car. However, it did come complete with an AM/FM radio, a dashboard electric clock, and a Magic Air heater which Estelle loved and kept running full blast until my parched father passed south of the Mason-Dixon Line on his way to Florida.

Once they arrived in Miami, they rented a room in a local boarding house, and within a week, they moved into a small, nicely furnished studio apartment in a complex inhabited by a good many Jewish families on 79th Street and 16th Avenue. This section of Miami was referred to as Liberty City, a name that sounded good to them.

With a handwritten letter of recommendation from Uncle Isaiah, my father was immediately hired as a car salesman at the largest Cadillac dealership in the area. His handsome looks and natural sales ability soon helped him build a loyal following, and referrals started reaping their benefits.

He was named "Salesman of the Year" in January of the following year, which included a $3,000 bonus, and he and Estelle bought a small two-bedroom, one bath home in one of the newest subdivisions in South Miami.

"Oh, Solly, we finally did it," she said with great enthusiasm and happiness. "This is all ours." My mother was finally settled and content, and my father was thankful for the much-needed peace in his life.

The young couple rejoiced in their first American home, my father's successful job, and the blissfully beautiful Florida weather. Now, Solomon thought, maybe his wife would be ready and willing to provide a child—their own creation—and then their life would be perfect.

Estelle, however, was not anxious to start a family. Deep-rooted scars still lingered from the brutal rapes she had suffered from the Nazi SS soldiers while in the camp, and my father, though anxious, expressed his empathy and love by not pressing the issue.

Having grown up in a large family of rowdy boys, he constantly dreamed about having a son. He would name him Solomon in memory of his father, and he would become a doctor or a lawyer.

"I must have a son while I am still young and healthy enough to enjoy and teach him," he would, in weaker moments, plead with his anxious wife.

36

Early Days

We settled into a very comfortable ride on our cushioned seats with the salt air and wind gently blowing across our faces. Sophia appeared most anxious to continue.

Four years later he got part of his wish, as my mother nonchalantly made an announcement over coffee in the lanai one morning before he left for work.

"Solly, what color do you want to paint the nursery?" she casually asked while he was drinking his second cup of coffee. This "casual bomb" had its effect.

He jumped up, spilling his coffee and screamed, "Really, Estelle? Really? Don't kid with me, now. Really?"

"Yes, really!" she shouted, and he swooped her up in his arms and danced around the lanai, holding her while she giggled.

He sent her three dozen, long-stemmed red roses throughout the day, an extravagant display of emotion that baffled her as Solomon was not prone to that behavior.

He was certainly able to afford it as he had taken over a failing Cadillac dealership a year earlier and turned it into one of the hottest properties in town by using the new medium of television to advertise his beautiful line of America's favorite expensive car. With his charisma and ease in front of the camera, the television commercials made my father a little bit of a local celebrity, something he enjoyed to the hilt.

At the same time, my poor, overweight pregnant mother was soon suffering from edema, severe back pain, leg cramps, hemorrhoids, constant retching over the toilet, and a total lack of sleep, while her semi-famous husband was bragging to everyone he knew that it was his anointed time to have a son. After all, he had waited all these years.

My father insisted the nursery be completely decorated in masculine blue and my mother insisted they add a hint of yellow, just in case. It was apparent that he could not wrap his mind around the idea of having a girl.

Nine months after the announcement, the "sacred son" did not appear as my father had boasted to friends and employees, and it was a bitter disappointment to him. I later accidentally learned from my mother that he was so angry I was not a boy that he tossed all of the "It's a Boy" cigars he had bought to share with his buddies into the trash can and stormed out of the hospital. She was so upset at his actions that she couldn't even breast feed me. And this, my friends, was the auspicious start of my life.

From the very beginning, I was a handful. Unfortunately, taking after my mother's sister, I was a short, gangly, clumsy child with extremely curly, brown hair. I always had a fit with that hair, and it was only later in life that I learned how to straighten it. I also had a nose only a mother could love as it was bigger-than-life to me, and it would be my quest for most of my life to minimize it.

To further improve my looks, I had been blessed with a mouth the size of Martha Raye's, a great singer and comedian from the '50s, who was called "the mouth," a moniker I adopted in college. My fabulous plump, pear-shaped figure completed the picture, and I wondered in high school why guys didn't fall all over me. Many times, I wished I had inherited my father's good looks as I felt he might have liked me a little better.

All I can remember in my early formative years was my father constantly telling me, "Don't talk so loudly, please act like a lady," something I had obviously not been taught. He also complained, "You're an embarrassment to me, and you have pathetic manners." I don't remember too many kind words passing his lips with regard to his only child, but I will say this: although "the mouth" probably deserved it, he never once laid a hand on me, and for that I was grateful.

Unfortunately, Estelle's traumatizing pregnancy and birthing experience with me propelled her delicate psyche back to the horrors of Auschwitz, and she spiraled into postpartum debilitating depression, only later recovering. On many days she never left her bed, and from the time I was five years old, I would make a peanut butter and jelly sandwich for myself and soup for my mother on nights when no supper had been cooked.

On the few times Estelle ventured out of her dark sanctuary, I embraced the effort she put into even basic conversation, and I would hold her hands, searching those empty eyes for a clue to what lay inside there. Sometimes I would sing to her while combing her long, now-graying hair. There was a connection sometimes in the solitude between us.

She never once mentioned anything about the concentration camp and I was thankful, as I knew I wasn't equipped to help her should she relive any part of it. Or maybe deep down inside I wished she had; it might have taught me how to better cope. I would try not to stare at the numbers forever etched on her skin, a reminder of the inhumane treatment man can inflict on his fellow man.

There were many nights over the years when my mother would awaken, screaming and crying into the darkness, the result of nightmares I would never experience. I could hear through the door my father's muted words of compassion, and I could picture him cradling her and rocking her gently back to sleep. His abundant patience was not lost on me.

Somewhere along the way, my father lost a wife, and I lost a mother, and I was always haunted by those listless, flat-lined eyes that reflected the anguish I felt she dealt with on a daily basis.

I believe my father unconsciously blamed me for my mother's problems, and he threw himself into his business even more, working late several nights a week. I heard rumors over the years about his mistresses, and while angry with him, I believed deep down inside that he did deserve some measure of happiness. I reasoned that at least he hadn't abandoned my mother, although I am sure the thought had crossed his mind.

On my tenth birthday, I received the most wonderful and unlikely gift from my parents. After two years of literally begging for one, my father presented me with an adorable white toy poodle.

"Here's a list of instructions on how to care for the dog. Since this is your first pet, I felt it would help for you to have some basic information," he said, while handing me the leash with my new dog attached to it. At first, I was a little miffed at his exaggerated concern; however, on second thought, I imagined he was nervous that I might accidentally kill it.

I have to tell you, though, having something all my own to love and nurture was like giving sugar to a diabetic. I truly overloaded on this dog, watching its every move from the moment we both woke up in the morning in my bed to the minute we laid our heads back down on it at night. We literally became inseparable.

As an only child, for the first time, I was sharing my life with something else.

Here was this delightful little "fur ball" that captivated my every thought, and I promptly dyed her coat a subtle pink color, painted her toenails hot pink, and tied bright pink ribbons in her hair.

Needless to say, my father was mortified and accused me of ruining a perfectly good dog. I, however, ignored his rants and proudly paraded Frances around in front of my friends, and they all loved her. It was great to have something unique to call my own.

It was a whole week before my friend's mother pulled me aside and pointed out, "Uh, Sophia, you might want to change Frances' name to Frank. The anatomy suggests that little pink Frances is indeed a Frank."

Having never owned a pet before, and certainly not yet being acquainted with any part of a male's private area, I had no clue what was going on down there.

My friends swore for a long time that my poor dog suffered from gender confusion for the rest of his life. And by the way, the name was changed, but the pink color stayed.

I loved school and excelled in my classes, finding more

acceptance from my teachers and other students than I did from the two people who were responsible for my existence. I literally devoured everything the textbooks had to offer, finding myself magically transported to other places, times, and lifestyles, sometimes continents away.

There was such a stark difference in these life-escaping adventures on paper compared to my listless and dull existence at home. I was especially drawn to the fashions of all eras, finding myself as a teenager in the birthing stages of what I hoped to be a future career in fashion design.

I imagined myself living in England in the late 1830s when Queen Victoria reigned. It was an elegant time when beautiful women with powdered wigs dressed in the most current Victorian fashion, characterized by narrow, sloping shoulders, low and pointed waistlines, and bell-shaped skirts that hid layers of petticoats, tight corsets, and ankle-length chemise-like skirts. Specially designed wide-brimmed hats were enormous and covered with flowers and feathers, and sometimes fruit. It was a time of pomp and circumstance and protocol, and I was enchanted by it all.

The Roaring '20s also fascinated me, and I could almost hear the staccato rapid-fire sound of the tommy guns as both gangsters and G-Men battled one another, sometimes while standing on the running board of a 1920s Ford Model-T, with long coats flapping in the wind, hanging on for dear life, while dodging a hail of .45 caliber bullets. I imagined myself as Clyde's Bonnie, minus the killing, of course.

I always thought I wasn't a very good Jew as I rarely observed Shabbat, and I certainly didn't eat kosher foods. My non-Orthodox parents rarely observed it as well as that was one of the busiest days at the dealership, and my father felt he could do more for his fellow Jews by working that day, rather than staying home, and it was too much of an effort for my mother. He had been quite generous with donations to his synagogue, so it appeared no one really minded.

We did, however, celebrate *Hanukkah*, *Rosh Hashanah*, *Yom Kippur*, and Passover, and we attended the bar and bat mitzvahs held for the children of their friends.

My own bat mitzvah at the age of thirteen was held at our synagogue and was well-attended by dealership customers, family, and friends. Uncle Isaiah, who was nearly seventy years old now, surprised me with his presence.

"Uncle Isaiah," I squealed, hugging his neck. "You came!" I was overjoyed.

"What, I would miss my favorite girl's bat mitzvah?" he remarked, with a sparkle in his eye.

I insisted he sit at the head table right next to me at the over-the-top party my parents threw at the local country club.

Everyone that night made me feel, for the first time in my life, like a true "Jewish-American Princess." I was still awkward, pimply-faced, loud, and boisterous, but it was my time to shine, and shine I did.

The large gifts of cash I received were immediately placed in a college fund to be used after I graduated high school. I always felt my father spent more money than most fathers would have on that party in hopes of atoning for his indifference to me over those thirteen years. He was "loaded," after all. My mother even found it in her heart to get out of bed and celebrate the occasion with us. It was a great day.

37

Life on my Own

Rashid spoke what we all were thinking by this time in Sophia's timeline. "Sophia, you really had it rough growing up. I'm so sorry." We all added an "Amen" to that. Little did we know, things would get even worse for her.

As I continued to excel in high school studies, I began looking into colleges and universities. My father felt I was still very immature (and I was), and he commented one day, "I want you to continue to live at home and attend the University of Miami. It's close by."

This, quite frankly, shocked me, considering I had been shipped off every summer of my life to health camp; however, his concern deeply touched me.

"Okay, Dad, this is the deal. I will agree to two years at the University of Miami, only if I am allowed to spend the last two years at the Miami International University of Art and Design." This was somewhere I could put my love and talent for design to work, something my father never fully understood but, nonetheless, agreed to.

"Also, part of the deal is that I live on campus in a freshman dormitory." The relief on his face was almost comical as he eagerly accepted.

On a final note, I insisted that, with me now out of the house, he would hire an in-home health care professional to attend to my mother's needs on the nights he worked. He had already thought of that, he informed me. Now I could truly move on with my life.

Once I was enrolled, I found college life perfectly suited to me. I was a small fish in a large pond, and I enjoyed blending in with the huge number of students on campus. One of the bonuses included the fact that my two closest friends also attended the same university, shared a dorm room with me, and all of us experienced the newness of college life at the same time. The three of us were together so much, our Cuban friends called us "las très amigas." I was happier than I could ever remember.

Once, while visiting my parents, I watched a Saturday late-night special with comic George Carlin performing "Seven Words You Can Never Say on Television" on the small television in my bedroom. Not one who was normally enthralled with profanity, I found his monologue on the subject totally engrossing and hysterical. Here was a true rebel and one with whom I could identify.

A comic was born that night as I bought the record, learned the entire routine, and performed it occasionally for friends on campus, who would roar their delight. It appeared that Mr. Carlin and I both viewed life pretty much the same at this point.

It was at my nineteenth surprise birthday celebration held by my friends at school that everything in my world turned upside down, and I found love in an unexpected way.

Her name was Holly. A petite brunette with a winning smile and great attitude, she had moved from Dallas to attend the university and was also taking prerequisites for a degree in fashion design. My friends had invited her to my party, and we found ourselves drawn to each other in a way I couldn't understand or explain.

"Howdy, I'm Holly," she greeted me. "I'm from Dallas." She had this interesting twang in her voice. She certainly wasn't from Miami.

"Gee, I would have never known," I replied, and she easily laughed. I found a connection in that, and I was eager to know more about her.

"Did you take a wrong turn or something?" I asked.

Another endearing giggle. "No, I'm going to school here, silly." Then she took a step toward me, put on a tough face, and said, "So, you have a problem with that, mister?"

"Yeah, maybe I do, mister," I taunted her back, making a mock fist with my hand.

"Well, okay, then," she said, surrendering. She was adorable and I was hooked.

Having such a weird home life had prevented me from having a serious boyfriend. Few friends or dates were allowed to visit my home because of my mother's fragile condition. I dated sporadically (mostly geeks) over the high school years, always having to meet dates at their car outside my home. I was hardly a "Marilyn Monroe look-a-like," so the phone wasn't exactly ringing off the hook.

In all those years not one boy had caught my serious attention, and I began to wonder why. Now I knew. No guy had ever made me feel the way this attractive young woman did, and I was eager to explore the future with her. I also knew I was treading on forbidden and unknown ground.

Holly and I began exploring the area together, attending concerts at Penrod's on the Beach where we used altered drivers' licenses that showed us to be twenty one years of age and where we saw Meatloaf and The Drifters perform. Afterwards, we walked on the beach, drinking illegally obtained Pabst Blue Ribbon beer, while singing the songs we had just heard, in perfect disharmony.

Sometimes on warm nights, before the summer heat became unbearable, Holly and my dorm mates and I would pile into the used 1970 Chevrolet Chevelle Malibu trade-in my father had bought me and go to a local drive-in theater, armed with popcorn, snacks, and iced-down canned Cokes we'd brought from our room. I even sneaked in a time or two, hiding inside the large trunk of the car just for the thrill of it.

Eventually Holly and I began exploring more than just a friendship. and I had my first lesbian relationship, something I hid from everyone but my two closest girlfriends, who were not surprised. I don't even remember exactly how or when it happened, but I do know why.

I wish I could say I felt guilty that first time, but I'd be lying. I'd never felt so loved before in my life. Unconditionally loved. I wasn't even sure I understood what was happening, but I was happy and content with my new sexuality, and time with her became more and more important to me.

The main thing I worried about was that word would get back to my father. I feared his stellar reputation would take a direct hit if customers knew about it. The gay lifestyle was not as accepted back then as it is now, and I was extremely concerned that he would find out and make my life with them even more miserable or, worse yet, disown me. I mean, here is his not-so-attractive, loud-mouthed, lesbian daughter whom he already feels destroyed the woman he loved. I was most certainly not the perfect, handsome surgeon son he had dreamed of. Thankfully, Miami was a huge city, and university life far removed from my father's eyes and ears.

I was happy my dorm mates totally accepted my new relationship with Holly and, over the next several months, the four of us partied and studied together, and I found myself becoming more and more obsessed with her.

I shared my fears with my roommate Jessica. "If I'm not with her, I'm dreaming about her. If I can't find her right away, I fear something has happened to her. I know this can't be healthy." I was dealing with powerful new emotions I had never felt before.

One night while we were sitting on the patio of Holly's apartment and, after we had both drank way too much Boone's Farm wine and she had smoked a joint, something I couldn't even think of doing because of my asthma, she shared something with me that took the wind out of my sails.

"I had a dream last night. It was about Leslie, the first girl I had a lesbian relationship with. She was the first person who showed me what true love is all about. You would have liked her."

Liked her? I probably would have liked to hurt her. My jealousy wheels immediately went into motion.

The next thing out of her inebriated and stoned mouth was, "Believe it or not, I still have feelings for that girl. I can't seem to get over her. What do I do?" All of a sudden, she wasn't so adorable.

I indignantly replied, "What do you do? Have you forgotten who you're talking to?" It was as if she punched me square in the face. I felt extreme jealousy for the first time in my life, and my big mouth let her know it. I can't recall exactly what I said, but it was vile enough that she ordered me out of her apartment and out of her life. It was an early lesson in bad behavior for me, and I hated myself for attacking her so viciously.

To say I was devastated would be an understatement, and I found myself inconsolable,. I was unable to concentrate on my studies, and my grades began to suffer. My roommates suggested maybe I should try dating guys but that didn't appeal to me any more now than it had in high school.

I believe the fact that she wrote me off so quickly hurt more than anything else. Jessica gingerly suggested, "Maybe some of the things you said were more directed at the confusion and guilt you were feeling deep inside yourself, rather than toward Holly." Through the haze of my pain, I somehow heard her and agreed.

I knew I had to seek help, or I would totally lose it, so I began a twice-weekly session with Constance Rubenstein, Doctor of Psychotherapy, and the same trusted "shrink" I knew my mother had briefly seen years before. Lord knows, she needed to see somebody.

I explained to the good doctor that in no way was my father to know of these sessions and that I would pay her cash out of the generous monthly allowance he provided. She reminded me about her professional oath of confidentiality and said my records would never be made available to anyone but her. I then felt safe and free to share without inhibitions. The woman was like a cool oasis in a very hot desert.

The channels of communication we opened during that time together helped me begin to understand that the anger I had been building inside me was a result of the rejection I had suffered from the two people children trust more than anyone in their formative years—their parents.

"Your father's disappointment in you has become a way of life for him and a door that he hides behind so he won't resent your mother. Through no fault of her own, she had closed her own door on their marriage vows years earlier," the good doctor explained.

I then shared with her, "I never understood why he didn't hate and blame the Nazis more as they were the ones who took the best of his wife from him, not me."

"We'll try and explore that over time," she soothingly replied.

I had suppressed my own rejection over the years as I never felt I could trust just anyone with the truth of my feelings. I also didn't want friends and classmates to think I was weird because of my dysfunctional home life. I began to understand that a lot of the reasons I had rejected guys all my life was the awkward and impersonal relationship I shared with my father.

Unfortunately, all four of my grandparents died at Buchenwald, a concentration camp located five miles north of Weimar, Germany, which was set up in 1937 by the Nazis. Over 54,000 people lost their lives there from 1937 until 1945 when the Allied forces liberated the camp. Sadly there wasn't even one photo left of any of them.

There had never been any family member for me to talk to and confide in. What had been simmering inside me for so many years was a cesspool of deep-rooted anger and resentment, which I covered up with comedy and making fun of myself. Sometimes I experienced such profound pain that I would find myself sobbing uncontrollably during these meetings.

"Please, just make it go away, once and for all," I cried out more than once. I grieved most for my mother, who had totally withdrawn into herself to escape the memory of the indescribable horrors she had suffered for years at the concentration camp. That had been her only salvation, and it was a big part of my problem.

After a few weeks of putting most of the pieces back together again, I got over the loss of Holly, my grades picked up, and that summer my father insisted I spend a month in Europe before entering design school in the fall. He would pay for one of my friends to go with me, and I opted for Jessica, who had stood by me through all my anger issues, a just reward for having done so. This trip would be like a breath of fresh air for both of us.

Dr. Rubenstein called me before I left and said, "I would like to suggest that you attend the Holocaust Museum in London. Maybe you will more deeply understand and accept your mother's condition. Let me warn you, though, the pictures are very graphic and the stories compelling and depressing."

I knew that visit was paramount to my understanding both of my parents' behavior toward me, and I planned it for the final part of our journey.

~~ 38 ~~

The Great Adventure

Sophia had taken to pacing back and forth on the junk, totally immersed in her life history. Her story was quite compelling.

Jessica and I chose five countries to visit, and the coordination was definitely out of our league. We selected a travel agency my father had used before and, with their help, the two of us planned the first great adventure of our lives. I was counting the days until we embarked, and with the stifling heat of Miami persuading a swift escape, we gloriously flew into our new adventure on a late August day.

Our first stop was Madrid, Spain's capital city, where we booked tickets for a bullfight upon arrival and check-in at our hotel. It would be our first and last bullfight.

I was amazed at the beauty of this centuries-old city. We visited the Parque de Retiro, which was built in the seventeenth century for aristocracy, then strolled throughout the three art galleries located there. Because it was a weekend, we were entertained by mime artists, painters, jugglers, puppeteers, singers, dancers, and fortune-tellers in the park. Although we didn't understand a word of it, the experience was fun.

The bullfight was another story.

"I honestly didn't think the slow destruction of such a magnificent animal as a 1500-pound bull by a 200-pound toreador, armed only with a sword, would turn my stomach as it did," I moaned to Jessica.

"I don't think I'll ever eat beef again," she replied.

After one more less enthusiastic "Ole!" Jessica and I left the arena, hungry for anything that didn't include beef. Madrid's nightlife was exciting, and we sampled tapas at a couple of popular restaurants. We drank our fill of Spanish beer and danced until the wee hours at several late night hot spots. On our last night there, a couple of really drunk Spaniards tried to pick us up as we were leaving one of our favorite nightclubs. It was most certainly a night to remember.

Our next stop was Barcelona. One of the first things we did was to take the gondola up to the famous hill of Montjuïc (also known as "Jew Hill"), which has excellent views of the city. From our vantage point, we were awed by the city's ornate Spanish-style architecture, framed by small hills in the background, and buffeted by the mesmerizing Mediterranean Sea.

While on top of the famous hill, we visited the Museum de Catalunya, the grand Palau Nacional and the ornate Font Màgica fountains, with the grand staircase leading up from the foot of Montjuic.

I had always been enchanted by Italy, and I could already feel my waistline expanding as I knew the centuries-old recipes of Venetians, Romans, and Florentines would soon be explored by both of us foodies. I would not be disappointed.

One does not see Italy as much as inhale it. It is a sensory experience that could be easily classified as spiritual. We devoured homemade pasta and sauces from recipes that had been passed down through families for hundreds of years, at times closing our eyes and moaning with delight.

We considered ourselves wine connoisseurs and most weekends at school we had several empty bottles of our "nectar of the gods" to prove it. Therefore, since Italy has been one of the leading producers of wine worldwide for over 2800 years, exploring a winery was a must.

With so many vineyards to choose from, we had a hard time selecting just one, but we finally settled on one in Tuscany, known as the true birthplace of the Italian Renaissance and located just outside Florence.

We stayed inside the vineyard in a quaint hillside villa with a fantastic view of the Apennine Mountains. One of the interesting things that sold us on this particular vineyard was that part of our stay included sampling and learning about various types of Italian cuisine and wines under the guidance of a charming professional Italian chef. It was a gastronomic experience of a lifetime, and conversations with this knowledgeable man were delightful.

"Now, this is authentic I-talian food," Jessica bragged one evening, while slurping up pasta from her spoon. The chef just shook his head.

"Look, we've got sauce all over us," I commented, and Jessica almost choked on her food. "It's kind of like eating watermelon, isn't it?" We could have stayed there the entire stay, but it was time to move on.

From the beautiful gliding gondolas on the myriad of canals of Venice, to the sacred Vatican City in Rome and its famed Coliseum, to the rich heritage of Florence's art and sculpture, we saw and tasted as much of this endearing country as time allowed.

While on the plane trip to Paris, Jessica and I started

boning up on our French language skills, which were pitiful. We arrived at night and were literally transfixed by the twinkling beauty of the lights, especially those on the Eiffel Tower. All I could say was, "This truly is 'the city of lights.'"

I believe Paris must be like no other city on earth. We very quickly learned some dos and don'ts in the restaurants as we weren't aware one shuts the menu to indicate readiness to order or to request the bill after finishing the meal, rather than waiting for it. We learned that Parisians take their dining very seriously, and we learned to pace ourselves over a couple of hours for dinner, always dressing up much more than we would have at home. In fact, we noticed that our version of casual varies greatly from theirs.

We spent a full day exploring as much as possible of the Louvre Museum, and I was spellbound when I gazed upon the innocent face of *The Mona Lisa* and the armless *Venus de Milo*, magnificent works I had only read about and that I now had the luxury to gaze upon.

We marveled at Napoleon's magnificent Arc de Triomphe, and the 800 plus year old, gothic-styled Notre Dame Cathedral, where we gazed upon Paris from the same high platform of legendary hunchback, Quasimodo, the bellringer of Victor Hugo's *The Hunchback of Notre Dame*.

"Hey, Jessica, look, I'm Quasi," I quipped, while bending over and sticking my elbow up to make a hump.

"Then come on over here and ring this bell," she retorted.

"Coming dear," I said, while dragging a foot behind me. She loved it.

For a moment, I wished Holly could be in Paris with me,

then the thought left as quickly as it had come. I was on the road to recovery.

Our adventure would not be complete without a trip to the top of the 990-foot Eiffel Tower and a stroll along the Champs-Elysèes, the world's most beautiful avenue, where we longingly gazed into specialty shops and boutiques that displayed magnificently designed dresses, capes, gowns, purses, jewelry, and shoes we couldn't afford.

Jessica and I fell totally in love with Paris and everything about it. We sampled almost every type of Parisian pastry at unique sidewalk cafes and found the French cuisine even more tantalizingly delicious than famed French-style chef Julia Childs had promised.

The French also lead the world in cutting-edge fashion design, and as a future student at a design school in Miami, I was invited to visit with apprentices to such haute couture fashion greats as Pierre Cardin and Coco Chanel at their design houses right in the city. It was a day I would never forget as I watched designs on paper translate into actual exquisite pieces right before my eyes.

When it was time to pack, we knew we would miss Paris and were reluctant to leave, but Germany was beckoning.

Berlin was next on the itinerary. It was a city that I especially wished to visit, hoping to try and understand a race of people who would do what they had done to the Jews.

Although Dr. Rubenstein had suggested that I attend the London Holocaust Museum, I opted to tour the actual concentration camp of Auschwitz, where my parents had been held prisoners of the Third Reich. More than see it, I needed to experience it.

The train trip from Berlin would take several hours, and I would be spending all day the next day at the camp, so I booked an inexpensive room for two nights at a small inn in Krakow, Poland, which is located two hours from Auschwitz.

Jessica decided to stay in Berlin. "This is something you need to do by yourself. I feel like I might be in the way." Truth be told, I was thankful for the respite, and she wanted to go on a city tour and shop for souvenirs anyway. I was beginning to see that we would need to buy another suitcase just for the gifts we had bought.

We truly had a unique friendship as we respected one another's space, and she had been a joy to travel with.

I read a little on the train ride, indifferently viewing the uninteresting landscape speeding quickly by, and we arrived at Krakow without incident. I was delighted to find that the ivy-covered, brick, family-owned inn I had selected also provided breakfast. I slept like a baby that night on an extremely comfortable down feather bed.

A cool gray mist blanketed the city and surrounding areas the following morning, which only helped to contribute to the chill I felt upon our arrival at Auschwitz by tour bus. As I walked down the long entryway, flanked on both sides by thirteen-foot-high barbed wire, the hair stood up on the back of my neck as I could actually sense the presence of death still lingering there.

Even after decades, all the propaganda in the world could not erase the atrocities that had been inflicted on human souls from 1942 to 1945. Over one million Jews were systematically annihilated in this camp alone in just three years' time.

I had reserved by phone a space on the six hour English-speaking study tour of Auschwitz II/Birkenau, which included a general tour of the site of the Birkenau camp, with a special emphasis on those objects associated with the mass destruction of the Jews.

I wasn't sure how well I could handle this, but I figured if my parents could survive it for those few horrible years, I could certainly survive it for one day.

There were ten of us on the tour. Six of us had relatives who had either survived or perished there, and the other two couples were there out of curiosity and respect.

We visited the ruins of the gas chambers, crematoria IV and V, and then Bunker No. 2.

Our young guide pointed out, "Bunker No. 2 was called "the little white house" and it was used for gassing Jews before new gas chambers in the Birkenau crematoria buildings were completed." I shuddered at the thought and a deep cold feeling came over me.

"Although the buildings were destroyed by the Nazis when the Allies were advancing, photos still exist that prove of their existence. There are also photos that show Jews, Poles, and Russians waiting in long lines to enter these death chambers, totally unaware they are about to be gassed to death. You will see their grim expressions belie the horror they will face beyond those doors.

"Women with small children, pregnant women, the elderly, the infirm, all would meet their fate in the gas chambers, their bodies burned afterwards in one of the crematoriums. This was all part of 'The Final Solution,' Hitler's plan for the complete annihilation of all Jews, regardless of age or gender."

It was a shameful period in our history, and I was sickened by it.

I hated the train tracks that still exist as I remembered the stories in school about cattle car trains arriving daily at Auschwitz, packed like sardines from front to back with terrified prisoners. I could easily imagine the initial frenzy as men, women, and children of all ages clamored for space inside those stifling, hot boxcars after the doors slammed shut.

These unsuspecting souls were then classified upon arrival at the camp as "fit" to work, where they immediately were assigned to a building in the camp; or "unfit," and targeted for the gas chambers.

Another part of the tour included an area called Kanada, which was used for sorting and storing confiscated property of Jews who had just been delivered to the camp's gas chambers by transport train. Photos showed piles and piles of suitcases, clothing, toys, shoes, eyeglasses, baskets of all sizes, bedding and pillows, as well as other personal items stacked several feet high. It was mind-boggling and depressing.

I wondered if any of those items in the photos belonged to my family. For the first time in my life, I began to understand what my parents and grandparents had gone through. Their entire past had been trashed and tossed away as if it never existed. That alone was reason for indignation. What I learned next sickened me.

Our tour leader explained, "German physicians and medical researchers used Jewish and Roma women as subjects for sterilization experiments. Women were especially vulnerable to beatings and rape, and many died or took their lives because of it. Pregnant Jewish women often tried to conceal their pregnancies or were forced to abort their babies upon discovery."

It was a horrible place for them all. The level of despair I felt at that moment, when I finally understood, was almost overwhelming.

Now I knew. Because of her beauty, my mother had been singled out to survive; but also, because of it, she had more than likely been raped on many occasions. I was sure of it, and now I began to understand her withdrawal. What she had endured, I did not know, but it had drained the very life out of a once beautiful and vibrant young woman. Somehow, I would have to find a way to help bring her back to an existence she clearly needed and deserved. This would be my mission when I returned home.

I now understood why the Holocaust was never mentioned in my home. I asked my father about it once, and he replied, "There are some things in life that are better left unsaid. Please do not ask me that again." I never did. But now I understood why he couldn't speak of it for it had already depleted too much of his soul.

Jessica was thrilled with my decision and vowed to help in any way she could. She was one of the few who knew what really went on in my household, and she had always been supportive of me.

On a happier note, the balance of the Germany phase of the trip included the great city of Frankfurt where we sampled at least thirty different brands of "real beer" and danced the polka with an over-exuberant accordion player, who jumped around the floor like his clothes were on fire. Not being a dancer by nature, I was surprisingly jumping all over the place as well. Of course, it could have had something to do with the beer sampling.

I've always loved the royal family, so the last part of "the Great Adventure" included a visit to London, where we rode a double-decker bus and toured Buckingham Palace (the home of the queen), Kensington Palace, the Tower of London, Westminster Abbey, and Hyde Park.

We also took a ride on the tube, London's rendition of our American subway, which is guarded by bobbies or cops, as we say in the good old U.S. of A.

When we returned home, I was both exhausted and refreshed at the same time, and eager for two things to happen: One, to prepare to enter school and two, to research organizations available to help survivors of the concentration camps. Somehow, I would make it happen for my mother. She deserved that.

Buying schoolbooks, supplies, and clothing for the next phase of my education went without a hitch; my father's credit card could attest to that. Finding information on the concentration camp syndrome took a little more time and work.

With the help of my rabbi, we located a couple of organizations that specialized in this syndrome, and I contacted them for information that could help me understand it. It felt really great to take that first step, and this added new purpose to my life as well.

The next step didn't go so well. My first year of fashion design school was tough as I found myself becoming disenchanted with the entire fashion industry. What I had perceived it to be and what it actually turned out to be were two vastly different truths. I just couldn't get a firm footing in it.

I was eating lunch in the cafeteria at school one day and overheard a conversation between two other students that sent up a red flag.

"Did you know that a lot of the students who graduated this past year and the year before cannot get jobs?"

"Yeah," the other girl replied, "the word is that the world is becoming more casually dressed and haute couture is not quite as popular as it used to be." Uh, oh, that didn't sound good.

There was no way on earth I was going to give up my apartment and move back home after graduation. I knew I needed to quickly find something I would enjoy doing that offered better earning opportunities.

It was one night soon after that I caught "The Tonight Show" on NBC with Johnny Carson. The guest that evening was Joan Rivers, an up-and-coming comedian at the time. I laughed so hard that night, my sides were hurting. Here was a beautiful, young Jewish woman with serious *chutzpah*. I decided right then and there she would be my role model. I was now seriously hooked on comedy, and in no time at all, I worked up a strong routine that could be performed at any "open mic" comedy night.

For the first time, I felt like someone who had taken complete control of her destiny, and I was ready to give it a shot.

39

Just Make 'Em Laugh, Sweetheart

To say we were blown away by the life Sophia had lived would be an understatement. She was a rare person and someone who had turned sadness into real joy. It was quite a testament to the power of the Holy Spirit. We were encouraged when she continued her story.

I developed my own shtick, which had to include comments about my overgrown nose. Borrowing a few lines from other comics, I said, "My nose is always on time . . . but I'm fifteen minutes late," "Laugh and the world laughs with you. Sneeze and it's goodbye, Seattle." "It must be wonderful to wake up in the morning and smell the coffee . . . in Brazil." I literally killed with that segment.

Over time, I found myself accepting my big "honker," as I didn't want to spend the money to get it fixed. I learned how to manage my unmanageable hair, and I accepted my pear-shaped figure. I basically became satisfied with who I was, and it was quite liberating.

While finishing out my first and, thank God, final year at fashion design school, I started working weekends as the opening act for well-known comedians in comedy clubs around Florida. I also performed in a couple of gay bars that had comedy night once a week.

In the early days, the sound of laughter coming from my audience started building a sense of success inside of me. I was determined to become the best at this business, and I studied methods of some of the greatest comics in the industry, which helped me fine-tune mine. I learned about the four basic parts of a joke: the set-up, the punch line, tag-ons, and call-backs. Over time, I realized the importance of reading an audience, of timing, and delivery.

Within no time I developed a following, and I moved into being the feature act, which was better money and one step before headlining. With another comic's recommendation, I signed up with a seasoned manager who specialized in comedy gigs.

"Why don't we bill you as 'The Jewish-American Princess,'" Herb, my manager suggested.

"Sure, it fits," I replied.

I could tell he liked my cocky attitude, and we became close friends over the years. I was thrilled with my promo CD, and he kept me constantly booked, which meant increased income.

I was finally doing well enough to remain independent while doing something I enjoyed. The next big hurdle would be the meeting I would have with my father when I discussed dropping out of school.

His comments had sarcasm dripping off them, "So, you're now a big shot comedian. Another bad career choice. I pay thousands of dollars for design school. Do I have a daughter who is a designer? No. Now she wants to throw everything away to make people laugh. What's next, are you going to tell me you're gay? Oy vey, what is going on here?"

Once I could talk, I replied, "What is going on here is that design students who have graduated are not finding jobs. It appears that high end fashion is being phased out. I didn't know that going in. With regard to your comment about me making people laugh, it wouldn't hurt you to try it once in a while. And, just so you know, great comics make great money."

"Well, Miss Great Comic, go make your great money. You will need it, for you will no longer receive any financial help from me. I cannot keep financing your whims."

This I had expected. He had never supported the "frivolousness" of fashion design, and for me to now choose something as reckless as a career in comedy was beyond his understanding. What stung the most was the fact that he had never encouraged me in anything, so why did I expect things to be different now?

He had his first scream fest, and I had my first hissy fit, and I was drained when I left the house.

It hurt to the core of my being that I now had no one to count on, and that is when my serious drinking problems began. I kidded myself that I didn't have a problem even though I started with Bloody Marys or Screwdrivers in the morning then kicked the afternoons off with a few highballs, which carried me to performance time. The balance of the night was spent drinking whatever was available with fellow comics and fans until the bar closed. It had to be the grace of God that kept me from serious harm during those days.

Ready to date again, I joined a couple of gay dating websites that specialize in "that perfect someone." However, the only women I got involved with would end up ditching me after becoming disgusted with my drinking habits (I suppose throwing up all over one's date isn't all that cool), or their insanity would send me packing. I was told by more than one of them that I was a mean drunk and, had I been sober, I most certainly would have disagreed.

I knew my life was rapidly spiraling out of control, so I returned to the warm, non-threatening couch of Dr. Rubenstein who, after learning of my daily alcohol regimen, prescribed Alcoholics Anonymous for me.

"Do it, it works, I know firsthand," she insisted, while pressing a sheet with AA locations and times into my hands. Now I was going to one of those meetings.

I like to kid that "I went kicking and screaming into that first meeting" but truthfully, it most probably saved my life. I sat in that small, windowless room on a hard, cold, metal chair, surrounded by complete strangers, drinking hot coffee while reading "The Twelve Steps" and "The Serenity Prayer" posted on the wall. I started warming to the plan as there was nothing else positive going on in my life, and I was sick to death of myself.

I raptly listened to stories from others like me whose pain had driven them to alcoholism and down the same dead-end road. I knew I was not alone. Now I had a support group, and I would have a sponsor. I picked up my white chip that night and made the commitment to read The Big Book and attend a meeting every day for the rest of my life. I felt better than I had in years!

Rachel walked into a meeting and into my life a few months later. She was a slight woman, about my age, who walked with a limp—the result of an accident on her Harley. She immediately captivated me with her genuine smile, sparkling eyes, and warm handshake.

We became acquainted over donuts and coffee after the meeting and shared a comfortable peace. She had caught my show a month before.

"What a natural comic you are," Rachel said with a big smile on her face. "That was one of the best shows our biker group has been to. You're great!"

"So, guest host on 'The Tonight Show' great?" I inquired.

"Have they asked?" she breathlessly asked. "They should!"

"Nah, just wondering."

"Sophia, you have spunk and a unique routine. Jewish women would eat you up. You should at least have your manager send them a short video."

"I'll have Herb do that. Thanks." This woman believed in me. It was nice to have her as my friend.

After a comfortable silence, Rachel asked me, "Listen, why don't you attend Shabbat with me this coming Saturday morning? I attend a messianic Jewish synagogue in Ft. Lauderdale. I really think you'd like it."

"Why, sure, I'd love to," I quickly accepted, although I really didn't have a clue what that entailed. I was just thankful to have someone to spend some time with that wasn't slobbering all over me.

The service was liberating with its freedom and ease of worship. We sang, clapped our hands, and danced to age old songs I had heard over the years. This was a celebration like I had never experienced before, and I knew I could definitely get used to it.

I discovered that these fellow Jews who accept *Yeshua* as

the true Messiah, study the Torah and the Hebrew language, strongly support the nation of Israel, and celebrate all of the Feasts of the Lord. It was everything I needed and more. I became a "completed Jew," and like everything else in my life, I threw myself into it with great fervor.

Rachel became my mentor, helping me learn the ways of Christianity. I couldn't learn fast enough.

"You are such an eager seeker," she kidded me one day. "You almost wear me out, but I love it!"

"I love it too!" I soaked it up like a huge sponge and found myself wanting to become a better person.

Part of the change in me had to do with my comedy routine. I was never really considered a "blue" performer, but I did have some reservations now about some of my material. This prompted me to start developing a routine that could be performed not only on the comedy circuit but also at religious gatherings as well. I was still the "Jewish American Princess" but my "still funny, but now clean" routine paid off, and I was constantly booked.

Another change that happened gradually over time was how I dealt with my sexuality. The more I delved into the scriptures, the more I was convinced that perhaps the lesbian lifestyle was no longer something I embraced. At the same time, I didn't judge those who still did as I felt that was between God and them. I remembered how hurtful it had been when wisecracks were made toward me by thoughtless people.

After feeling comfortable enough at a Wednesday night Bible study to share my mother's plight, Ruth, one of the older female church members met with me after the meeting and volunteered to counsel her.

"I too am an Auschwitz survivor. Over time, I developed a method that helps others recover from concentration camp syndrome and become capable of living a normal life," she told me. "Please, let me help your mother."

"Yes, please, we would be most grateful," I replied. "My father will be more than happy to pay for your services."

"There is no need. He has already paid enough."

My father was both shocked and pleased that something could be done to help Estelle, and he eagerly accepted Ruth's offer. I saw hope shine in my father's eyes for the first time ever.

Over time, this loving woman worked magic on both my parents, helping my mother finally blossom into the vibrant woman she had once been and the wife my father desperately needed. They both made several efforts to restore and improve our relationship, and it worked. We started functioning as a family.

This messenger from God never told them she was a Messianic Jew, knowing my father would have disapproved.

"No need," she said, "It's God working the miracle, not me."

I was thankful this had worked out, and I knew *Yeshua* had put His blessings on it. I had finally fulfilled the promise I made to myself in Europe to help my parents in their recovery. Thank God, He sent an angel to help me, and this act alone helped me enjoy the time I had left with my wonderful parents.

Over the years I never met "that perfect someone" and

accepted it as my fate. The friends I developed through my relationship with *Yeshua*, however, lasted for a lifetime.

My demise, as they say, is one for the books.

It was a beautiful summer day, and I had just met with my agent to see if I could be sued for the comedy skit I was doing called "Weird Walmart Customers." Basically, I was planning to copy a number of the photos from e-mails that had been sent to me by friends; then I would flash the photos on a screen and comment on their bizarre outfits. My agent assured me that since the photos were now considered public domain, I could proceed as planned.

Herb added, "That might be one of your funniest routines yet."

"See, I told you, "Clean is mean.'"

Herb had thought I would fail after changing so much of my routine, but I had proven him wrong. God had backed me up.

I was just praying one of those Walmartians wouldn't come to the show, see me poking fun at them, then make my life miserable or, worse yet, pull out a .38 and go "postal" on me.

After leaving his office on South Tamiami Trail, I decided to jaywalk in the middle of the block rather than wait for the long traffic light down the street. This would obviously prove to be a bad decision.

Herb had just walked over to the window to watch me leave and saw the speeding 2008 Mercedes-Benz S550 come out of nowhere, hitting me before I made it to the sidewalk. Those who witnessed the accident say I performed a perfect 180-degree arc over the car and I "stuck" the landing; unfortunately, it was on my head. My neck was broken, and I was killed instantly.

One of my friends would later comment at my memorial that it was definitely my style to go out with a bang and in such a dramatic way.

"Okay, I'm done. That's all there is, folks."

We took turns hugging Sophia to show our support and thanked her for her ability to make us all laugh.

It was my turn to share my story and, I have to say, they were all shocked at the violent manner in which I died. The support from them was there for me as well when I finished, and we were soon docked and ready to return to the garden of Tranquility.

The bond between the five of us was now greater than before, as we recognized that we had survived the devil's lies to wind up in the most beautiful place one could imagine. Things were getting better and better.

40

Mount Transfiguration

After exiting the boat, we stood once again on the shores of the Sea of Reconciliation, remarking to one another about the unbelievably beautiful homes we had seen on the way back from the Other Side.

Wisdom then shared with us, "We are now going to Mount Transfiguration. You will all need to hold hands once more and close your eyes. You are getting used to this, right?" Before we could answer, we had already transported to the mountain.

"Okay, everyone, open your eyes," Wisdom commanded.

When I did open my eyes, I was bowled over by the vista that stretched hundreds of earth miles before me. This mountain was the highest I had ever been on, and the rock outcropping we stood upon provided an amazing view.

Wisdom explained. "We are standing on Mount Transfiguration, the tallest point in heaven. As you may recall, the entire countenance of Jesus was transformed as He stood on this mountain outside Caesarea Phillipi with Peter, James, and his brother John.

"Matthew 17 says, *His face shined like the sun and his raiment was white as the light. And behold, there appeared unto them Moses and Elijah talking with them.* It happened right here."

I knew now why Jesus glows with such brilliance, and His transfiguration had happened right here on this sacred place. I could almost feel the intensity of such an act, and I felt as if I could fly at that very moment, a thought that brought a chuckle from Wisdom.

"In due time, Miss Julie, you will be transporting around the galaxy just like me. But you must take these things in easy-to-swallow doses right now. I know that's easier said than done," he finished, which now brought a chuckle from me.

There was a lot to take in, and I could see forests in the distance, thick with giant sequoias, evergreens, redwoods, and cedars reaching hundreds of feet in the air. Monkeys and orangutans swung and swayed from leafy, thick branches, and many types of colorful birds were also present, flying from tree to tree as if impatiently visiting.

An arid section much like the Serengeti Plain with its open, lush grasslands and wooded hills was home to a menagerie of animals and birds that lived together in total peace, without fear of attack. I could hear the roar of lions and tigers, and the trumpet call of elephants with legs the size of tree trunks and enormous ears flapping in the wind. It was the first time I had actually experienced anything like this, and I was enthralled. *My eyesight has to be better than 20/20 now*, I thought, as I could see for miles without squinting.

"Look," Wisdom said, directing our attention to an open field right below the mountain. "You're going to enjoy this. It's great competition and good for the soul."

Fawn-colored gazelles with horns almost three feet in length and ostriches with two-toed feet, scrawny legs, and oddly shaped bodies were lined up on one end of the field. There were a few hundred altogether, and no one was moving.

All at once, several elephants trumpeted their call, and the racers took off. Within seconds, they appeared to be going over forty miles per hour. The drag racing part of me was quickly surfacing; I looked at Wisdom, and we both smiled.

"They're running almost as fast as I used to when there was a sale at Macy's," Sophia commented, winking at us girls. Abbie and I looked at each other, then at Sophia, and we said in unison, "Or Stein Mart!" I remembered how crazy it could get on holiday shopping days when the crush of humanity eventually drove me out of the stores and into the ease of online ordering.

"I've heard both can reach speeds of over sixty miles an hour," Tiny replied.

As quickly as he had spoken, the gazelles and ostriches ratcheted it up and very shortly disappeared from sight. We were speechless.

"Any prize for the winners?" I finally asked.

"Just bragging rights," Wisdom replied.

I could see a large, clear lake nearby and found it almost surreal to see buffalo, wildebeests, and rhinos comfortably drinking water from it side-by-side. Yet, I knew that's how God had planned it from the beginning.

I watched as tall, stately giraffes, with their long, graceful necks, nuzzled one another, basking in their simple love, and, again, I thanked God that He had given me Bobby.

It was clear from my vantage point that all of the Plain's inhabitants were enjoying one another, and I couldn't wait to see these magnificent creatures up close.

"That reminds me a little of my homeland, you know, when it was a little more innocent," Rashid quietly spoke, a wistful sigh inadvertently escaping. "I must believe that Fila and my family are okay."

"They are, Rashid," Wisdom kindly replied. "Remember, your prayers are powerful here in heaven. Put them to use."

"I shall never stop praying for them," Rashid responded with much conviction. "When the time is right, they must be here with me."

We all said an "amen" to that.

"Is that a rainforest, Wisdom?" Abbie asked, pointing to the far right.

"Yes, Abbie, it is," he replied.

The rainforest was awash with a vibrant and beautiful forest green color although a fine mist lightly blanketed it. An abundance of two-hundred-foot-tall trees were alive with playful spider monkeys and guarded by bald eagles with bulging eyes that watched you from their nests in high places. Bats hung upside down from tree limbs and would occasionally let go and fly... just for the fun of flying.

A thick canopy served as the forest's primary cover and temporarily hid enormous snakes—a fact I was thankful for—as well as tree frogs, and toucans, which I didn't fear.

As if he had read my mind once again, Wisdom spoke. "You all will visit the rainforest and observe anacondas, monkeys, alligators, and crocodiles in a new and different way."

"We're not talking alligator wrestling, are we?" Sophia playfully asked.

"Only if you want to," he playfully retorted, and we all laughed at both of them.

Wisdom continued, "There is so much to the heavenly realm, it will take you quite some time to see it all. As I said before, you will be introduced to every part of it throughout our journey."

Our viewpoint was so high that huge, puffy, pinkish clouds floated beneath us. Every now and then angels flew by, wings outstretched and riding the currents like birds, no doubt on a mission somewhere for God. Condors with wing spans of over six feet, along with hawks and falcons, flew by occasionally, dipping their wings at us in greeting. I was quite sure my jaw had dropped to the ground by now.

Wisdom smiled at our wonderment. "I never tire of seeing new heavenly beings' expressions here. It is a spectacular sight."

To put this in proper perspective, the only other time I had gasped aloud at a view was at my first sighting of the great Rocky Mountains. Bobby and I had rented a car for a ski trip to Breckenridge, which is about forty-five miles north of Denver. As we came out of the Eisenhower tunnel, enormous, snow-covered mountains, some stretching 16,000 feet into the air, dominated every line of our sight. It was phenomenal!

This was so far beyond that day that I would be hard put to even describe it.

As we enjoyed the eye treat, Wisdom continued, "Heaven, as I have mentioned, is designed to give you access forever to all things that you have enjoyed throughout your life.

"Do you see the snow-capped mountains in the far distance? Those mountains are inhabited at all heights by individuals who love their permanence and strength. The same is true for those who wish to live a nomadic desert life, a busy city life, or experience the peace and tranquility of waterfront living. Eskimos are provided with igloos, and jungle dwellers inhabit tree houses, never worrying about poisonous snakes or wild animals destroying them.

"God does not make junk either. Every home is designed with tender, loving care in appreciation for faith shown throughout one's life. The things you will notice missing are shanties, shacks, or broken-down dwellings. There is nothing negative here, my friends.

"Your home was designed by God in answer to the desires you expressed in prayer over the years. Other angels and I watched as God lovingly constructed them all. Attention to detail is always paramount to Him."

We all spoke over one another, expressing our gratitude. I couldn't wait to hear about my new friends' homecoming parties and to visit their new mansions, but we would have plenty of time for that later.

Tiny spoke up. "I have to tell you guys that when I saw the home of my dreams, I cried like a little baby, and I have thanked my Father God many times over for His faithfulness to me at those times when I had none for him."

"Well said, Tiny," Wisdom replied. "Just remember you all are here because you had faith, not because you were perfect."

"You know, I was always thankful for whatever God gave Bobby and me. Even when I lost him, I still had a warm and comfortable home to share with my son . . . not to mention the memories inside our home. But I always secretly wanted that Southern mansion on a hill—and I got the water view to boot. My goodness," I said, while shaking my head at the wonder of it all.

Wisdom continued. "Heaven provides an atmosphere pleasing to all who dwell here."

"I think we're starting to understand," Sophia commented.

"I see. But the best is yet to come. So, did everyone enjoy the view?" Wisdom finished.

"Absolutely!" we all exclaimed in agreement.

"Great. Now, all of you, close your eyes and hold hands again," he instructed, "for what I am about to show you is like nothing you have seen yet. Don't say I didn't warn you."

I couldn't even imagine what was waiting to be seen at this point in time. When I finally opened my eyes, I gazed upon a walled city so dazzling in its glory, so breathtakingly beautiful, that I couldn't speak. What I had experienced to date had been fulfilling, new, and definitely exciting, but this City of God, which glittered with golden walls and thousands of gems was absolutely indescribable. This was exactly what John described in Revelation 21:

It shone with the glory of God, and its brilliance was like that of a very precious jewel, like jasper, clear as crystal. It had a great, high wall with twelve gates and with twelve angels at the gates. On the gates were written the names of the twelve tribes of Israel. There were three gates on the east, three on the north, three on the south, and three on the west. The wall of the city had twelve foundations, and on them were the names of the twelve apostles of the Lamb.

The angel who talked with me had a measuring rod of gold to measure the city, its gates, and its walls. The city was laid out like a square, as long as it was wide. He measured the city with the rod and found it to be 1400 miles in length, and as wide and high as it is long. The angel measured the wall using human measurement, and it was 200 feet thick. The wall was made of jasper, and the city of pure gold, as pure as glass.

The foundations of the city walls were decorated with every kind of precious stone. The first foundation was jasper, the second sapphire, the third agate, the fourth emerald, the fifth onyx, the sixth ruby, the seventh chrysolite, the eighth beryl, the ninth topaz, the tenth turquoise, the eleventh jacinth, and the twelfth amethyst.

The twelve gates were twelve pearls, each gate made of a single pearl. The great street of the city was of gold, as pure as transparent glass.

What John had experienced in his vision at Patmos was what I was now experiencing. It was incredible!

I saw heavenly beings passing in and out of the mammoth gates and much activity going on outside the city as well. Beautiful parks were dotted with jungle gyms filled with laughing children and overflowing with fruit trees and vibrant foliage. Fountains percolated throughout the parks, and the River of Life powerfully flowed alongside golden streets and into the heavenly realm, its banks filled with mature and budding foliage. There were guardian angels escorting heavenly beings and winged angels flying off to unknown places.

Although I couldn't see inside the city, the exterior was so breathtakingly beautiful I could only gaze in wonder. The city literally glowed like a bright light bulb. I had dropped my hands and put them over my heart, as it was almost bursting with excitement.

I can't even imagine what goes on inside the walls of this splendid place, I thought with fascination. I then realized the reason my heart was beating stronger was because I was getting closer to the throne of Almighty God. I would finally gaze upon the One who created me and who had forever been the lover of my soul.

"Thank you, God," I said aloud, "I am so blessed to be in this amazingly beautiful place." I could see the others were also caught up in their own spiritual moments, and I heard a few "amens."

On the right of the walled city, I saw a massive military installation, with a two-story white brick building and a tournament-style outdoor arena where colorful flags fluttered in a light breeze from sharply pointed towers. It reminded me a little of jousting tournament arenas at some of the castles in Scotland.

I watched as enormous, powerful Clydesdale horses, at least twenty-four hands high, pranced into the arena, heads proudly tossing alongside athletically fit twelve-foot-tall angels. These fearsome looking warriors were decked out in practice gear: thick vests, shin guards, and lightweight helmets. I couldn't wait to see their actual battle armor.

"That is Warrior's Field," Wisdom pointed out. "Constant training is required of these devoted warring angels as their task is to protect God, their Supreme Commander, and the entire heavenly realm. They perform their tasks unwaveringly, obeying their superiors without fail.

"I will take you there, and you will meet the army's leaders: General Victorious, one of the few in God's inner circle, and Colonels Majestica and Splendorous, officers who serve directly under the General. Warriors Field is a training arena for the Supreme Commander's army preparing for Armageddon, the final showdown, when God's angels will rise up against Lucifer's demons, and defeat Satan once and for all."

"Can we get advance tickets to the event?" Sophia asked.

"Ringside seats if you want," Wisdom playfully answered.

"Wow," was all Abbie could say, and Tiny responded, "Cool."

I, myself, was ready to experience everything Revelation had described, without mounting one of those enormous horses, of course.

"Holy schmoly!" Sophia shouted out, and we laughed at her outburst. "I am actually gazing upon the very place that God lives. He's there, isn't He? Right now?"

"In answer to both of your questions, yes," Wisdom replied. "However, there are two things you all need to know. First and most importantly, God is omnipotent, which means He is all-powerful, and He has unlimited authority. No one questions that, just ask Lucifer. Number two, He is omnipresent, which means He is present everywhere simultaneously."

"Whoa," Sophia said. "And I used to think my schedule was busy."

"Where do you come up with these things?" I laughingly asked her.

I heard sobbing and turned to see Rashid on his knees, his face in his hands.

"Rashid, are you okay?" Tiny asked as he knelt to comfort him. We all crowded around Rashid as well.

Rashid replied, "Don't worry, my friends, I am okay. What I have just gazed upon is the most glorious sight I've ever seen. You have to understand that I grew up with no electricity, running water, or even the basic comforts so many others take for granted. There was not even a window in our home. I am so profoundly grateful to be here that I am overwhelmed."

It was at that moment that a large cloud formation morphed into an oversized, interesting face. It had the same kind eyes I had seen when the Holy Spirit welcomed me at the River of Life. While drawing close to us, it blew a soft fragrant wind upon our faces, and I knew it was Him, visiting in yet another form.

The Comforter reached out His arms and wrapped them around Rashid. This act of divine love brought us all to our knees. Rashid kept saying, "I love you," over and over, and we could feel strength and power emanating from God's tender spirit.

As soon as He left, we returned to our feet, revitalized, and even more eager now to move on.

"When do we go there?" Abbie asked eagerly, voicing all of our thoughts.

"Excited, huh?" The big guy was toying with us. He certainly kept things interesting.

"First, we return to the garden of Tranquility, then we go to the City of God. Just wait until I share with you how Lucifer created the mutiny in heaven and the horrors of hell that my best angel friend Divine shares with me. Divine actually got fooled by Lucifer and was taken to hell with him. You will find it disturbing yet fascinating."

"Oh, Wisdom," Abbie mused, "We are actually going to hear about the mutiny. Were you there?"

Wisdom replied, "Yes, unfortunately I was. And there's even more amazing stories to share about that time. Are you guys ready to go?"

"Yes!" we exclaimed in unison.

I looked once more at that glorious city and realized I was beginning to feel like Dorothy in *The Wizard of Oz*, when she first beheld the Emerald City. I even looked down to see if there were ruby slippers on my feet. However, I had not gone through a tornado to get here, but rather a kaleidoscopic trip through a tunnel, and I had ended up in heaven, not Kansas. And Jesus Himself had personally welcomed me here. I was both humbled and grateful.

I would now traverse the heavenly realm, experiencing those things I had so rapturously gazed upon, then enter into the City of God, where the King of Kings and the Lord of Lords reigns.

I was thrilled, excited, and a little apprehensive.

Like I used to say on earth, "Throw me something, mister!" I was more than ready to catch.

STUDY GUIDE

This novel was written based on the Word of God's interpretation of heaven and visions given to the author. Studying these scriptures will give you a better understanding of what God has in store for us in His glorious heavenly realm.

Angels

Psalm 91:11—*For He will command His angels concerning you to guard you in all your ways.*

Matthew 16:27—*For the Son of man shall come in the glory of his Father with his angels; and then he shall reward every man according to his works.*

Luke 4:10-11—*For it is written: He will command his angels concerning you to guard you carefully; they will lift you up in their hands, so that you will not strike your foot against a stone.*

Our Heavenly Home

Hebrews 13:14—*For this world is not our permanent home; we are looking forward to a home yet to come.*

2 Corinthians 5:1—*For we know that if the tent that is our earthly home is destroyed, we have a building from God, a house not made with hands, eternal in the heavens .*

John 14:2—*My Father's house are many mansions; if it were not so, I would have told you. I go to prepare a place for you.*

Feasting

Revelation 22:2—*In the midst of the street of it, and on either side of the river, was there the tree of life, which bare twelve manner of fruits, and yielded her fruit every month: and the leaves of the tree were for the healing of the nations.*

Matthew 26: 29—*I tell you. I will not drink from this fruit of the vine from now on until that day when I drink it new with you in my Father's kingdom.*

Matthew 8:11—*Many will come from the east and the west and will take their places at the feast with Abraham, Isaac and Jacob in the kingdom of heaven.*

Friends and Family

Matthew 17:3-4—*And, behold, there appeared unto them Moses and Elias talking with him. Then answered Peter, and said unto Jesus, "Lord, it is good for us to be here: if thou wilt, let us make here three tabernacles; one for thee, and one for Moses, and one for Elias."*

Hebrews 2:9-13—*But we see Jesus ... bringing many sons to glory. Both the one who makes men holy and those who are made holy are of the same family. So, Jesus is not ashamed to call them brothers. He says, 'I will declare your name to my brothers. Here am I, and the children God has given me.'*

1 John 3:2—*Dear friends, now we are children of God, and what we will be has not yet been made known. But we know that when Christ appears, we shall be like him, for we shall see him as he is.*

1. We will be ourselves and have emotions

Ezekiel 34:28—*They will live in safety, and no one will make them afraid.*

Galatians 5:22-23—*But the fruit of the Spirit is love, joy, peace, patience, kindness, goodness, faithfulness, gentleness and self-control.*

2. We will maintain our newly regenerated and improved heavenly bodies.

1 Corinthians 15:49—*Just as we have borne the image of the man of dust, we shall also bear the image of the man of heaven.*

Romans 8:11—*If the Spirit of him who raised Jesus from the dead dwells in you, he who raised Christ Jesus from the dead will also give life to your mortal bodies through his Spirit who dwells in you.*

About the Author

Sue Campbell began receiving amazing visions from God as a teenager. She has acted on those visions throughout her life, one of which was to create Praise Unlimited, the world's largest Christian toy company, with thousands of toy missionaries worldwide who spread the gospel through Christian toys.

Her foray into writing began while living on Cozumel Island with her husband, Will. The vision to present heaven in a new and exciting way was shown to her and the "Conversations in Heaven" book series was born.

Whether at home in Georgia with her large family or traveling around the country spreading God's Word, she is thankful for the gifts and talents God has given her.

Sue's website: www.sue-campbell.net
Facebook: Conversations in Heaven
Contact Sue: suecampbell4448@yahoo.com